"I'll tell you what," Kit said, "you just give orders, and I will follow them."

"Speak for yourself," Shelby said.

"Would you rather take orders from me?"

She looked away from him quickly, and he realized that he'd stepped into something. Because she didn't fire anything right back at him, and he almost felt guilty about that.

And then she looked up at him, dark fire banked in her eyes. "I'd like to see you try."

He held back his answer. He held it back because everybody was here. He held it back because he didn't know how to make it not explicitly sexual.

He held it back because the last thing in all the world he needed to do at this wedding preparation party was declare his sexual intent with his brother's future sister-in-law.

Especially when he knew that he couldn't have any intentions toward her at all.

* * *

Best Man Rancher by Maisey Yates
is part of The Carsons of Lone Rock series.

Books by Maisey Yates

The Carsons of Lone Rock

Rancher's Forgotten Rival
Best Man Rancher

Gold Valley Vineyards

Rancher's Wild Secret
Claiming the Rancher's Heir
The Rancher's Wager
Rancher's Christmas Storm

Copper Ridge

Take Me, Cowboy
Hold Me, Cowboy
Seduce Me, Cowboy
Claim Me, Cowboy
Want Me, Cowboy
Need Me, Cowboy

For more books by Maisey Yates,
visit www.maiseyyates.com.

You can also find Maisey Yates on Facebook,
along with other Harlequin Desire authors,
at www.Facebook.com/harlequindesireauthors!

NEW YORK TIMES
BESTSELLING AUTHOR

MAISEY YATES

Best Man Rancher
and
Want Me, Cowboy

HARLEQUIN
DESIRE

Recycling programs for this product may not exist in your area.

ISBN-13: 978-1-335-67996-3

Best Man Rancher & Want Me, Cowboy

Copyright © 2022 by Harlequin Enterprises ULC

Best Man Rancher
Copyright © 2022 by Maisey Yates

Want Me, Cowboy
First published in 2018. This edition published in 2022.
Copyright © 2018 by Maisey Yates

For questions and comments about the quality of this book, please contact us at CustomerService@Harlequin.com.

Harlequin Enterprises ULC
22 Adelaide St. West, 41st Floor
Toronto, Ontario M5H 4E3, Canada
www.Harlequin.com

Printed in U.S.A.

CONTENTS

BEST MAN RANCHER

Chapter 1

"Six inches is too long!" Shelby Sohappy glared across the table, across all the flowers piled on the table, across the tulle and the candy strewn over the table, to her older sister.

But it wasn't Juniper's reaction to Shelby's words that caught her attention, and held her there.

She felt it before she saw it. His response. *His*, always his. The change crackled through the air. And she told herself not to look. She told herself to keep her focus on Juniper, the bride, her sister, her best friend, and direct all wedding preparation complaints to her.

But she turned her head anyway.

As if he'd put his finger beneath her chin and swiveled it toward him. That's how powerful the impulse to look was.

Kit Carson.

Damn Kit Carson.

Her eyes clashed with his, electric and upsetting. And his mouth curved—even more upsetting. "Six inches is too long? Maybe that's why I'm still single."

That earned a round of groans from the table—and Shelby should also groan. But instead she felt like her body had been lit up.

She had learned a lot since middle school.

That you didn't actually need algebra. That body glitter wasn't worth the hassle. That the girls who wouldn't let you sit with them would—in fact—peak once school ended and spend their adult years trying to reconnect with people they had once been mean to so that they could sell them lip gloss, leggings and the secrets of success and wealth and sisterhood, as long as you bought their weight loss shakes.

She'd learned that she was stronger than she'd imagined. That loss wouldn't kill you, even if you might wish it had.

But she hadn't learned how to control her physical response to Kit Carson, a man who was soon to be practically family, the best man to her maid of honor, her longtime, shame-fueled object of lust.

Yeah. She hadn't learned that.

"That's not why you're single, bro," said Chance, her sister's fiancé, and everyone laughed.

So Shelby laughed too. What choice did she have?

She felt like a foreign tourist pretending they understood what was happening around them. She was just lost. In ribbon curls and Kit Carson's excess of six inches.

How *many* inches more?

She didn't need to know the answer to that.

She didn't even need to *wonder* it.

Nope.

"Six inches," Juniper said, holding up a ribbon and a pair of scissors, and letting the edge glide effortlessly across it, resulting in a rather impressive curl, "is not too long at all."

Shelby ignored Chance and his brothers chuckling at that.

So did Juniper.

Shelby wondered, not for the first time, how the hell this had happened.

The Carsons and Sohappys had been enemies for generations. To the degree that the first time she'd spotted Kit Carson at a football game when she'd been in seventh grade and he'd been in tenth, she'd felt a deep, instinctive recoil in her soul.

At least, she liked to tell herself that's what it was.

Because it couldn't possibly have been anything else. She'd been dating Chuck already by then. Well, *dating* was a strong term. They'd been twelve, after all. They'd walked down to the diner in Lone Rock and had shared a milkshake with money Chuck had gotten collecting bottles and taking them to the can return.

They'd gone down to the river and skipped rocks.

They'd held hands. And he'd kissed her.

They'd started having sex when they were way too young, but hey, she'd been certain she'd marry him so the moral risk had seemed worth the reward.

And she'd been right.

She'd married Chuck pretty much as soon as high school had ended. She'd been so ready for that life. She'd loved him. Deep and uncomplicated.

And if she'd sometimes… If she'd been unable to

keep herself from thinking of the man who'd first created a shiver of awareness inside her before she'd known
what it was, she'd just blamed it on having been with
only one man. Dismiss it as adventures she'd chosen
not to have.

There had been moments in her marriage when she'd
wondered if they'd done it too soon. If not dating other
people had been a mistake.

When Chuck had died, she'd been so glad they'd had
that life. That whole brilliant life.

From twelve to twenty-six. Thank God for all those
years, because they hadn't gotten to grow old together.
Just older.

She really didn't need to be thinking about any of
this now.

But it was a wedding, so it was unavoidable.

And it was her sister's wedding, which made it more
poignant.

Her sister's wedding to a Carson. That's what tipped
it over into improbable.

"Who would have thought you'd be a bridezilla,"
Shelby groused.

Juniper was an EMT, and in general a very practical and nonsentimental soul. Before her engagement
to Chance, anyway. Now suddenly it was all sentiment
and fluffy dresses and ribbon curls.

"I haven't even begun to bridezilla," Juniper declared
from her end of the table, which had all the Carson men
looking worried.

The lone Carson girl—Callie, who had gotten married a while back and moved to Gold Valley, Oregon, a
few hours away—was grinning. "I love this! I need more
women in the family. To cause chaos and mayhem."

"You don't need any help with that, sis," Boone Carson said.

"I'm happy to contribute to family chaos!" Juniper said.

And Shelby couldn't help but feel just a little bit outside of all of this. It wasn't anyone's fault. Especially not Juniper's. Her sister deserved happiness. So much happiness. She had been there for Shelby in a profound way when Shelby had lost Chuck. And in all the time since. Juniper was her best friend.

But that didn't mean that Shelby couldn't find a way to have complicated feelings about this.

It made her think about her own wedding. And the terrible thing was... She didn't have a very clear memory of that day.

Which had seemed fine in the decade since it had occurred, when Chuck was still with her. She'd had the marriage. She hadn't needed more than good feelings and a few photos of the day.

She couldn't remember if they had sat around making wedding favors. She didn't think they had. Nobody should get married when they were eighteen. That was a whole fashion disaster. Shelby had worn a princess dress and a tiara. The entire thing had been a debacle. But of course, when you were eighteen, what you wanted out of the wedding was to be a princess. You thought a lot more about the wedding than you did the marriage. Not that her marriage hadn't been good. It had been. It had been great. Chuck had been her best friend, well, her other best friend, apart from her sister.

It was just, when you were eighteen you didn't really know what the rest of your life meant.

You still don't.

No. She didn't. Because her husband had gone and died and made her a widow in her midtwenties. But what the hell was she supposed to do with that?

Make ribbon curls, she supposed.

"We need to have all the wedding favors ready by tonight," Juniper said.

"Or heads will roll," said Chance, looking at Juniper as if seeking approval.

"That's right," Juniper said. "Heads will roll."

"Good luck with that," Shelby said.

"Yeah," Kit agreed, and she did her best to stop herself from looking at him, but much like her first best, this was not enough. Because she ended up looking at him. And he smiled. And she felt it. Hot and slow as it moved through her.

"If you make my bride upset," Chance said, looking right at his brother, "it'll be your head."

"If your bride can be upset about ribbon curl... I don't know, man."

"When was the last time you ever loved anything?" Chance said to his brother.

"I had a pretty damned good cheeseburger at about one o'clock today," Kit said. "I think I might've loved that."

She couldn't help it. She found herself laughing. And their eyes clashed again. This time, the electricity sent a shower of sparks through her, settling down between her thighs, and it made her twitchy.

This was the problem. When she had been in middle school, she had been able to write off the things that Kit Carson made her feel, but as she had hurtled toward adulthood, it had been impossible to pretend she didn't know.

But it was… It was wrong. It had been wrong because he was her enemy—by virtue of his family connection, nothing personal—and then it had been wrong—very wrong—because she was in love with another man.

Married to another man.

She gritted her teeth together. No. She wouldn't even think about it. She got up from the table, heading over to one of the coolers that were set around their little gathering. They had tables placed all around the yard, where different family members were helping with wedding favor assembly, and all around that were coolers with different beverages, and there was also a table full of snacks. She decided that it was definitely refreshment time.

She felt hot and unwieldy. Lost in the memories of the past, and the debate over ribbon curls, was the double entendre that had passed between herself and Kit. Well, not lost. It was just not the big thing that remained in the forefront. But the slow burn of it was left behind. She was uneasy, and she needed a moment with it.

She reached into the cooler and took out a bottle of beer. And then she heard footsteps, and straightened, looking across the cooler to see none other than Kit himself.

"Anything good in there?"

"They have the kind of beer that you would expect from a couple engaging in this level of wedding frippery. Does that answer your question?"

"Oddly, yes it does." He grinned, then reached down into the cooler, and took out the first beer his hand closed around.

She felt like saying something sharp. She felt like being mean and making him walk away from her. But the truth of the matter was, all of this stuff… This stuff was one-sided. He didn't know that she had a long-standing hated attraction for him. And yes, they had clashed on a few occasions. So there was… There was a thing.

Though, she denied it. And had denied it on multiple occasions. In fact, she could remember clearly one time when they had been down at the Thirsty Mule, and he had been goading her, while offering to buy her and her friends a round of drinks—it had been girls' night out. And Kit had kept on making comments about how Shelby and he *didn't normally get along*. There was *a whole situation with her*, and she *didn't like him*. On and on. Until she had screamed at him at the top of her lungs: *you and I do not have a situation*.

Of course, for the rest of forever, everyone in town had convinced themselves that there was a situation.

Chuck had just laughed about it. Thankfully. And he had written off her umbrage as the normal sort of umbrage that her family felt whenever the Carson name was mentioned. And she had never had to admit that it wasn't just Kit's name that made her feel all out of sorts. It was the man himself.

He grabbed one of the bottle openers from the top of the cooler and popped it easily. Then he reached out to grab her beer out of her hand. A few things happened simultaneously. The first was that his fingertips brushed hers. They were hot and rough, the way a man's hands were when he worked the land.

She didn't comprehend what was happening in the moment, and she did not release the hold on her beer.

Each of those realizations and moments occurred in

one breath, and she found herself being dragged over the cooler into Kit.

"Easy," he said, taking hold of her arms. And she got an even more intense taste of the roughness of his hands. The heat there.

Oh, Lord. Oh, Lord, save her.

She was being tested, and she was failing. Here, at the preparation for her sister's wedding, she was having a full-blown attack of lust for a man who was about to be family-by-marriage. The man whom she had spent all these years pretending she had no situation with.

It was a situation.

"What the hell were you doing?" she asked, still clinging to her beer, still being held on to by him.

"I was gonna open your beer, Shelby," he said, peeling the bottle from her hands, while he set her back onto her feet. "Just a beer. Not a situation."

That bastard.

He had gone over that same night. Those same words.

It did something to her.

Meant something to her.

She wished it didn't.

"I didn't say that I needed help with the beer," she said.

He moved the edge of the bottle opener beneath the perforated cap and flipped it up. "No, you didn't. But I'm nice like that. A real gentleman, some might say."

"Who? Who has ever said that?"

"Not entirely sure."

"No one has ever said it."

He shrugged. "Someone must have."

"Not me."

"You're the president of my fan club. At least I thought so. If not, this is awkward. Because I thought…"

"You did not."

And she felt herself getting red, because… Because, all this banter was just a little bit too close to reality.

"We're not enemies anymore, or did you miss the memo."

"I missed *zero* memos. Believe me. And I tried to talk my sister out of this whole thing. You know, back when she lied to your brother about being her ranch hand when he had amnesia. And then fell in love with him. Yeah. I tried to interfere with all that."

"When you put it like that, it sounds vaguely ridiculous."

"It does," she said.

But ridiculous or not, it had occurred. That could honestly be the subtitle of a movie about her life. *Ridiculous or not, it had occurred.*

He lifted the beer bottle to his lips, and she couldn't help but watch the movement of his mouth, his throat working up and down as he took a long pull off the bottle. Why was he so damned compelling. Why? He didn't have any right to be. He was just a cowboy. They were a dime a dozen around here. Hell, he was one of six boys. There really was no call for him to be all this compelling. She had been married to a rancher. This one shouldn't stir…

She didn't want to think about this. She didn't want to be anywhere near Kit Carson while she was dealing with marriage and wedding feelings. She didn't want to think of him in a game of compare and contrast with Chuck and what she had felt for him.

She had loved Chuck. The love of her life. That

phrase couldn't be truer about anyone or anything than it was about Chuck. She had loved him from the time she was twelve years old. And was certain that she would marry him from that same time. She had loved the man until the day he had died, and in all the days since. Kit Carson wasn't owed the same mental airspace as Chuck.

"You got your speech all nailed down?" he asked.

"Yes," she lied. "It's going to be the best speech."

"And you're ready for the bachelorette party?"

"More than ready."

They would be hosting the bachelor and bachelorette parties at the wedding venue. Which was going to be at a ranch about an hour away, up in the mountains, Green Springs Ranch. They were all going to stay in the different buildings on the property, and the wedding would take place in one of the main barns. As maid of honor, it was up to her to plan the bachelorette party. As best man, it was up to Kit to do the bachelor party.

"How did you end up being the best man, anyway?" she asked.

"I drew the short straw."

"What?"

"It's true. We never really figured on any of us getting married. Not us boys. I mean, there's Callie, but… Well, we didn't really figure on her getting married either. But she did. But you know, as far as the best man thing goes, we drew for it. I drew the short straw."

"Doesn't that imply that it's a bad thing?"

"I'm paying for the bachelor party. I'd say that's the short straw."

Suddenly, she felt boxed in. Observed by too many people, or maybe it was just him. The way that he always looked at her. Like he knew. But nobody could know. Nobody could ever know.

"Better go," she said. "The ribbons aren't going to curl themselves."

"Nope."

She turned away from him, and she ignored the way she could feel his gaze resting between her shoulder blades. Like a touch. A caress. Yeah. She ignored that because to acknowledge it would mean acknowledging the spark between them. And she absolutely refused to do that.

Chapter 2

Kit Carson wasn't an idiot. Despite reports to the contrary. In fact, he had a pretty damned good head on his shoulders. He might make dumbass decisions out riding the rodeo, bold and rash and dangerous when he flung himself on the back of an angry bull, determined to see him in an early grave, but that recklessness had netted him a damn good portfolio, personal wealth and a hell of a lot of prestige in the rodeo community.

Not to mention the attention of a great many buckle bunnies. And so, it was to his great and eternal mystery that Shelby Sohappy got underneath his skin to quite this degree.

And it wasn't recent. The woman *always* had.

Dating someone else, engaged. *Married.* He had felt drawn to her like a moth to a flame. Like a deer in headlights. Like some other cliché he couldn't think of right now. All he knew was that he really wanted to see her naked.

He could have his pick of women. He had. But there was something about her. About the way they sparked heat off each other, the way that he flustered her, that made him interested. But she was off-limits. She'd been off-limits for a long time, but in all honesty, he figured another man's marriage was that man's responsibility. He had never made a move on Shelby, but he figured whether or not her marriage put her off-limits was up to her. Now that the Carsons and the Sohappys were no longer enemies, well, that changed things a fair bit. Now she was going to be essentially family. And that meant there could be absolutely no... Nothing. Anything.

Because that would make things difficult for Chance. And Kit didn't want to make things difficult for Chance. They had had a difficult enough life as it was.

Chance had found love, and good for him. Kit didn't have it in him.

Losing their sister Sophie when they were kids had just been too much for him. The loss, the feeling of failure when all the caregiving he did couldn't save her...

He'd been twelve and that weight had never shifted.

And more than that, the ongoing grief in the family.

He loved his mom, his dad, his brothers and his youngest sister, Callie, so damned much. And losing Sophie to a terminal illness had underlined how dangerous that love was.

Then there was Buck, his oldest brother, who'd been involved in a horrible car accident that had left him scarred, distant from everyone. They hadn't seen him in years and there was nothing Kit had been able to do to fix it.

There was just so much pain to manage in his family. Lord.

He didn't want more of it. He never wanted a wife or kids. He didn't even want a dog. He didn't want to love any new thing.

That was the thing. He didn't love Shelby Sohappy. He wasn't even really sure if he liked her. He just wanted her. He was a man who knew that chemistry superseded common sense pretty much any day of the week. He had accepted that what they had was some kind of superior chemistry. The kind you couldn't manufacture even if you wanted to. And you wouldn't want to, but if you could, you would definitely direct it at somebody you'd never see again. Or someone who wouldn't get tangled up in your life. At least, that was what was ideal to *him*.

So yeah. Nothing much had changed. He couldn't have her back when she'd been married. He couldn't have her now. There had been a very small window where he might've been able to have her, but she'd been grieving. Fair enough.

He knew about grief. He knew how it changed you. How it fucked you up big-time. Changed the way that you saw the world. Broke down all the landscape inside you and didn't bother to rebuild the damn thing.

Yeah. He knew about grief. And it was knowing about that kind of grief that made him all the more determined to stay the hell away from this woman.

Too bad they were going to be in proximity for the planning of this wedding. They wouldn't be most of the time. He assumed that for holidays Chance and Juniper would go back and forth between the families, and Shelby didn't have anything to do with the Carsons specifically. But just for right now the woman was squaring his path.

He did his best not to think about how soft her golden brown skin had been beneath his fingers when he held her there. Dammit she was beautiful. Her thick black hair was cut into a chin-length style that highlighted the heart shape of her face, her high cheekbones, her deep brown eyes. Her lips were full and dusky, a caramel color that he wanted to lick.

And he needed to not think of that. Not right now.

"There's dessert."

He looked across at the table where all the food was, and saw his mother setting three giant cheesecakes covered with caramel down onto the tabletops.

Dammit all. Caramel. That was really what he wanted to think about right now. In context.

Everybody made a grateful noise and he gathered around the table along with all of them, getting his piece and returning with it to the assembly point.

"The wedding is in just three days," Juniper said, as if they needed reminding. "And we need to get everything up to the venue and get it all set up."

"I don't know why the hell you didn't just get married at the Carson ranch," Kit said.

Juniper gave him a scathing look. "I'm not letting you win like that."

"Getting to host the wedding would be winning?"

Chance held up a hand. "Believe me. I have had that conversation. Back out now. You won't win."

"Now that's what I like," Juniper said. "A Carson admitting when he's beaten."

"It's just a Carson admitting he knows how to choose his battles," Chance said, grunting.

"Well, it's no problem," Kit said. "There's no shortage of pickup trucks between us. We can carry whatever the hell you need up that way."

"I got a pickup truck too," Shelby said. "And I'm the maid of honor."

"I don't think we need all the pickup trucks we have between us," Juniper said.

His eyes met Shelby's again, and she looked away, faint color on her cheekbones. She felt it too. He knew she did. He'd always known that. What he didn't know was what story exactly she told herself.

It didn't matter. He might want Shelby, but there was no way in hell he would ever do anything to make her his. She was the marriage-and-family type. She'd been in love, and she lost that love. He didn't want to step into that. Not even a little.

"I'll tell you what," Kit said. "You just give orders, and I will follow them."

"Speak for yourself," Shelby said.

"Would you rather take orders from me?"

She looked away from him quickly, and he realized that he…stepped into something. Because she didn't fire anything right back at him, and he almost felt guilty about that.

And then she looked up at him, dark fire banked in her eyes. "I'd like to see you try that."

He held back his answer. He held it back because everybody was here. He held it back because he didn't know how to make it not explicitly sexual.

He held it back, because the last thing in all the world he needed to do at this wedding preparation party was declare his sexual intent with a woman he was inextricably linked to through his brother's relationship with her sister.

Especially when he knew that he couldn't have any intentions toward her at all.

Shelby was exhausted, carrying all the baskets of various things into her cabin.

Juniper was helping, basket after basket of different wedding favors coming in after the other.

"You know," Shelby said, "I'm trying not to be nosy, or in your business, but aren't you marrying a super-rich cowboy?"

Juniper laughed. "What's your point?"

"My point is, you had to make all of this. The guy could *buy it*. Why are we doing favors for every table, and ribbon curls?"

Juniper looked at her, confusion etched into her features. "You really don't know?"

"I mean, your pride, I assume."

She shook her head. "I don't have any of that with Chance. We're getting married. We have a partnership. We don't divide things up, and we certainly don't keep score on what's his and what's mine or any of that. It isn't that. It's just I wanted to do this because this is what we did for your wedding."

Shelby blinked. "Is it? I was just trying to remember. And I couldn't. I just remembered the wedding dress. Which, by the way, you should've talked me out of."

"I loved it."

"Well. You were also a teenage girl. Neither of us were trustworthy."

"Do you really not remember? We wrapped all those different terra-cotta pots that we found for cheap down at the dollar store in pretty paper, made paper ribbons, and you had those potted plants up all around in the wedding venue."

She frowned, her forehead creasing. "Yeah. I do remember that. It's weird. I just don't... I don't think about it much."

"I'm sorry. I didn't mean to bring up a painful memory."

"I've been thinking about Chuck all day." Truth be told, she thought about him most days. "It's unavoidable."

Juniper looked worried. "You didn't say anything about it."

"I don't want to make your wedding about my issues. It isn't about my issues. Your wedding is about you. And I'm so happy for you."

"You seem like you maybe aren't sometimes."

"It's not that. I think it's a little bit strange that you're marrying a Carson. All things considered. But I'm coming to terms of it."

"And it has nothing to do with Kit?"

She narrowed her eyes. "Don't push it." Juniper had never mentioned Kit, or Shelby's non-situation with Kit, until recently. Shelby didn't like the new development.

"Did something happen between you two?"

"No! When would anything have ever happened?"

"I don't know. I've never known. All I know is that when you see him..."

"Please don't finish that sentence, because my pride is hanging on by a thread, because I nearly fell down into the man tonight, and I don't need anything to compromise what remains of it. It is tenuous. At best."

"I don't think anyone else can tell," Juniper said

quickly. "It's just that I know you. I know you really well."

"And you know me well enough to know that if I don't want to talk about it I'm not going to talk about it."

Juniper nodded. "You're right. I do know you well enough to know that. Sorry."

"It's fine. Like I said. I'm a little bit surprised, both because of his family, and the circumstances…"

"Oh, the thing that I did that you absolutely disapproved of because it was really messed up?"

"Yeah. That thing. Where you lied to the guy about who you were? And who he was?"

"It worked out," Juniper said. She winced. "Believe me. I have apologized many times over. And I do feel bad about it. Though, forgetting who he was… And me treating him like he was somebody different… It was the only way that we could really get to know each other. I know it sounds imbalanced. But… It's just how it works."

Shelby couldn't help it. Right in that moment, she sort of wished that she could have that. A moment to be somebody new. Maybe she needed to leave town. She had never really considered it before.

Losing Chuck had been destabilizing in every way. Leaving Lone Rock, leaving their land…leaving her parents, her grandparents—that was something that she couldn't even fathom. But it was hard to be here. Hard to be in a place where everybody knew who you were, where everybody knew your life story. So they looked at you like you were sad even when you had never exchanged three words with them, because they already knew through the grapevine exactly what you'd been through.

"I can see how that would work," she said, her voice feeling scratchy.

"It did work," Juniper said. "So are you going to head up to the venue early?"

Shelby looked around at all the things. "I don't see how it will work if I don't. I need to get everything set up for the bachelorette party, and I need to get all the party favors up there for that. Plus the wedding."

"He has six brothers. He will absolutely handle whatever needs handling."

"I'm your only sister," she said, fiercely. "And it means more to me now than it ever has. Your... You and Mom and Dad and Grandma and Grandpa are all I have. I was supposed to make a family, an expanded family with Chuck. And I... I want to do everything for you. Just trust me."

Juniper looked at her, her dark eyes steady and level, and filled with compassion, and it put Shelby back to that night three years ago when Juniper had come over to tell her...

When Juniper'd had to be the one to tell her Chuck was in a car accident, and he hadn't made it.

Her sister was real. Genuine. When she said she wanted to be there for Shelby, it wasn't an empty gesture. She'd proved it that night. She hadn't passed the job off on someone else. She'd been the one to do it. She'd been the one to hold Shelby while she'd cried like she'd never stop.

"Oh, Shelby," Juniper said. "I'm so sorry that this is hard."

She loved that Juniper cared so much, but she really didn't want to take the focus off her either. This was her moment. Her love story.

Shelby was happy for her.

"I don't want this to be about me. I really don't. This is about you and your happiness. And I am thrilled for you. Yeah, weddings make me think about my own wedding. But don't think for one second that you're causing me any sadness. You couldn't. I live with the loss. Every day. He was part of my life for so long, and then just one day having him gone completely… It's awful. But it's different than it was right at first. And it isn't… I don't know how to explain this in a way that makes sense, but it isn't your wedding making me sad. It's making me think about my wedding. But that isn't thinking about him more than usual."

"Thanks. I love you."

"I love you too."

They hugged, and Juniper left. Left Shelby with all these baskets.

Yeah. She was going to have to get them up to the venue, but actually, maybe that would be a good thing. It would give her a little bit of time to herself. A little bit of time to reflect.

The thing that made her feel guilty, really guilty, was that sometimes she was just tired of grieving. Just tired of… Of living with loss. She wanted to be done with it. But that was hardly fair. Chuck couldn't really stop being dead.

She laughed. She needed to move his things out of their bedroom. His clothes. She had gotten some out when Juniper had borrowed them for Chance. She hadn't taken them back. Hadn't put them back in the closet when they'd been returned to her. It had felt like a baby step. An important one.

But this house that she lived in alone still had the

hallmarks of a home that was shared. And at some point she was going to have to change that.

There were other things that probably needed to change. She should make a crafting room out of that spare bedroom. Even though she didn't craft. She should make it a reading nook. Because it was never going to be what she had dreamed of it being. Even with Chuck, they hadn't been able to turn that spare room into a nursery.

There was no way that was going to change.

But letting go was just so hard. And sometimes… Shelby didn't understand why she had to be the one to let go of so many things.

But her sister was getting married. And they were going to have a bachelorette party. One of epic proportions.

If Juniper wanted to hearken back to Shelby's wedding… Well, Shelby owed her a little bit of revenge, actually.

She smiled.

Oh yes. The bachelorette party was going to be an epic night to remember.

Chapter 3

Kit, Jace, Flint and Boone were all down at the Thirsty Mule getting drinks. The ramshackle old saloon had been the heart of Lone Rock since the late 1800s. It had the original saloon doors still swinging between the entryway and the bar. It was rumored the hole up at the top had come from a bullet that had shot the piano player stone-cold dead back in 1899.

Kit had it on good authority that it was actually from a jackass who put a pool cue through it in 1980.

Jace's best friend, Cara, was serving beers gamely from behind the bar, and Kit would be remiss if he passed up the chance to make a sly comment about his brother's friend in his presence. "Cara is looking pretty good."

Jace didn't look at him. "I will kill you. With my bare hands. And I'll enjoy it."

Jace insisted he was only friends with Cara. Kit believed him, mostly. Jace was also very protective of Cara, so whatever the reason, Kit's commenting on Cara's beauty often caused chaos. And Kit lived for it.

He grinned. "Why don't you just marry her already?"

"What are you, eight?" Jace asked.

"No. I am not eight. If I were eight I would be suggesting you marry the beer because you love it."

"I hate you."

"Hey," said Flint. "We are here to discuss our brother's bachelor party."

"Right, right. I'm the best man," said Kit, "so this is primarily my responsibility."

"Strippers," said Boone.

"Hell no," said Jace.

"I'm sorry, why are you opposed to exotic dancers?" Kit asked.

"Since this is the kind of event people are going to hear about." He tilted his head toward Cara.

"Again," Kit said, "if you are so beholden to Cara and what she thinks, you might as well marry her."

Cara began to walk toward them then, her blond hair pulled back in a ponytail, a short, spiked leather jacket making the point of her general demeanor for her. "What's that, Kit?"

"I said," Kit responded, grinning, "if Jace is going to be whipped by you, he might as well marry you."

"I won't marry him," said Cara. "I can't be tamed."

"I'd be happy to tame you for a while," Kit said, which earned him a glowing smile from Cara. All in with the intent of pissing Jace off.

"I will kill you," said Jace.

"Jace," said Cara. "Please. If anyone is going to kill Kit it'll be me. Or Shelby Sohappy."

The mention of Shelby's name was like a firecracker going off in his gut. "She doesn't have it in her."

"Yes, she does," said Boone. "She would kill you with a smile on her face. And she's got enough land that they'd never find your body."

Boone was a terminal smart-ass. He and his best friend in the rodeo, Daniel, had a reputation for being hell-raisers. Though Daniel was married and had settled in theory, rumor had it he hadn't changed at all.

He often wondered what Boone thought about his friend's behavior. It was tough to tell what Boone thought about anything.

Too much of a smart-ass, that was the thing.

"Well, good thing she has no reason for wanting to kill me."

"That's not really what I've observed," said Cara.

"Ah, right. I forgot. The all-seeing, all-knowing bartender," Kit said.

"You guys have a thing."

"We do not have a thing," Kit said. "In fact, she once told me that we have no situation at all."

"You don't say that to someone you don't have a thing with," Cara said. "If there's no situation, there's no need to remark upon the situation."

Kit shrugged. The fact was, they did have a thing, and he knew it. That *thing* was chemistry. But Kit liked his chemistry with women the way he liked his chemistry classes. Over quickly. Handled. Done. Graduated from. He was a satisfy-them—multiple times—and leave-them type. He had done serious way early on in his life. He knew what it was like to have the burden of taking care of someone, and he never wanted it again. He had a huge family, and he loved them. All of them. Even Buck, who was gone. It was exhausting. He didn't need to love anyone else. Not ever.

"Whatever you say, Kit. But anyway, why are you assuming that Jace is beholden to me? He can do whatever he wants."

"He wants to hire strippers for the bachelor party."

Cara looked at him, her eyes like daggers. "I'll never speak to you again, Jace Carson."

"Just a second," said Kit, peering behind Cara at some of the jars at the back shelf of the bar.

"What are you doing?"

"Checking to see if you have Jace's balls back there."

Cara was unmoved. She planted her hands squarely on the bar and leaned toward him, staring.

"And what are you doing, Cara?" he asked.

"Checking to see if you got any human decency in there. Because Jace has it. He is almost a gentleman."

Boone laughed so hard he nearly fell off the bar stool. "Jace Carson. A gentleman. That's because you only see him here in Lone Rock. And you never see him on the road. You've only seen a piece of him, sweetheart."

"Call me sweetheart one more time and you can find out whether or not the spikes on this jacket are a decoration or for practical purposes."

"That's my girl," said Jace.

She walked away from them, and Kit was just mad that she had managed to redirect his thoughts right back to Shelby.

Right. Like they were ever all that far from her to begin with.

That was the problem with Shelby. She was under

his skin, and he couldn't even really say why. Just sex. That was the thing. He wanted her, and he had never been able to have her. Maybe he wanted her in part because she was so... So decidedly off-limits. Actually, it should be a little bit more resolvable these days. She was single, and the barrier had been broken between their families. Juniper and Chance were already getting married. There was nothing forbidden about an association between the two of them at all. That should make her less interesting. That should make him entirely less aroused by the thought of grabbing her and pulling her up against his body, lowering his head and tasting whether or not her lips were sugary, salty caramel like he imagined...

Dammit.

"So, what is the bachelor party plan, then?" Boone asked.

"Well, because I don't want our mother to kill us, I was never planning on hiring any strippers. However, I was thinking skeet shooting, some drinking. Darts. Pool. There's kind of a bachelor pad house up there, all outfitted for this kind of thing. And, we need to have a camping trip."

"A camping trip?" Boone questioned.

"Yeah. Like we did when we were kids."

They didn't talk about why. It was just one of those things. But the boys had gotten sent out of the house quite a bit when their sister Sophie had been sick and recovering from different treatments. Having the campout in the backyard was a way to get the house quiet for her.

It wasn't a bad memory. Not really. But that time would always be bittersweet.

It was something that they shared. All of them.

"All right."

"Yeah, I figured it would be good. Hell, we didn't get to send Callie out into the world with any warning. She just went and eloped."

"Yeah. With Jake Daniels. Of all the things."

"She seemed happy enough."

She was taken care of. And that was a big load off Kit's mind. When she had first come back to the ranch with him, Kit had been… Not very happy. He knew Jake from the rodeo circuit, and as far as he was concerned, Jake was a bad bet. He had been the kind of guy who was… Well, he was like all of them. He was a ho. A shameless, uninhibited man ho. And, the idea of him marrying Kit's sister had gone down like a lead balloon. But he had proved to Kit that he loved Callie. And more than that, he had proved that he was committed to Callie's safety. And that mattered. It mattered a whole hell of a lot. Because he had spent all of Callie's childhood worrying about her safety, and then she had gone and gotten the rodeo bug. And she couldn't do something sane like riding barrel horses. No. His sister had gone and gotten the bug to ride saddle bronc. And she had been insistent about it. Their dad had done basically everything in his power to block her from doing it, but she had gotten around that by marrying Jake and getting access to her trust fund.

But, the thing was, she was great at it.

She was great at riding saddle bronc. And she really brought something fresh and new to the event. She had invigorated rodeo-goers. And he had to be proud of her. From a feminist perspective even. But as an older brother, not so much. And there were just two different kinds of things that existed inside him. He was all for equality. But a lot less so when it came to the health and safety of his little sister. Let somebody else blaze trails. Blazing trails was dangerous, and he had a hard time admitting that it was all right for Callie to be out there doing it.

But Jake cared about her safety so much that it gave Kit some room to breathe.

"I'm planning to go up to the wedding ranch and check things out tomorrow," Kit said. "Get some supplies delivered, get the house opened up and set to go."

"I've got a date," said Boone. "So, I won't be up till a little later."

"You have a date," Kit said. "With who?"

"You know, I don't remember her name. But, she's one of the rodeo queens. She's coming through town, and I'm not gonna miss it."

"Great. Enjoy your booty call."

"I promised Cara I'd help her with a few things. But I'll be there the day before the wedding."

"You better the hell be. That's when the party's happening."

"Great. Well. We'll see you out there in a couple of days," said Flint.

"Yeah. Assholes. See you in a couple of days."

Shelby had somehow managed to get all the baskets of favors into the back of her truck, and all of the favors for the bachelorette party into the back seat. She was feeling pretty good about everything. She had some great favors for the bachelorette party, and she had been mean.

Because Juniper had been mean to her.

The problem with having your equally young and

immature sister plan your bachelorette party when you were getting married at eighteen was that *everything* was immature.

Penis everything.

And so, Shelby had retaliated. Meanly. And with grown-ass adult money and the full power of the internet, that meant she'd been able to take what Juniper had accomplished and turn it up to the tenth power.

And she didn't care if her sister liked it or not.

Now, there would be real decorations too, but she'd had to get penis straws, a penis crown and, best of all, a very large vibrator to be the centerpiece of some flowers. She figured that Juniper and Chance might appreciate the gift.

They could take it on their honeymoon.

For just a moment, that stopped her short. She really didn't want to think about her sister hooking up and having sex. But the subject of honeymoons, and the thought of the vibrator, brought it all close to mind.

You don't need the guy. Just the vibrator.

And she had her own, thank you very much. She had invested in a pretty decent collection of them during this stretch of single time.

Eventually… Eventually there would have to be a guy. Wouldn't there? Eventually there would have to be one just so she didn't go crazy.

Except, she couldn't imagine it. Couldn't imagine being with anybody except for…

Unbidden, an image of Kit popped into her mind. No. She had spent way too many years being disciplined about him. She had never fantasized about him, no matter how it had hovered around the edges of her consciousness. Not while she was with Chuck, and not since. She was not going to undo all that good moral fiber in a moment of weird weakness.

So she shut that out of her mind. She was fine. And she wasn't envious. If she wanted to hook up, she could go hook up. It wasn't even flattering. Men were disgusting. They would literally hump a tree if given half the chance. It wasn't like she wouldn't be able to find somebody. There was nothing wrong with her.

She stood there in the driveway of the farmhouse where they would be having their girls' night. And she felt like that thought fell a little bit flat. It wasn't like there was anything wrong with her.

There was something sad in her.

Something a little bit dampened.

Broken.

Something that wondered if it would ever feel *alive* again.

Yeah, the thing about grief was, it changed. It didn't go away.

But there was a hole in your life where someone had once been, and the passage of time didn't make it stop being there. It didn't make that person not gone. For a while there, the grief had gotten worse.

Because it had been even longer since she'd seen Chuck. As silly as that sounded. For a few months it had been like… Maybe he was on a trip. Maybe he would come back. But at six months… She remembered very distinctly realizing she had not been away from Chuck for that long ever. Not since she had met him. It wasn't a vacation amount of time. It was significant. And it left her feeling raw and hollow.

That had gone away. That part of it. There were all those firsts she had to get through.

And there is a first you haven't gotten through yet.

She just didn't want to. Not yet.

She had kind of underestimated how her sister's being in a relationship would bring a bunch of stuff up to the surface for her, and she didn't want it to poison this experience. She wanted her sister to have this. Wanted her sister to have a good time. Wanted it to be all about her. Wanted it to be special.

She did not want it to be about her pain. She just... She couldn't bear her own pain. She was sick of herself.

So she focused on her immaturity, her amusement at it all. And started taking trips from the house to the car.

The ranch was beautiful, set high atop a mountain overlooking the valley below. It had a gorgeous little farmhouse, a huge barn where they held all of the events, very rustic, and different from the one on Carson land, which was a bit too slick, according to Juniper.

There was another house spaced out in a different part of the property that Juniper had mentioned the men would be staying in.

The men.

Well, they weren't here right now. Shelby was by herself.

As if that's remarkably different from every other day?

No. She supposed it wasn't. But at least she wasn't alone in her house. It was a different kind of alone. It almost felt like a vacation.

She saved the load of penises for last. And she did laugh, when she pulled the big laundry basket that contained all those party favors out, and began to cart them toward the house.

"Well, fancy meeting you here."

She turned around, her eyes wide, and jostled the basket, one phallic straw springing out and down to the ground below.

Great.

Her basket of cocks overfloweth. In front of Kit.

"What are you doing here, Kit?"

"Same thing as you, I imagine." And then, he seemed to realize what was in the basket she was holding. "Well, no. Not the same thing as you."

"Did you not have a basket of dick paraphernalia for the bachelor party?"

"Suddenly I feel remiss," he said.

She was doing her level best to cling to what little dignity she had and it was tough. It was real tough.

"It's not too late," she said.

"Do you have an extra?"

"Do I have an extra… Penis?"

A smile spread, slow and dirty over his face, and she wanted to… Punch him. She really wanted to punch him. "I just have the one, that's all."

She felt like she was going to choke. On horror, heat, arousal, or maybe all three. "Wow. Well, this has been delightful. How long are you up here for?"

"Until the wedding."

"You're not serious," she said.

"I am serious. I'm here to the wedding because there are some things to set up."

"No," she said. "No, because… I'm here until the wedding."

"Is that a problem?"

"No," she said.

"Good."

"Like I told you. We don't have…"

"We don't have a situation," he said, his eyes giving off way too much heat.

"Not even a little one. Not at all."

"Good to know. I'm glad. Because I want the wedding to be perfect. And I would hate for anything to interfere."

"Nothing will interfere."

"Good. In fact, we could probably be of some use to each other. What do you think?"

She blinked. And really, she had no reason to refuse him. If there were things that could be done, things that they could do collaboratively… It actually just made sense. Because the truth of the matter was, nothing had ever happened between them. Nothing beyond a few warmish exchanges that had left her feeling flustered. And that was all her. Kit was Kit, which meant that he was a flirt, because he didn't know another way to be. It was simply how he was, and that was the way of it. She knew that. There was no reason to go getting heated up.

So yeah. Why not. But not now. Because right now was awkward.

"Well. I'm just going to… Take my basket of penises and go."

"Okay."

"Maybe I'll have a bath."

"Okay."

And suddenly she felt overly hot, because it was like her mouth was just saying things, and she didn't have any control over it.

"I'm out of practice," she said. "With the talking to people. That I'm not related to. Sorry."

He nodded slowly, and right then, his expression did something sort of genuine. "I'm sorry," he said. "I'm sorry about your husband."

That he linked her lack of social skills with her loss was…weirdly touching. His awareness of it, of her as a person, was sort of unexpected. She didn't know what to do with it.

"Thank you."

She swallowed hard, and went into the house, and just as she did, she remembered what Juniper had told her about their family. That they'd had a sister. And she died when they were kids.

That was why he looked at her like that. That was why he said it with that kind of gravity. It was why he knew *I'm sorry* was enough. Because there were no platitudes that made it okay. There was no grand speech to give that was going to magically make it all less painful. It just… Was. It was lost. The loss was lost. You couldn't fix it. Couldn't go back. Couldn't change it. Couldn't hold on to him for five more minutes before he walked out the door to change the timing so that when the other pickup truck crossed the yellow line his car wasn't there. No. She couldn't go back. She couldn't fix it. She wasn't prescient. She hadn't been able to prevent it. She hadn't even had a bad feeling about the day.

No. She'd been over it a hundred times. Magical thinking didn't have any kind of place in the grief sphere.

And the way he'd said that. All practical. He knew. He knew. And she really appreciated that.

Who would've thought that she would appreciate an

encounter with Kit. Well. And who would've thought that she would be standing in front of him with a basket full of phalli. But, it was that kind of day. It was just that kind of day.

And she really was going to take a long hot bath and put all of it out of her mind.

Chapter 4

The bachelor house was a big log cabin filled with animal heads and cowhide everywhere. He loved it. This was the kind of place where he would like to settle down. They all had cabins on their parents' property, and there really was no reason to buy up, especially when he was still traveling with the rodeo during the season. But the places at his parents' house were slick. They weren't this country. And he really liked things being this country.

He paused at the doorway and looked across the expanse of fields. It was dark now. But he could see a light on in the window of the farmhouse just across the way.

Shelby Sohappy.

They were on the same mountain. And there was nobody else around. That really was something. And he needed to stop thinking of her that way. It was difficult, considering she had been standing there with a whole barrel of sex toys.

He did not need to think about Shelby and sex toys. Not in the same sentence. Not in the same… Oh, the same fantasy. And it was getting there. It was getting there quick.

This was the problem with small towns. It was like they'd been engaging in foreplay for years on end. But he really was sorry about her husband. He tried to focus on that. He had liked Shelby's husband. He'd been a nice guy. He used to run into him out on occasion. He'd sometimes even sit with the Carsons and have a beer. He had just always told them never to tell his wife, considering the family had such a rivalry. But, being outside of the family, he hadn't internalized it to the degree that Shelby and Juniper did.

Yeah. He had been an easygoing guy. Short and stocky with dark hair and an easy smile. It really was a shame. A tragedy.

Too bad Kit had always wanted the guy's wife.

Didn't make it not a tragedy in the abstract, though.

It was one of the things that Kit would never understand about the world. The way that the good seemed to die young and terribly. And leave voids in the world that nobody could ever fix.

It was why he preferred to have as few connections as possible.

Well, *preferred* wasn't even a strong enough word. He lived his life by that code. By that creed. He hadn't fully appreciated the connections that would end up being built, though, when his siblings started to get married. He just had so many damn siblings. Callie had gotten married, and Jake Daniels had been brought into the fold. If they ever had kids, there would be nieces and nephews. And then there was Chance and Juniper. And the same went for them.

Babies.

Babies freaked him out.

They were so soft and vulnerable. When Callie had been little, he didn't think he'd ever gotten a wink of sleep. That was the problem with being a kid who'd watched his sister die.

You didn't trust anything. That was just it. He didn't trust anything, so it was better to just not love much.

He hadn't had any choice when it came to his family. They were big and boisterous. And he loved them with everything he had.

But he didn't have to add more people to the list.

While he was looking out across the way, the lights turned off. And he would've thought nothing of it, except there were lights on on multiple floors and in multiple windows, and they all went out simultaneously. So unless there was some kind of smart-switch situation happening—and out here he seriously doubted it—he had reason to feel a little bit concerned.

He hustled out the front door without thinking, and jogged across the field, heading toward the farmhouse. And just as he was about to knock on the door, it opened up.

"Oh," she said.

"Hey," he said. "What happened?"

"The lights went out," she said, her cheeks illuminated.

"Oh. Well. I can come in and take a look if you like. I got a flashlight out in the truck."

"Thanks, I…"

"Alternatively, you could come stay in the bachelor pad."

"Oh," she said. "No."

She didn't like this. His pushing her. But she needed help, and he didn't see why he shouldn't offer it. He didn't see why there needed to be such a big wall built between the two of them. Not now anyway.

"There's like ten rooms in there. And they're all vacant. And then, in the morning, we can sort out whatever the hell happened here. Seems better than stumbling around in the dark."

"Yeah, I guess so."

"Go get your suitcase."

"It's just an overnight bag."

She disappeared, then came back a moment later. She looked… She looked afraid. At least, as far as he could tell with only her cell phone flashlight lit up.

"You don't *have* to come with me. I can try to figure out why the lights went out here."

"No," she said. "No. You don't have to do that. It's fine. Let's just go. I'm starving. And with the lights out I can't cook any food and…"

"Do you have stuff in the fridge?" he asked.

"I have it in a cooler."

"I brought some steak. And I do have power. So I'm happy to grill for us both."

"I don't want to eat your steak," she said, wrinkling her nose.

"Hey. You offered to lend me a penis. So… I feel like it's a fair trade."

She choked, and tried to cover it with a cough. "Well, I didn't bring any of them with me."

"I'll take a rain check."

"That's very reasonable of you," she said, still wheezing.

"I'm very reasonable."

He reached out and took the overnight bag from her hands. But this time, he was careful not to touch her. When he had tried to help with the beer, he had touched her. And it had set off a whole thing.

He didn't need to go setting off whole things. Not again.

So they walked across the field together in relative silence, toward the bachelor pad.

And when they walked up the front porch and inside, she made a scoffing noise. "Well. I can see why they were putting you all up in here."

"Yeah. Who was all staying in your place?"

"Your sister. My mother. A couple of friends from high school. But this is going to be…"

"Oh yeah. There's a lot of us. And it's a lot of testosterone."

"Sounds great."

"I don't really think you mean that."

"Well, since you're offering to cook me steak, I'm actually not going to push you."

She hung back, though in the doorway, as he went inside.

He went into the kitchen, and got the steaks out of the fridge. They were sitting in a marinade, because he wasn't an animal. The thing about being a bachelor was if you were committed to that kind of lifestyle, then you needed to learn how to take care of yourself. And Kit liked good food.

He didn't see the point in living like a trash animal just because in many ways he philosophically was one.

"I'm grilling anyway," he said. "I had it preheating outside."

"Wow. I feel kind of honored."

A strange, haunted look crossed over her face. He had a feeling she was thinking about another time. Another man.

And that is why you don't want to get involved.

"Yeah. You like… Grilling?"

"Obviously I don't," she said.

Dammit. He had been trying to ask an innocuous question, and he'd gone and stepped right into it.

"Yeah. No. I mean…"

"Yes. My husband used to grill."

He was still here, that guy, even though he wasn't here. Kit knew how that worked. He felt bad that he'd missed a connection here, with her. That he hadn't been more careful.

"Right. Sorry."

"You don't have to say *sorry*. It's… I mean, it's not as painful now. I just think about it all the time. You know, because you realize how absurd it is you can't turn and say something to someone who used to always be there. But they'll never be there again. It's ridiculous. So how can you… Not think about it?"

"Yeah. I know."

She nodded gravely. And he had a feeling she really did know that he knew. So that was good. He didn't have to explain it. He was not looking to have a heart-to-heart with her. Nothing that was personal. He wasn't looking to have a heart-to-heart with anybody.

"Grill's back here," he said, pushing open the double doors that led out to the grand outdoor kitchen area. It was a lot spiffier out there than it was inside.

"Wow," she said, looking up. It made him look up too. The stars above were a brilliant blanket of diamonds, and he really figured he didn't take enough time to appreciate that sort of thing. But he just didn't think much about it. Miracles and wonders and all that kind of stuff had been rendered pretty moot for him back when Sophie had died.

He had hoped.

That was the thing. Because he thought that the good guy won. And there was nobody better than his beautiful, tough little sister. And then it was like the safety net in everything had been pulled away. It hadn't made them afraid. Because Sophie hadn't done anything risky to get sick. He'd figured if death was out there… Well, then it would come for you when it felt like it. That was actually worse than becoming a shut-in or an agoraphobe. Just believing that no matter what, it might get you. So you might as well do whatever. He'd been hell on his parents during his teenage years.

And it had been hell on his soul.

Because it just… Everything felt tenuous. All the time.

But the stars were still there. He wasn't sure how many years it had been since he'd thought to look up at them before Shelby had just prompted him to.

It was a hell of a thing.

"I can see why they chose to get married up here. There's so little light pollution. I mean, I'm about to pollute it all with my flame in my grilling. But you know."

"The cost of progress," she said.

"True."

He put the steak on the hot grill, and watched as the flame rose up.

"Is there a salad or anything?"

"Of course. And baked potatoes. I did them before I came up. I'm not an animal."

"Well, that's kind of a revelation."

"There's one baked potato. We're going to have to split it."

"You brought up two steaks?"

"I don't take chances with steak," he said.

"Fair enough."

Silence lapsed between them. "This is very nice of you."

"Well," he said, shrugging as he looked down at the grill, "we are about to be family and all that."

"Not really. I mean *we're* not. It's not really like that."

"I guess not. But functionally it kinda feels that way."

She turned a small circle, then separated from him and went and sat down on the couch nearby. Her hands clasped in her lap.

"So," he said. "What is it you do exactly?"

She laughed. "What is it that I do?"

"Yeah. Your sister's an EMT, and you…"

"I make jewelry. I bead things. I sell a lot of it online. But… Yeah. You know. Things like that."

"Really?"

"Yeah. Do you not frequent the farmers markets around here?"

"No."

"Well. I'm very good. But mostly, I'm lucky to have family land, which I also work."

"Yeah. That is nice. I also benefit from that."

"And you're still riding…bulls?"

"I am indeed. Still riding bulls, and traveling around when I can."

"How long does a person do that? The bull riding thing."

He shrugged. "As long as your body can take it. Though, I admit it's not as easy as it used to be."

"What makes a person want to do that?" She was looking at him, something bright and mysterious burning in her eyes just then.

"Family business."

"And that's it? You do it because you saw the people before you do it?"

She looked a little bit disturbed by that fact. "Aren't we all doing that to some degree or another? I mean, it's easiest to take a path that you've seen forged, isn't it?"

"Maybe," she said.

"Why?"

"I don't know. I was feeling like maybe I'm not all that adventurous. But… You make bull riding sound the same as deciding to get married and have kids just because your parents did it."

"In a lot of ways, it's the same. You do this thing that seems like a legacy, I guess." But he felt a strange pang in his chest, and he didn't want to think too deeply about why.

"Except, you haven't done that part."

"No interest in it. So yeah, I guess it's not exactly the same. I knew how to get into the rodeo because it's the family business. But I don't have a whole lot of interest in the domesticity part. I have enough of it with the family I have."

"Makes sense."

"And you?"

"I think it's obvious what I wanted with my life, isn't it? I got married when I was eighteen. You don't do that if you don't want... That same thing. That thing your parents had. You don't do that if family isn't your dream. But I don't have it anymore. So... I guess maybe that's why I asked. How long you're going to do the bull riding. And when it ends, then what?"

"I don't know. And I'm not really sure I get how it connects."

"Because I'm living in this...*and then what* space. The first thing I wanted is gone. So what do I do now? And I don't know the answer."

He didn't know why she'd chosen to ask him that. Maybe because they were relative strangers. Maybe because he was something entirely different to her, and to her family. Maybe just because the steak was good, or because the stars were bright.

Maybe to scare him off, because she felt the same heat burning between them that he did.

Whatever the reason, he found himself wanting to give her an answer. And he didn't have one. He wasn't deep. Not by any metric. But he wished that he had something to offer her.

"Maybe that's the secret," he said. "Maybe nobody knows what to do with that second choice. Because the fact of the matter is, we all end up living with the less-ideal scenario at some point. Whether it's work or family or... We all have to face it at some point. And maybe you never quite know what to do with that part of your life as clearly as you knew what to do with the first part."

That cut close to his bone. But it had nothing to do with bull riding.

"Eventually everybody loses someone. And the older we get the more someones we lose. And you're always living in that and after. Always." He shrugged. "It takes away little pieces of the life that you knew. Of the things that you imagined. And the more of those pieces you lose, the more you have to rebuild. I'm not sure that the answers ever get clearer or easier to see."

"So what then?"

He looked at her then, and he noticed a necklace around her neck. Made with fine little beads. "Did you make that?"

"Yes."

He did something he knew he might regret, and took a step toward her, reaching out and touching the center of the necklace. "And how do you make something like this?"

"With a thread, a needle and these little seed beads and…"

"Right. But do you throw them all on all at once and see the big picture?"

"No. You go one bead at a time. But you have some idea about where you're headed."

"Right. But maybe in life sometimes we just have the one bead. We don't know how it fits into the bigger picture. So we just have to keep going. One bead at a time. One step at a time."

"I didn't realize that you were a philosopher," she said, her breath quickening as she looked up at him.

"Neither did I. But you suddenly made me want to try it out."

She cleared her throat and turned away. "Don't overcook the steak. I like it medium."

He cursed and went over to the grill, poking one of the steaks with a fork and slicing it so that he could get a look at the color inside.

"Not overdone."

He stuck the meat on plates, and they went back in the house, where he added the baked potato and salad. "Want to eat outside?"

She nodded.

They went back outside and sat opposite each other on the patio furniture, the plates in their laps.

"I guess my worry is that maybe it's not making a picture. I haven't done much of anything for the last few years. Maybe I haven't added a bead at all. You know. So to speak."

"Well, grief is like that. And that's different. You need to give yourself time."

"Right."

"You know about my sister."

"Yes. I do. I'm sorry about that. It's hard. I can't imagine what it must be like when it's a child."

"Loss is loss. You don't need to go ranking it. But yeah. I… She wasn't well for a long time. And I took care of her. We all did but… I just wanted to make her comfortable. And sometimes that was impossible. But it obsessed me. Distracting her, trying to do things to make her happy… And when I lost that, I didn't really know what to do. For me, that looked like a lot of years of bordering on juvenile delinquency. But eventually I figured that wasn't a very good tribute to Sophie. And that was when I got serious about the rodeo. And it just gave me something to do that was… That was something. I'm not going to say I made anything for the greater good, but it brought me closer to my family again. Because that's what we do. So it seemed like a worthy enough pursuit.

I guess bull riding is my 'and then.' There will be another one too. Because I can't do it forever."

"How many new lives are we supposed to live?"

"As many as we need to, I guess."

"I guess."

They ate in relative silence after that. He couldn't remember the last time he had a conversation that was so… It brushed up against all the difficult things he preferred not to think about. And yet, he wanted to talk to her because she was asking him those questions. Because it didn't come from a place of gawking at pain, but of sharing it. Because she knew what loss was, and… And that was the thing. If he could make the loss of his sister mean something, he was always willing to take that opportunity.

If it could be used to help her, well, that seemed like a decent enough tribute. At least, the best he had.

When they finished up, they carried their plates inside and put them in the sink. It wasn't all that late, but Shelby picked up her bag and began to sidle out of the room. "So just… Any of the rooms upstairs that don't already have your stuff in them?"

"Yep. I took the first one, because I'm lazy. So any of the others…"

"Great." She walked slowly up the stairs. "Thank you. For giving me a place to stay."

"Thank you for… Eating dinner with me."

"Yeah. See you tomorrow."

"See you tomorrow."

And then she disappeared down the hall, and he couldn't help but feel that he had let an opportunity slip by. But he couldn't quite say exactly what it was.

Chapter 5

When she woke up the next morning, she was breathing hard. Because the lingering effects of the dream that she'd had last night were still making themselves known in her body. She was tingling. All over. Because there had been a moment downstairs right before she had gone up to her room when she had imagined what it would be like if she crossed the space and kissed Kit Carson. She didn't let herself have those thoughts. She'd had them, yes, but she considered them to be intrusive thoughts. In the minute she was aware of them, she shut them down. But he was under her defenses, and he had been nice to talk to, which was maybe the most surprising thing. And that had opened up this floodgate. And her dream had been about a whole lot more than kissing. Her dream had been about scorching, hot, naked…

No. No. She wasn't doing that. She wasn't indulging

it. Because she was going to have to go downstairs and head back over to the farmhouse, and she was probably going to see him. And she really didn't want to. She really did not want to have all this in her head when she did see him. That was going to make things impossible, and awful, and she really wanted to avoid impossible and awful.

So she got up, and got dressed, and shoved all of that out of her mind.

As she looked in the mirror, clipping a beaded barrette into her hair, she just stopped for a moment and stared at herself. Why had she shared all of those things with him?

It was being out of her house. Out of her empty house, and realizing that she hadn't done that in far too long. That her life was divided so firmly into this before and after that she had lost a lot of different pieces of herself. She didn't go out with her friends anymore. She'd done that when she was married. Had gone out sometimes with the girls, had dinner, had drinks. She had gone on weekends to vacation houses, and hung out and talked and laughed and ate food. She'd gone on dates with Chuck, and even though she wasn't… Even though she didn't have him, and even though she didn't really want to date, it just represented another thing that she had lost along with him. Because she had stripped herself down almost so she could focus on what she didn't have. Almost so she could hold the loss keenly against her chest and simply cling to it. Because who was she without it.

She hadn't known who she was without Chuck, and somehow that had morphed into her life being about the lack of him. And sitting in this completely different environment with Kit Carson, of all people, had spurred those questions. Maybe because she did know he knew about loss. And he'd been so surprisingly giving with what he'd said.

Well, don't go romanticizing it.

You think he's hot. You think he's hot, and that is a little bit dangerous.

She hoped that she would listen to her own scolding.

She shoved her pajamas into the duffel bag and went downstairs. And she didn't get a chance to breathe, didn't get a reprieve at all, because there was Kit, standing by the coffee maker, a mug in his hand.

"Good morning, sunshine."

"Good morning to you too."

"Busy day of wedding prep ahead," he said. "Though I figure we ought to check and see what's up with the power at your place."

"Yes. That would be good."

"Probably the fuse box."

"I wouldn't know where to find it or what to do." She felt slightly embarrassed by that.

"I was married for a long time. My husband did all of that. And now my dad does it because he feels sorry for me and I lean into that."

He laughed. "I have to say, I kind of respect that."

"If you have to go through something terrible you might as well take all the help that comes your way."

And she had shrunk her life so fiercely, down to just her family, down to that house, that it seemed fair enough to take all the sympathy that her parents were willing to dole out.

The field was bright green in the daylight, the sun illuminating each blade of grass, fiery-gold-tipped green all around them. There were purple flowers scattered throughout, and she wondered why it suddenly felt like she was waking up along with the world.

Like she hadn't really breathed or seen these things around her in the years since...

She looked over at Kit. And he was just as striking as all the natural beauty around them. He was wearing a black cowboy hat, a black T-shirt. It outlined his broad shoulders, his muscular chest and slim waist. He was tall. She was tiny next to him. Chuck had only been a couple of inches taller than her.

Kit Carson had always seemed like an entirely different species to her. The kind of man who could just as easily be on the silver screen, he was so much larger than life. He was not the kind of guy you could say vows to, live a life with in a modest home. Dream of warmth and comfort and children with.

He was a mountain. And she was not a mountain climber by nature.

But then, that was the before Shelby, she supposed. She had never needed to climb a mountain.

Why are you thinking about mountain climbing? It sounds sexual.

Yeah. It did. But there was a part of her that was still humming with feelings that were decidedly sexual. So why not?

They didn't speak as they crossed the field. And the only sound when they approached the house was their shoes on the porch steps.

It was a stark contrast to the bachelor den the guys were staying in. It was white and delicate, with a wraparound porch and lace curtains.

The kitchen was all done up in a cheerful yellow,

and it made Shelby imagine what it would be like if she lived in a different house. If her view changed. Or her life changed.

There was nothing holding her here. Not really. There was nothing holding her in place except herself. She could just start over. She could do whatever she wanted. She was still living like Chuck was in her life, but without any of the benefits. She had taken everything but grief from herself.

And it was just so… Starkly clear when she began to imagine what life might look like. She tried to take a breath, but it was hard. Her lungs felt too small. Or maybe it was her that was too small.

Her life.

And Kit Carson was large in the feminine space, and he seemed to fill up everything. Everything around her. Everything she was.

"I'm going to check the mudroom for the fuse box." He slid past her in the kitchen, and her breath caught when his warmth and scent tangled around her.

She didn't take a full breath again until he was out of the room. And then suddenly, all the lights came on. "There," he said, coming in. "That was easy. Just had to find the one that was tripped."

"You probably could've done that last night," she said.

"Yeah. I could have. But then you wouldn't have been able to have steak with me."

She felt herself smiling, felt her cheeks getting warm. Was he flirting with her? She wouldn't even know what to do with that. She never flirted. Not in her life.

Guilt hooked around her insides.

Because he was a forbidden object. She had made him a forbidden object all those years.

It was why she was so antagonistic to him usually.

Because what was wrong with her? She had the most wonderful man. He was everything. He gave her everything.

But Kit had always felt like sex and danger, and she hadn't trusted him.

Hadn't trusted him to care that she was married if they encountered each other in a bar.

And her deepest fear, her deepest unspoken fear, was that if he had ever drawn near to her... She would forget what mattered. She would forget that she had everything with the man at home. And throw it all out for this one burning, bright thing.

You wouldn't, though. Because you didn't. You never did. You never let him get close enough, it never happened. And it still hasn't. Not even after Chuck died.

So there. Her resistance of him, even now, was evidence of her purity. Of the fact that she wouldn't have done it. And it made her feel exponential relief. So there was that.

He might not be forbidden anymore, but her ability to resist him proved something. Something that mattered to her. Something valuable.

"I was going to go over to the barn today and start getting the favors in place and things like that." She looked down the hall toward where she had stashed all the baskets of things.

"I'm happy to help with that," he said.

"You don't have to."

"Yeah. I know. But you know what they say, many hands make light work and all of that."

And she really might as well say yes. Because truth be told, she enjoyed his company, and all of her issues that were swirling around inside her were her issues. So that was that. She didn't need to treat him like he was an enemy. Like she was afraid of him.

In fact... Why not be around him? Why not... Keep testing it?

"Great. I figured I would save some of the bachelorette party stuff, in part because I don't really want to live amongst the decorations."

"What?" he asked. "It's not your chosen decor motif?"

"I cannot say that it is. But, my house is more functional than decorative."

"I think I have the same straws at home."

"I don't think you do," she said.

He walked past her and into the hall, where some of the laundry baskets filled with favors were stacked. "Shall we carry these out to the truck?"

"I really should've left them. Instead of unloading them in the house."

"No big deal."

He grabbed them, in one stack, and stuck them in the bed of the pickup truck. Then they got inside the truck, and she felt a little bit less confident than she had before. In her decision-making.

Because suddenly being in such a tight space with him made her feel... Warm. And made her feel very tingly between her legs.

This was dangerous. He was dangerous.

She swallowed hard.

"Let's go."

She was trying to untangle her own motivations.

What if she wanted to test herself and see if she was pure? Or did she want to fail the test?

None of it sat comfortably with her.

She felt scratchy.

Very, very scratchy.

She wasn't used to having to figure out her motivations. She was just used to existing. Get up, help her parents with chores around the ranch, work on her beading for a few hours, watch TV. Eat sometimes in between those things. Visit with Juniper maybe. Her life was simple. This wasn't simple. And she didn't know what to do with this more complicated calculation of behavior.

It was a short drive to the barn, and when they got there, they pushed the doors open and found it set for the ceremony. There were chairs, and in the back part of the barn there were tables for dinner.

"Wow. I really didn't think Juniper would ever get married. She was more of a love-them-and-leave-them kind of girl."

"Chance wasn't any different."

"I guess it makes sense that they'd end up together, then. Similar mindsets. And neither of them prepared for it."

He chuckled. "I suppose so."

She and Kit were different. Shelby was a lifer. That was the problem. She had wanted to be committed to one person forever. It was her ideal. It was what sounded like life.

She didn't want to go to bars and hook up. Didn't want to get to know anyone. The idea of having to fall in love all over again was... It actually just sounded exhausting. She had married a man who had known her since she was a child. He understood her. Melding their lives together had been easy. And now she was firmly set in her ways, and... The very idea of trying to figure out how to shape her life around somebody new made her want to lie down.

So maybe she wasn't a lifer anymore. She didn't want to date particularly, for all the afore considered reasons, but... She didn't really want love again either. She couldn't even imagine it.

"I'm glad they found each other. Either way. Expected or not," she said. "It's a... It's a good thing for them."

"Yeah," Kit agreed.

She cleared her throat and started to get all the little tulle-wrapped bubble bottles out of the laundry baskets. With their glorious ribbon curls trailing from them.

"There's supposed to be one for each seat at the table," she said. "Because everybody is supposed to blow bubbles when they walk through to go cut the cake."

"That seems very fluffy for Juniper."

"Yes. But apparently the wedding has made her fluffy. At least, she's fluffy in regard to the decorations. I don't think she would appreciate being called fluffy in general."

"No, of course not."

They got them positioned on the table, and then she looked down the aisle. "There should be everything to put the canopy together in the back of the truck."

"A canopy?"

"Yes. She's going to walk under a canopy to go down the aisle. We made a frame for it and got some tulle to wrap around it. I know how it's supposed to go together. She didn't say that we needed to get it set up, but I think we could."

"Sounds like a lot of work."

"Well. My sister is being high-maintenance, and I guess she's entitled to it. She was the bridesmaid at my wedding, and it was pretty damned high-maintenance."

"So this is payback?"

"I believe it is payback in part, yes."

They went out to the truck, and she found the metal poles in the bed, and then she took the carefully wrapped tulle out as well, and with Kit's help they took it into the barn. She directed him, telling him where to lay the poles out in the aisle, because she had seen Juniper's sketches of it all.

She had done some beading on the tulle, just to add some sparkle. To add a little bit of them.

She had done the same for Juniper's veil.

"Is there something to anchor these?"

"Oh, right. I forgot. There's a couple of cement forms in the bed of the truck."

"I will get them."

He left, and returned a few moments later, with big cement bricks in his hands. The poles were meant to sit down inside them, and they held them in place. They were really heavy, and he made lifting them look like it was a breeze.

And she couldn't help but watch. The play of his muscles. His forearms, his biceps. She watched as he made every trip, and she just stood and kind of stared. Openly.

He was… He was glorious. Kit Carson was the most beautiful man she had ever seen, and she felt it was a traitorous thought, one that made her feel as much guilt as it did excitement. And it brought her back to her dream. Because in her dream, she had crossed the kitchen last night instead of retiring to her room. In her dream, she had put her hand on his face and kissed his mouth, and then he had put his hands all over her body. He had taken her against the wall, his arousal hard and thick and devastating, and she had screamed her pleasure in a way that she had always thought was fake, and found nowhere this side of ridiculously overblown in movies and porn.

And hey, it probably wasn't to be found anywhere outside of adult entertainment. Because she had dreamed it. It hadn't really happened.

She had certainly never experienced anything like that.

She shifted uncomfortably.

This was the problem. She didn't have experience in the sense that she had only been with one person. So her experience wasn't broad. But she'd had all kinds of sex. Years of it. Steady. Because she had been in a consistent relationship for so many years.

And when you were in a long-term relationship, you tried things. All the things.

It was such a scary line to walk. Because she had no idea what it would be like with someone else, but she also knew what was possible. And she really wanted to test the limits of what was possible with Kit. Or rather, her libido did. Or better, her more critically thinking self didn't want to do that. But sometimes when she looked at him, it felt like her critical self did not exist. It was just her replaced by a horny monster that she didn't recognize.

And again, she had to question what her motivation had been in doing this with him.

And why she was watching his muscles.

Did she want to resist? Or did she want to throw herself headfirst into something different?

Into something new.

"Can I help you with something?"

She blinked. And she realized she was standing there gaping.

"No. No. Sorry. I'm just… My sister is getting married. I'm just a little bit overcome. Emotions. I'm very sentimental."

She actually kind of was. She knew that most people wouldn't characterize her that way, but a woman who still had all of her late husband's belongings could hardly be considered anything but sentimental, she supposed. A woman who hand-beaded a bunch of details that no one would ever see, but she would know were there, could not be characterized as anything but sentimental.

"All right. Let's start getting this thing up." They started placing the poles, the supports and the different sections.

He found a ladder in the back of the barn, and they set it up, him working by stretching as tall as he could go and using the full length of his arms, and her needing the ladder every step of the way.

She showed him how the tulle was supposed to wrap around the frame, and she had to admit, he made a very skilled laborer.

"You would be handy to have around the house," she said, not thinking until the words escaped.

He looked at her, lifting a brow. "Would I?"

"To reach tall things. And open jars."

"I do know how to do both of those things."

"That's all I meant by it."

"I didn't think you meant anything else."

"Somehow I don't believe you."

"That is between you and your God. And not my concern."

"Everybody else is coming up today."

"Yep."

"I guess we better get that bachelor and bachelorette party thing ready."

"Definitely."

He took a step toward her, and she found herself scrambling back as if he had physically touched her.

He didn't react strongly, but it was the slight jolt in his frame that told her she had surprised him with her response.

"See you later, then. At the barbecue."

"Yeah. See you then."

And she had never needed to get away from another person so badly in her entire life. Especially not while feeling the intense desire to stay with him.

Chapter 6

Everybody gathered around the catered barbecue just outside the newly decorated barn. Family was here, and there were many friends thrown into the mix. The pre-wedding party was a big one, and he had a feeling tonight was going to be a pretty wild celebration.

But for now, the men and women were joined together having a potluck, and it was pretty damned good.

But he was still fixated on what had happened between him and Shelby earlier.

She had jumped away from him like his fingertips were on fire and he might burn her.

You know why.

Yeah. He could say that nothing had been happening. It hadn't been, strictly.

And yet, everything had been.

There was an undercurrent between the two of them that was difficult to ignore.

And need that was growing in his gut.

And it was complicated by the fact that their siblings were getting married, and she was vulnerable. He could see it. She was at a crossroads in her life, and she was looking for something, anything to hold on to.

And he was all right being a temporary mistake. Hell, maybe that was what she needed. But he couldn't be anything else for her.

So he needed to watch himself. And he wasn't all that good at watching himself. She was sitting with her sister, talking and laughing and eating, and he found himself a little bit overly fascinated by her.

"I can't believe how much you got done," Chance said. "You didn't have to do all the work. We were planning on getting some of it done tonight and tomorrow."

"Yeah. But I'm the best man. I wanted to do it for you."

"I have all these brothers. What good are they if they don't all help out?"

"Well, Shelby was in here doing it all, and I figured I shouldn't leave her to her own devices."

Chance looked at him, a little bit too sharp. "No. I suppose not. Awfully nice of you to assist."

He looked back over at his brother. "I think we both know that I'm not that nice."

"Yeah. So... Don't mess things up with my sister-in-law, please? She's been through enough."

Irritation stabbed at Kit. Primarily because his brother wasn't off base on things. But it was still offensive that he felt he had to tell him that.

"Yeah, I wasn't really planning on closing the loop in the family tree."

Chance chuckled. "Well. See that you don't. Honestly, the issue isn't… The issue is just that you and I both know that you don't want anything permanent. And she's been through a lot."

"Who hasn't?"

"Good point. Look, man, if the opportunity comes up for a little bit of fun, and that's what she wants, that's different."

"Are you warning me away from your sister-in-law, or are you giving me permission to have a one-night stand with her?"

"I'm actually not doing either one. You're both grown people. She gets a say in things. I am expressing my preference for you not making my life difficult."

"Got it. You don't want your wife to get mad at you."

"Correct. Or, my wife's grandfather, who scares the ever-loving shit out of me."

"Fair. Look, it's nothing I didn't think of already."

"How long have you two…?"

"Nothing's going on between us."

"No, I get that, but you're into her."

He shrugged. "I just think she's hot."

"Right. Well. Hey, whatever. Things are set up for camping tonight?"

"Hell yeah. Epic camping. It's going to be great."

"Good. After we play pool."

"Of course. We gotta make use of the house too. I just figured a little bit of sleeping in the woods was also in order."

"You thought of everything."

"I try to."

And he realized how true that was. He did try to think of everything. To the best of his ability. He tried to take care of everyone. Protect them.

He just knew how desperately short a person could fall with those things. And it haunted him. He had a feeling it always would.

But tonight was about celebrating his brother. Sending him off into a new life.

Kit might never be able to see having a new life of his own, but he could definitely be happy that Chance would have one.

Definitely.

The party in the farmhouse was raucous. Luckily, their mother hadn't planned on staying in the farmhouse for this part, which was good, because if she had, they all would've died of embarrassment.

The alcohol was flowing freely, and Juniper, their friends from school and a couple of the EMTs whom Juniper worked with were all giddy and lessening their inhibitions. Shelby had opted for sobriety since she was running the whole show, and felt like she wouldn't be a great host if she let herself get too loose.

Are you just afraid of imbibing too much with Kit in the vicinity?

Well. It didn't matter if Kit was in the vicinity or not. He was out with his brothers, so it didn't matter. She was safe. They now had a buffer of all these people.

Still. Keeping her wits about her was probably the better part of valor.

But Juniper was living it up. She had her phallic crown placed on her head, and had a bright pink drink with a straw of the same color.

"This is immature," she said, lifting her glass to Shelby.

"I know," Shelby said. "That was the idea."

"Well, excellently done," Lydia, one of Juniper's friends, said, reclining back on the couch and laughing.

They had all put on club dresses, as if they were going out for a night on the town, and not just sitting in a farmhouse playing games with a group of women. But it was fun. Shelby hadn't done anything like this for a long time. It was fun to dress up just for herself. Just for a group of women. She had gone a little bit overboard. She was wearing a short emerald green minidress that had lived in the back of her closet for at least ten years. It did not fit the way that it once had, and her more generous curves made the hemline ride up higher, and it clung to her breasts and her stomach in a way that made her self-conscious now. Except... She looked at herself in the reflection of the window just quickly. If she saw it on another woman, she would think the woman looked great. So why she was being hard on herself she didn't know. Maybe it was just that harsh reminder of the passage of time. That she wasn't an effortlessly willowy teenager anymore, and that she didn't have a husband who just loved her through all the changes.

Love yourself, then.

That was the point of tonight. All the women were dressed up, just dressed up to please themselves in this group.

And yet, Kit was on her mind.

She really needed to get a grip.

This night reminded her a lot of her own bachelorette party, and she felt guilt at the way she seemed unable to separate Juniper's happiness from her own all those years ago. Maybe it was normal. Maybe it would've been like this no matter what. It was just that it should've felt happy, and not ominous.

Not strange and sad. This heavy reminder of the ways in which life can take unexpected turns.

She suddenly felt outside of the festivities. Being the sober one probably didn't help.

"Next game," she said.

She moved quickly into explaining the rules of the card game that had them matching up certain phrases with other phrases, creating the most outrageous combination that they could.

It quickly had everyone dissolving into fits of laughter, and she had beauty queen sashes with dubious honors printed on them to pass around to the women she deemed winners.

It was going on one in the morning, and they had music pumping, and everyone started dancing.

And Shelby couldn't escape that feeling that she was just… Standing outside, looking in. Participating, yes, but not really there also.

She could remember so keenly the night before her wedding.

Young and so filled with hope for the future.

And then… And then they'd been married. And it had been good. But there had been hardship. Figuring out how to pay bills in this small town, how to get enough work to cover it all, while knowing that they were lucky they had the house on her parents' property to fall back on.

The fact they hadn't been able to get pregnant, and didn't have health insurance so they hadn't had the luxury of going to a doctor and finding out why. They just kept hoping it would work.

It was supposed to. They were young, and they were healthy. And hell, they'd spent their teenage years trying desperately not to get pregnant, doubling up on all manner of contraception to make sure that it didn't happen before they were ready, and dammit, why couldn't it happen when they were?

They'd been happy still. It was just… She was ready. For that next part of her life.

They'd been saving. Saving enough money to go and get answers. To figure out what they needed to do. And then the accident had happened and…

She blinked, suddenly coming back to the moment.

It was like she had been watching a movie of her own life. From the night of that party to tonight. And it was… Jarring. To come back to this. Her sister was just starting down that road now. And Shelby had already walked on it.

She hoped it was better for Juniper in ten years. She really did.

But she suddenly just felt old, and like she really wasn't part of this for a reason.

There were no more structured games happening, people were just dancing, and she had a feeling they were all going to get sleepy soon.

She melted into the background of the room, and then slipped quietly out the back door. It was warm outside, not as hot and sticky as it had been inside, but pleasant, with a cool breeze blowing over the field.

She closed her eyes and let it wash over her as she walked off the porch down into the grass.

She felt tears slip down her face, and she didn't bother to wipe them away.

It was just a moment by herself. Just a moment to let all of this wash over her. Wash through her.

Just a moment.

And when she opened her eyes, she saw a figure, dark on the velvet blue horizon. And she knew immediately who it was, standing one hundred paces from her, with the bachelor pad to his back.

She didn't say anything. She just stood there, regarding him. He knew it was her. She didn't need to ask.

They had both left their respective parties.

She wondered why he had. Wondered why tonight was too much for him.

She took a step toward him, at the same time he took one toward her.

Until they had closed almost all the distance between them.

And she didn't know what she should do. If she should speak, or if they were past words.

They had talked last night when talking wasn't what either of them had wanted, and she'd known it. They had talked today, when all she had wanted to do was look at his fine form.

Sure, there was a lot of talking that could be done. A lot of concern about consequences and fallout. Disclaimers and things like that. But she had a feeling they both knew them. That they both lived in the pocket of the same sorts of concerns and there was no reason to put voice to them. No reason to break the spell of the moment with language that could never capture what was happening inside her anyway.

The truth of the matter was she wanted Kit Carson.

She had wanted him when she was a middle school girl and he was in high school, standing across the field from her looking like everything she had never thought she'd ever see in real life. She had wanted him as a grown woman, her heart firmly engaged in her marriage, her vows happily and meaningfully spoken. She had looked at him and seen the promise of desire fulfilled in a way she had never imagined. And she had turned away from it, because she had promised she would. Because love outweighed desire.

She had wanted him amid all the dark lonely days since, and hadn't even let herself fantasize about him because she was still testing herself. And why?

Suddenly, it was like she had let go of a burden that she'd been carrying all this time.

Why. Why was she still carrying it? What was she trying to prove? Why was she still trying to be… Strong? To be better? Why? What did it matter? What did it matter what she did? What did it matter whom she was with now? Her house was empty, her bed was empty. He was dead. Death had done them part. That was it, it was the end. And she wanted so badly in some ways for it to not be the end that she just couldn't…

But Kit was here. And she was so tired of being better than this fire that had ignited itself in her veins all those years ago.

She wasn't better than it. She was it. Entirely. Utterly. And tonight she wanted to burn.

She was the one who made the move. She knew that she would have to be. It was a fraction. A breath. But he saw it for what it was. And suddenly, she was in his arms. Strong and certain and hot. His chest was a wall of muscle, and she pressed her palms flat to it, felt his heartbeat raging there. He was tall, so tall, and she was disoriented by the height difference, but in the best way. She felt small and fragile, but it didn't undermine her. She was so used to being strong because she had to be.

And right this moment, it didn't feel like she had to be. It didn't feel like it at all.

It felt like he was holding her up, it felt like he was holding her in place. It felt like he might be holding all the world on those broad shoulders, just for a moment, just for her.

She smoothed her palms up and down, feeling the hard delineation of his pectoral muscles and reveling in the answering kick of need between her legs.

Yes. She was a grown woman. And she knew what the hell she wanted.

She wanted Kit Carson.

No explanation. No apologies.

No disclaimers.

And he seemed to be of the same mind.

And just when she thought she might die of the frenzy that was whipping up inside her, he lowered his head. And finally, finally that hard, uncompromising mouth was softening over hers.

It was demanding, and he parted her lips roughly, sliding his tongue against hers as if he was voracious, hungry. Starving.

She whimpered, wrapping her arms around his neck and pressing her breasts flush against his chest.

And then she felt herself being lifted off the ground, like she weighed nothing, and she supposed to him maybe she did. And all of her insecurities from earlier tonight just melted away. Because her body fit against his. Because the years had changed her into the sort of woman who could withstand this. Because the years had brought her to this moment. Stripped away everything that had ever prevented it whether she wanted it to or not.

She was here. And she was the woman whom she was. The woman who could have it.

So she had to honor it. The changes. The aging. The weight. The loss. She had to honor it, because it was why she was here. And she couldn't hate herself, or second-guess, or warn herself off about consequences.

Because it was like this moment had been destined to unfold from the beginning.

And she refused to feel guilt over that thought either.

If the moment felt like fate, she was going to take that too. Because no one had asked her if this was what she wanted. If this was where she wanted to stand. If she had been able to pick her own life she would be back at home with her husband and the children they'd had years before, but she had been denied all of that, so she would have this. Unreservedly.

She would have it.

For the Shelby who stood here now. The Shelby with the thicker ass and thighs and rounded stomach. That Shelby. The Shelby who had loved and lost and felt so broken she didn't think she could ever stand again.

The Shelby who had always done the right thing in the face of temptation because doing right and being right and loving right had mattered.

But now only this mattered. Not tomorrow, and not yesterday. Only this.

And he was everything. Everything she had never allowed herself to fantasize about and more.

His lips were hot and all-consuming, and she felt his kiss burn through her like a wildfire. Burn through her without compromise.

She throbbed between her legs, excitement blooming in her midsection, her breasts growing heavy. Her nipples demanding his touch.

She had never kissed another man. And yet, it felt like because it was Kit it just fit.

And it was a good moment for it. For him. Because she knew what she wanted. She knew what to demand of him. She knew where she wanted to be touched and how.

And suddenly, he moved his big hands down her back, down to cup her ass, and he squeezed her hard, commanding and possessive in a way she never experienced, and she realized that even if she might know what to demand, there were other things that he knew.

And suddenly, that feeling of inexperience, the lack of understanding of how he might touch her. Taste her. Of what he might choose, made her feel giddy with excitement and nervous like she was a virgin.

Because she knew where this was going. Wherever they had to go. Wherever they had to go to make it happen, she knew that this wasn't ending in the field. That it wasn't ending at a kiss.

With her legs wrapped firmly around his waist, he held her and began to walk back toward the bachelor house.

"You should put me down," she whispered, breaking the silence for the first time, and she regretted it. Because she had broken it with her uncertainty, and she didn't want to bring uncertainty into this.

But he did nothing but chuckle against her mouth, the way his breath filled her causing her to shiver.

"I'm good."

She realized that they were going into the house. "Everyone's camping," he said as he walked them up the porch, and she disentangled her legs from around his waist, feeling a little bit silly that he was carrying her like she was a koala bear.

But all he did was lift her up fully into his arms, opening the door and closing it behind them, before kissing her hard right there in the entry, deep and unending.

"This is what you wanted, right? You didn't want steak. You didn't want to banter with me about ribbon curls, or just stand there watching me drink a beer. Or even have me open yours. This is what you wanted."

She nodded slowly. "And it's what you wanted too."

"Back before we even had a situation," he said, the words rough and ground out.

And the explosion of desire that ignited in her was too all-consuming to deny. "Thank God," she said, and she grabbed his face and kissed him. With everything she had. With everything pent up and brilliant in her.

She kissed him. She kissed him because she didn't have another choice. She kissed him because he was everything. She kissed him because if she didn't she might die.

And then she realized they were moving again, that he was carrying her up the stairs.

"Good thing you chose the closest bedroom," she said.

He laughed, but it sounded strange. He pushed the door open, and then slammed it shut behind them, pushing the lock. "Just in case. You never know who's going to wimp out and try to use the indoor plumbing."

"Or notice that you're gone," she said softly.

"They are pretty wasted," he said. "And there are a lot of us."

"Yeah. My sister and her friends were pretty wasted too." She blinked. "You're not wasted." She just needed to check. Because if Kit Carson needed to be drawn to have sex with her, that was a little bit embarrassing.

"Haven't had a drop."

"Me neither."

And right then, as they stared at each other in the dimly lit room, she wondered if that was why neither of them had had any booze. Because if they were drunk, it would've dulled their senses for this. Would've created a gray area where one of them might have wanted to refuse because the other one was compromised. Or, they both could've been sloppy drunk, but then they wouldn't have remembered it. And there was one thing she knew for certain. This was her only shot. Because it was complicated, and neither of them wanted that.

This was just the fulfillment of a fantasy. And it was one she really needed. Because she was trying to find a way to move on. Trying to find a way to make a change, and this was it. It was what she needed. But it wasn't going to be a regular thing.

It was a singular gift that she was giving herself before she decided… If she was going to move. To change her scenery forever. To get herself out of the echoes of the life that she had before.

So yeah, she wanted to be present for it. And like he was reading her mind, he reached out and flicked the lights on. It was bright. Bracingly so, but she understood. He wanted to do this with everything lit up. With no mystery, with no fuzzy edges. And she found it was what she wanted too.

"Take your clothes off, Kit Carson," she said. "Because I have been wondering what was under them for far too long."

His mouth quirked up into a grin, and he set her down slowly on the edge of the bed. Her heart hammered at the base of her throat, throbbing insistently.

She shivered as he reached up and began to undo the buttons on his shirt. His chest was well muscled, covered with dark hair, and she squirmed in her seat, as her center throbbed, moisture flooding her, because she was just so damned hot for him.

Women weren't visual her ass. She could get off just looking at Kit Carson.

He shrugged the shirt off his broad shoulders, and her mouth went dry.

He was masculine perfection. His abs would have been highly regarded back when her family had first settled the area. They could've cleaned their clothes on them.

And he had those lines, narrowing down beneath his jeans, pointing down to that part of him that had hardened into an insistent bulge pushing at the front of his denim.

She moaned. She couldn't help it. And he laughed. But not her. He slowly undid the buckle on his belt, undid his jeans and kicked his shoes off as he shrugged his pants and underwear down. As he revealed the whole rest of his body to her, and damn. Just damn.

She had really never. Not even in her wildest fantasies. He was beautiful. Thick and long and just gorgeous. She had a healthy appreciation for the male form in general. She liked the look of a naked man.

But she liked the look of this naked man better than she had ever liked anything in all her life.

And then he did something wholly unexpected. He knelt down slowly on the floor in front of the bed, and looked up at her. The expression in his eyes was wicked, the curve of his lips a sin.

He smoothed his hands up along her thighs, beneath the hem of her dress. And he found her panties, grabbing them and dragging them slowly down, removing them, but leaving her shoes still. Then he moved his hands to the insides of her knees, parted her legs, and she felt her face ignite as he examined her, his expression one of filthy awe.

"Do you have any idea," he said, "how long I've wanted to taste you? You make me so hard. Do you know that? Do you know that I fantasized about you? I have a policy. I don't do the married-woman thing. Sorry. But it's been that long. And you tested me."

"Well, I didn't do the infidelity thing. So it's a good thing you didn't try."

"But now it's all good. And I have wanted you… I have wanted you."

He pushed her dress up, exposing her completely, and his gaze only seemed to get hungrier. Then he kissed the inner part of her thigh, and she started to shake.

She couldn't believe it was him. Kit Carson. Right there. Looking at her like that. Like he wanted to devour her.

And she knew he was going to. All of her nerve endings were at attention. Her whole body on high alert.

His mouth moved higher, pressing soft kisses on her thighs, and then, then, he put his mouth right over her, her center, and she let out a short, shocked sound, because even though she had known it was coming, the reality of it was just so much more. His mouth was hot and confident, and his tongue went deep inside her before he slid it over the most sensitive part of her, then sucked her deep into his mouth. He shoved his hands beneath her ass, and brought her hard against him, as uncompromising here as he was everywhere else.

And she lost herself. In the way his shoulders held her legs wide, and the rough feel of his fingers, digging into her flesh. And the white-hot pleasure that his mouth gave her. She lost herself utterly. Completely. She clung to him, and she felt her climax, quick and impossibly intense, building inside her, and she wanted to resist it. Wanted to stop it. Because once she had one, she wasn't going to have another, and she had really wanted it when he was in her.

But there was no fighting it. It was too good. Too enticing and tempting, so she let go. And she couldn't help it. She screamed. She rolled her hips in rhythm with the waves of pleasure that were moving through her. He rose up on his feet, growled and grabbed hold of her hips, lifting her back farther onto the bed as he covered her. He ripped her dress down, and then off completely, throwing it onto the floor. She was still wearing her shoes.

He kissed her. And she returned the kiss, wrapping her arms around his neck and giving him everything she had. He covered her, his chest hair rough against her breasts. And she moved her hands all over his body. His chest, his back, feeling all the muscles there, down to his ass. She parted her legs, encouraging him between them. And she could feel the hard press of his arousal against the entrance to her body. She moaned, rubbing against him, slippery with need, but he didn't give her what she wanted. Not quite yet. He lowered his head, and took her nipple into his mouth, sucking hard.

And she ignited.

He sucked her hard, and she wrapped her legs around his, arching against him, trying to assuage the ache between her legs. She was so close. Again. Already.

"Please," she whispered.

And then he thrust home.

She gasped. He was so big. And she hadn't been with anyone in a while. Years. So it was a little bit of a shock.

Sex toys were not Kit Carson. He was bigger and more. Hot and insistent. And he was in control.

He grabbed her hands and held them up over her head as he began to establish a steady, hard rhythm that rocked her. Utterly. Mercilessly.

She looked up into his eyes, looked right at his face. The lights were on. And she wouldn't let herself forget. As if she could have.

She was with Kit. Kit.

And then, it was like everything around her was fire, and so was she.

Her climax ripped through her. Her need overcoming her as she cried out his name. As she felt wave after wave of desire pulsing through her.

And then he growled her name on his lips as he shuddered and shook. And if there was one thing that was better than finding her own release in Kit's arms, it was watching him find it in hers.

This man, the object of her darkest and most shameful fantasies, was surrendering to her.

To them. To this.

It was everything. He was everything.

And they were something else entirely.

And when it was over, she lay there, sweat-slicked, her heart pounding so hard she thought it was going to escape her chest.

"Oh, well," she said.

Because it was all she could say. They weren't wrong. They weren't exaggerating, those movies. You could lose yourself, lose your head. End up screaming and not care who heard you.

It was a revelation.

One she had always been a little bit afraid she could only ever have with him.

And there it was.

"Good for you?"

"Extremely," she said.

They lay there, and she looked at him, at his body.

And she was sad. Because she could've… Well, she could want this for a long time. She could want this forever.

That made something like an alarm bell go off inside her. She wasn't supposed to be thinking things like that. Wasn't supposed to be thinking in those terms. Because there was no point to it. None at all. They both knew what it was. "Thank you," she said. "But I really should get back. Because…"

"I know. Same reason I should."

"You know that this can't…"

"I think we both know exactly what this was. That's why we didn't talk about it beforehand, right?"

She nodded. "Yeah. So… I'll see you at the wedding tomorrow."

He nodded slowly. "Yeah. See you at the wedding."

Chapter 7

It was tempting to be smug when he was the only one who woke up the next morning without a hangover. Except… He couldn't say with confidence that he didn't have a hangover of some variety. Of the Shelby Sohappy variety, in point of fact. Because that woman had turned him inside out. Had left him completely wrecked.

He had had a whole lot of sex in his life, but he never had anything quite like that.

He couldn't explain it. It was just her. The look of her, the feel of her, the taste of her.

"Hey, assholes," he shouted, experiencing a great amount of satisfaction when all of his brothers groaned. "Chance is getting married today, so you all better deal with the hangover situation."

"Do you think yelling at us is going to help?" Boone asked.

"I'm not trying to help."

"Why are you not hungover?" Chance asked.

"Superior genetics?"

"We have the same genetics."

It was his brother's day. He should be thinking of best-man things and being responsible, maybe even being happy perchance, but instead his mind was firmly fixed on the events of the night before. Of Shelby, and what it had felt like to finally touch her. To finally kiss her. To finally be with her. She had been everything, and they had been incendiary. It had been more than he had ever imagined being with her could be, and he had imagined quite a bit. She had been a revelation. There had been a connection between them for years. An ember that had burned bright, and last night it had exploded into a flame that had threatened to consume them both.

He knew that he was the first man she'd been with since her husband's death. He felt that. Like it was a weight to carry, a burden, and yet, he couldn't say he minded. Not really. If someone was going to be that man, it was better that it was him. Because he had wanted her for a hell of a long time, and there had been nothing he could do about it.

Well. Not again. And today they needed to focus on his brother and her sister. That's what it was all about.

So he rousted those idiots he called brothers, and got them fed, got everybody's suits ready to go.

Boone looked at him as he finished tying his tie. "Where were you last night?"

"What do you mean? I was with you."

"You see, I wasn't all that drunk. I noticed you leaving. And I noticed that you didn't come back for a couple of hours. So, where were you?"

"Maybe I was working on a surprise for Chance."

"Yeah. Maybe you were. Maybe you were working on a surprise for Chance, and that's all legit. But… I have my suspicions."

He narrowed his eyes. "Do you, now?"

"I do. I think that you found the maid of honor."

"And why do you think that?" he asked, his voice flat. Dangerous.

"Because you want her. Because you have wanted her for a record number of years. I think we all know that."

"That's interesting that *you* know that, Boone. Because *I* don't know that."

"Liar. Fucking liar. You want her. You know it. And I think something finally happened between the two of you."

"I think that I didn't ask for your opinion, Boone. That's what I think. So maybe you should take a little bow tie and get ready to go stand at the front of the church. Otherwise, we might recast you. You would make a charming flower girl."

"I would," Boone said. "I'm happy to tiptoe through the tulips anytime. But none of that deflects from the fact that I think you're a liar."

"Well. That is brotherly love, isn't it? You think that I'm a liar. What an asshole."

"Yeah. I'm an asshole. But hey, don't worry about it. I'm sure that Chance would be thrilled to know that you hooked up with his sister-in-law."

"Chance doesn't need to know. Does he?"

"Is that a confession?"

"You think what you think. What does it matter what I say or not?"

"Nothing. Just…"

"Yeah. I know. Be careful. Be careful with her because… All those reasons."

"Yes. All those reasons. Unless you're about to make like Chance and get everything together and make forever…"

"I get that you think she might want forever, but she doesn't. Not with me." He wasn't anything like her husband, and he didn't want to be. He wasn't ever going to be a forever guy, and if her past actions indicated anything… She was a forever type of woman. "That was just old business. Needed to be taken care of. It had been deferred way too long. Believe me. She doesn't want forever. She's had that. You know how it is. You lose someone… Nothing is ever the same again."

Boone got a faraway look in his eye. "Yeah. I know that." He cleared his throat. "I also know sometimes you…miss your chance with someone and regret it."

He didn't know what his brother was referencing, but it was clear something else was going on with Boone. And also that Boone didn't want to go into detail about it, or he would have.

"It wasn't about having a chance for me. It was just attraction."

"Whatever. I hope you had a good night."

"I fucking did."

"Good, then. As long as all involved were satisfied, I assume the day will go off without a hitch."

"It's not my day. It's Chance's."

"True. True."

And he kept that in mind as they assembled for the wedding. Kept it firmly in mind when the bridesmaids showed up. Kept it firmly in mind when Shelby, wearing a red dress that scooped low and showed off her stunning breasts, came to stand near him, because they would be walking down the aisle together.

"Hope you slept well," he said.

"Just fine."

"Did they notice you were gone?"

"When was I gone?" She looked at him with unfathomable dark eyes.

"Guess you weren't."

That was how they were going to play it. Like it hadn't happened. Even though they both knew it had. Even though he had a feeling they were both replaying scenes of the night before as they stood there regarding each other.

"Yeah. I know."

They linked arms, and walked down the aisle, taking their place where the bride and groom would stand.

The wedding was beautiful. Went off without a hitch. And he was glad. He was glad for Chance. Because the man deserved some happiness.

And Boone was right. Unless Kit was willing to make changes—big changes—unless he was willing to abandon his entire life, he had to leave Shelby alone. He just did.

But it looked like Shelby was more than willing to leave him alone. At the reception she danced with just about everyone but him. A knot of jealousy formed in his stomach, but it should be gratitude. Gratitude for the fact that she knew what had happened between them was temporary.

He just wished it was more than once.

Maybe. But it wasn't.

And when they saw Chance and Juniper off, away

from the barn, away on their honeymoon, he should have felt glad. Grateful.

Because their little dance together was done. Because the families could go back to being about as distant as they'd ever been. They would see each other occasionally. But not all that often.

Yeah. This was over. He had scratched the itch that was Shelby Sohappy.

And he should be glad that it had gone off without a hitch.

Shelby couldn't believe it. She really could not believe it. In a deep, profound way that had her ignoring the problem for four whole weeks. Until it happened again. She hadn't seen Kit Carson since the wedding. She had been telling herself that she was fine with that. But all the while, there was a growing unease, a growing sense of disbelief that had taken root inside her. She had a feeling it wasn't the only thing that had taken root. But it didn't seem possible. She had tried to get pregnant for years. Granted, she didn't really know what the source of her inability to conceive with Chuck had been. She had known that it could have been him, but she had just felt like the odds were with her. Women's bodies were tricky things. And it had seemed reasonable that the issue was her.

Yeah. It seemed completely reasonable, completely standard, really, that the issue would be her. They hadn't gotten to find out yet, though. And then in the end they hadn't. But this was two missed periods. Two. And that was two more than she had ever missed in her entire life.

She'd never been pregnant. Not once. She was as

regular as cows that needed feeding, and there was no doubt in her mind that this missed period was not a co-incidence. How could it be? How the hell could it be? And she knew that what she needed to do was talk to her sister. Confess everything. Figure out what the hell she was supposed to do. She wanted a baby. She had wanted a fresh start.

Those two things hadn't really gone together in her mind. Because, of course, she had wanted to be a mother in context with the marriage she had with Chuck. She hadn't really considered being a single mother. But here she was…

You don't know if you'll even be able to keep it. Eight weeks. It's not secure yet. You could just leave it. You could just keep ignoring it. You could not talk to any-one about it.

Except, she was already dialing her sister. Already time to find out where she was. As an EMT, Juniper was often on call, or in the far reaches of Lone Rock and the surrounding areas.

"Are you around?" she asked without introduction.

"Yeah. Pretty around. Are you at home?"

"Yes. I need to talk to you. I mean I really need to talk to you, and I need you to not tell Chance."

"Well, this is a little bit disconcerting. And I'm not sure what to do with it."

"Come over. Don't make any promises yet… Just come over."

Shelby started pacing. Pacing the halls of this house that still had her husband's clothes in it. It had been a whole thing coming back home after the wedding. Sleeping in the bed that she had shared with her hus-band, having gone to bed with someone else. And not just anyone else, Kit Carson, who had been a source of guilt and shame for her for all these years.

She had known that she needed to make a change, and she still hadn't done it. She had just sat in whatever all this was. Had just sat in her... Her fundamental misery, and she still hadn't made a move. Maybe this was her move. Maybe it was an answer to prayers that she hadn't had a voice for, hadn't had concrete words for.

"I'm here," she heard her sister call through the front door.

She scrambled back to the front of the house. "Thank God."

"What the hell is going on, Shelby?"

"I think I'm pregnant."

"Holy shit," Juniper said, staring at her.

"Yeah." She chewed the edge of her thumbnail. "I know."

"*How* pregnant?" Juniper asked, her eyes narrowed.

She felt heat creeping up the back of her neck. "Why is that the question?"

Juniper's expression went granite. "I think you know why."

Shelby coughed. "Well, that would be two months," she said.

"Coincides with my wedding date, doesn't it?"

"You can't tell Chance yet."

Juniper looked too all knowing, and it hurt. "Kit's the father?"

"You know he is," Shelby said, feeling defeated and seen and helpless. She knew that Juniper knew. That was the thing. Maybe that was why she wanted to talk to her sister more than anybody. Because she just already knew. And no matter how much Shelby had ever tried to deny it, Juniper had known that Shelby was attracted to Kit.

"You're pregnant though," Juniper said. "Really."

"I haven't taken a test. I've never missed a period. In all the time that I was married, and we tried. We were trying to have a baby, but I never got pregnant. Not one time. I was never late… Nothing."

"You didn't think about protection with Kit?"

"I didn't think about *anything*," she said, throwing her hands out wide. "If I had stopped to think about anything, I probably wouldn't have done it."

That was a lie. But it made her sound a little bit more thoughtful. A little bit more balanced and sane. So she was going to go ahead and go with that.

"Right. Well. You have to tell him."

"Why? He doesn't want… He doesn't want to have kids. He doesn't want to settle down."

"Neither did Chance."

"I don't think that I'm going to be able to contrive to give Kit amnesia so that he can forget all of his trauma and fall in love with me." Just saying that made her cringe.

"Anyway. I'm not in love with him. He's… He was this vaguely bad object that I had in my life and I… I don't know that I want to get married again. I don't know. I don't think that I love anyone else. I loved Chuck for all of my life. And it was special. I had this… This weird thing with Kit. And I hated it. I've never really known him, I've never especially liked him, and I just wanted to tear his clothes off. From the minute I first saw him. It's never been okay with me to feel that way. It's never been what I wanted. This thing with Kit has never been what I wanted. I do want a baby. I was even moving away, Juniper."

"You can't do that," Juniper said. "You can't give me a little niece or nephew and then move away."

She realized when she said that the moving thing wasn't feasible. Or fair. Moving away when she was having a baby. What would her parents think? Her grandparents? Well. What the hell were they going to think when they found out she was pregnant without a husband? That was the whole thing. It was a whole damn thing that she hadn't thought she would be dealing with when she was twenty-eight years old.

"Kit needs to know," Juniper said. "You need to give him a chance to do something."

"He's a Carson. He's an alpha male. What do you think he's going to do? He's going to storm in here and try to take over my life."

"So, tell him no. You're an alpha female, Shelby. And you know that. Why are you acting like he's going to run you over? He's not. You've got to handle this with honesty. You have to."

"Why?" Shelby said, knowing that she sounded petulant. "Why do we have to be grown-up about this?"

"Because you're going to have a baby. Maybe. The first thing you need to do is take a pregnancy test."

"Do you know if they expire?"

"I… I don't."

"Well, I have a few. In the bathroom. I was just avoiding them. I've been avoiding everything. I've been trying to pretend that it didn't happen. That all of it… Just didn't happen."

"Very healthy. But, it might be time to take a different approach. But I'm here. If you want someone here. I can also go if you don't want me here."

"I'm afraid to know," Shelby said.

"What exactly are you afraid of?"

"That it will be positive. That it will be negative." The idea made her want to burst into tears. Both of them. Seeing the results at all.

"Well, it's going to be one of those things. I'm sorry. That's just… A fact. But you want to know, right? So that you can start figuring out what you're going to do."

"I don't want to." She was about to say something along the lines of she had been working way too hard to figure out what she was going to do for too long, since she had been thrust into a change she hadn't asked for. But she hadn't been. She had just been sitting. She hadn't chosen to lose Chuck. It wasn't the consequence of anything. It was an accident. A car accident that had changed her entire life in the blink of an eye.

But this… This was her fault.

This was the direct result of her actions. It was… She'd slept with Kit without a condom. And she had put herself in the situation, and just suddenly that felt a little bit powerful. She wasn't sure she would ever be able to explain that to her sister. Because it sounded a little bit unhinged. But… This was her life. It was a choice she made. To be with him, to not take precautions. So… Here she was. At least she was doing something. Even if it was just a reaction to something else she'd done. She had earned this.

This moment, positive or negative. It was something new. It was, in a very messed-up way, that step forward that she had been avoiding taking. And now here she was taking it.

"Okay. I guess I'll try one of the tests that I have."

"Okay. I'll wait for you."

With shaking hands, she went into the bathroom, and got one of the tests. She had taken so many pregnancy tests. In spite of the fact that she never had a late period. She had done it just because she had hoped. She had kept them on hand just in case. But they were good for three days before a missed period, and she had kept them and taken them three days before more than once. And now they had just been sitting there for a couple of years. No reason to be taken.

It was such a strange, familiar routine. But in the past, she hadn't had a missed period. In the past, even though she had hoped, she had been certain of the outcome. She was not that certain here.

And when two pink lines came into view for the first time in her damned life, she could not believe it. She swallowed hard and exited the bathroom.

"It was positive," she said, standing there looking at Juniper, trying to gauge her expression.

"Oh, Shelby. You want this, though. I know you do. You want a baby."

Suddenly the intense misery that overwhelmed her was almost too much.

"I wanted my husband's baby," she said, her eyes filling with tears. "Why didn't we get to have that? All those years, and we didn't get pregnant. I didn't get to give this to him. He died and he never got to have it. And I'm... I'm going to do it without him. Because I had sex with someone else. Because I..."

"You're still alive, Shelby," Juniper said, crossing the space and taking her face in her hands. "You're alive. You're going to move on, you're going to do things that

Chuck couldn't do. And I know it's not fair. I know. I loved him too. He was like a brother to me. Shelby, when I came upon the scene of his accident, when I had to tell you… It was the worst day of my life. It is still the worst day of my life. There is nothing that will ever match that. It was hell. We both went through hell. But you're alive. And he isn't. So yes. You're going to have sex with other people. You're going to smile again. You're going to be happy. You're going to feel good things and bad things. And if you want to, you get to be a mother."

"I could still lose this pregnancy."

"You could. But you could still be a mother if you choose to be. You could still adopt, you could get fertility treatments until it happens. It's your life, Shelby. And nobody gets to tell you how to live it. And it doesn't have to stop. It doesn't have to stop just because you lost somebody. You don't owe him a half life."

"But it feels like I do."

"I know."

"And that it's Kit's makes it even worse."

"Why does it make it worse?"

She wanted to hide from that question. But she knew hiding was over. "Well, first of all, I can't keep it from him. And second of all… I feel guilty." She looked away, her throat aching. "Because it is wrong to be attracted to another person when you're married."

"No, Shelby. It's wrong to act on it. And you didn't. You never did. You can't help that you and Kit have physical chemistry. You could help what you did in response to it, and you did the right thing. You always did the right thing. You were good to Chuck. You were appropriate in your response to Kit. And you don't have anything to feel guilty for. You can't help your feelings. It's what you do with them."

"The sex was so good," Shelby said, breathing out hard. "I knew it would be. I knew it. I can't… I can't love him. I don't want…"

"Then don't. Don't. Like I said. It's your life. But if I'm going to strongly push you in any direction, it's to be honest with him. He is my brother-in-law. I cannot lie to Chance about this. I know who the father of the baby is, and I can't pretend that I don't. So… That just has to happen."

"I'll tell him," Shelby said. "It's another thing I don't really want to do. Or deal with. And that makes me a little bit tired."

"That's understandable. But you know, I did a pretty messed-up thing with Chance, and you called me out. I didn't let you in on my plans before I did it. If I had, I probably would've made a different decision because I would've seen the look on your face, and know that I couldn't lie to him like that. So let me be your conscience now. You've got to tell him as soon as possible."

"I need… I need a favor first."

"What is that?"

"Will you help me pack everything up here? I need to change the house. I need… I need new stuff. I need to get rid of the old stuff. Because it's been way too long, and it's starting to feel wrong. Really wrong. It's starting to feel creepy. I can't tell Kit that I'm pregnant with his baby with Chuck's clothes in my closet, okay?"

"Yeah. I can help you with that. I'll let Chance know I won't be home for a couple of hours."

"Don't tell him yet."

"I won't. I'll let you talk to Kit first. Just because I think that's the way it needs to go."

"Thank you," she said. "I really appreciate it."

And then, she and Juniper set about to make the clean slate that Shelby should've made for herself a long time ago. And it felt like more, like better than she could've imagined. Even though the sense of dread looming before her seemed nearly unmanageable. But all she could do was put one foot in front of the other, just slowly. One thing at a time. One piece of clothing at a time. One wedding photo at a time.

And she left one. Hanging on the wall, right in the center. Because there were fresh starts, and then there was ignoring the past in a way she simply couldn't. She would always be shaped by her marriage. By loving Chuck. She wasn't going to pretend otherwise. No matter what. And even though she felt steadfastly cowardly at the moment, that felt just a little bit brave. So she would take that. Cling to it. She didn't really have another choice.

Chapter 8

It had been a fairly normal day. He had only thought about Shelby and what she looked like naked five times. Before coffee. So it was going well. He had thought about her maybe ten times more in the hours since. She had wrecked him. He hadn't been able to get excited about another woman since then. Hadn't even really bothered. He'd considered it one night at the Thirsty Mule when he had gone down to have a drink with Jace, but had abandoned it pretty quickly.

But hell, there was no reason to obsess about her.

What he needed to do was get back on the road. He had been flirting with the idea of retirement from the rodeo, and had been picking up more responsibility on the family ranch. He liked it. Liked the idea of being here with his brothers more. He had decided to take this season off. And yeah, he figured that was probably one foot in retirement. But he was in his thirties. He might be avoiding that "and then" stage of things, but he was definitely there.

He looked across the landscape from his vantage point on the back of his horse, flat and rocky, scrub brush as far as the eye could see. This place was home. And he tried to imagine it being home in a more permanent sense. He hadn't been settled ever. Even when he'd been a kid, they'd gone around the circuit along with their dad, staying in an RV when they could. They'd only ever had stability when Sophie had been ill. And even then, it hadn't been a real stable sort of stability. Having a sister in and out of the hospital wasn't stable. Having a sister die wasn't stable.

His phone buzzed in his pocket, and he reached into it. He had a text from Jace.

Shelby is here to see you.

And suddenly, his blood went molten. Maybe she had been thinking about him too. Maybe she was here to… Maybe it was just as bad for her. Maybe one time wasn't going to be enough. *What the hell is wrong with you?*

He didn't know. And he wasn't going to allow that question to land all that deep. Because he wanted what he wanted. He wanted her. And he was clear on that.

So he urged his horse into a flat-out run, the dust coming up high, rocks and clumps of mud all stirred up in his wake. And when he came up to the front of the barn, Jace was standing there, alongside Shelby, who did not look like she had come for afternoon delight. Or indeed, delight of any kind. Her expression was flat, something steely reflecting in her eyes. Her lips were turned down. It didn't make her any less sexy, not to him. She was still a pocket-size package of absolutely everything he wanted in a woman. But she didn't look like she was here for what he wanted.

"I need to talk to you," she said.

"Yeah. Sure."

Jace looked at him with cool speculation, and Kit curled his lip and lifted his hands, giving his brother an expression straight out of their childhood.

He could tell that Jace wasn't going to let him off all that easy. But for now, he was going to have a talk with Shelby.

"The barn?" she asked.

"Sure. If you want."

"We need to talk alone."

"It may have escaped your notice, but a lot of people live here. Alone is kind of a tall order."

"Then let's... Go for a drive."

"Okay."

He walked over to where his truck was parked, just in front of the barn. "Care to get in?"

"Sure."

His brother was handling his horse, and Kit started the engine of the truck, heading out toward the remote part of the ranch where he had just been. He drove over to the edge of a ravine, the view down below of mountains that looked like they might as well be made of moondust, red and yellow and black paintbrush strokes. It was beautiful. Still not as pretty as her. Even when she was... Well, she wasn't glaring. She was just not looking at him.

"What's going on? I've had a lot of strange interactions with you, but none of them have been silent."

"I have something I have to tell you. And I don't really know how to do that."

And just like that, the view in front of him seemed to go sideways. Suddenly the mountains were to his right and the sky was to his left, and he didn't even know where his stomach was. Somewhere. Because there was only one reason for a woman you'd slept with to say words like that to you.

"Fuck."

"Oh, you guessed," she said.

"I need to hear you say it."

"I'm pregnant."

"Yeah. Well." There were spots in front of his eyes. A baby. A damned baby. And suddenly, all he could see was Sophie. Small and vulnerable and sick. Dying. And there was nothing he could do. The crushing weight that he felt every night when he went to bed. The need for her to be better. The knowledge that she wouldn't be.

And he just never... He never wanted to feel those things again. He never wanted to feel responsible for that sort of thing again.

He turned and looked at her. Hell. She was pregnant. Pregnancy was not an altogether safe condition. And so many things could go wrong. For her. For the baby.

"Have you been to the doctor?"

"No. I just took a test. I suspected... I suspected about a month ago. But I didn't want to jump to any conclusions. I've never been pregnant before. And I've tried. So... I didn't actually think that I could."

"Shit. I didn't even think about protection. I didn't even..."

"I didn't either," she said.

"It's not your fault. I mean, it's not your fault entirely. It's mine too," he said.

"Well, how generous of you to acknowledge your part in a process that I would be physically incapable of completing on my own."

"I'm not suggesting that I'm being heroic in taking responsibility. But you can't deny that some men don't or won't. And I'm not that guy. I'm not going to blame you or say that you should've said something or done something different."

But there was panic rolling through him. A sense of horror that he couldn't seem to shake, a sense of urgency. He needed to do something. He needed to take control of this somehow.

"I had to tell you, because I told my sister, and she can't not tell Chance. She told me there was a very tight clock ticking on that."

"Would you not have told me otherwise?"

She was silent for a long moment. That silence told him a hell of a lot.

"I don't know. Because I was thinking about moving away. And I feel like that offer still needs to be on the table. You don't have to be involved in this. I've wanted a baby for a long time. This isn't how I saw it happening. I told you. I didn't see it happening this way at all. I didn't think that I could. But I wanted a baby. I wanted to be a mother. You don't have to be involved. You can consider yourself an anonymous sperm donor."

"Like hell I will. Like hell I will. I'm not a sperm donor."

"What are you, then? We had a one-night stand, Kit. A one-night stand that might've been a long time coming, but you don't owe me anything. You and I do not owe each other anything. It was sex. Nothing more."

"I'm the father of the baby." And as soon as he said it he realized it was true. "The father, do you understand? Not a sperm donor."

"Do you want a child?"

"It's immaterial. I'm having one. That's how it is for me. I can't have a child walking around on this earth and know about it and not claim him. Bottom line. That's just how it is. For me, that's how it is."

He hadn't wanted this. Hadn't wanted this worry, this burden or this responsibility. But it was here, it was happening, and he couldn't contort it into something else. There was no way. Absolutely no way at all. For him, it wasn't a matter of whether or not he decided to step up. He would.

"I could still lose it."

"But it's here now."

And suddenly, the silence seemed to swell between them. The enormity of that. The reality of it.

Even though it was barely the promise of a heartbeat right now, they had… Made something together. It couldn't be nothing. Not to him. It could not be nothing. "We should get married."

"No," she said, the denial abrupt and sharp.

"Why not?"

"Because it's not 1950, you dope. We don't need to get married. This is not a reason to get married."

"It's about the only reason I can think that I would ask a woman to marry me."

"Well, I'm flattered. How many women have you had to propose to?"

"None. You've never been pregnant before. I've never gotten anyone pregnant before. I don't generally…or ever, have sex without condoms. It was very important to me to avoid this. I didn't. In this case. So... I think marriage makes the most sense."

"I've been married, Kit," she said, her voice suddenly soft. "We didn't have a baby. And we were married. Husband and wife. Childless the whole time. Kids are not what marriage is. Marriage is about loving somebody. Being in a partnership. Marriage is about choosing *them*. Not... Some version of a family."

"I think marriage can be either thing. Sometimes people get married for that reason. Sometimes people get married for convenience. Sometimes people get married for kids."

"Not me. Not me. I will never get married for less than what I had before."

And he didn't know why, but that stuck in his chest. More than a little bit. But he couldn't argue with her. Not really.

"I'm moving in with you, then."

"No," she said. "There's no reason to do that. I could have a miscarriage. Something could go wrong. I don't even have the baby."

"So we can move in together after you have the baby."

"Or we share custody. Like grown-ups. Or we decide what it looks like then."

All these things were foreign to him. And none of it was making sense. None of it was clicking. He wanted her with him. All the time. He wanted to protect her. He wanted to keep an eye out for her. He wanted to keep surveillance on the baby in utero and out constantly. To make sure that everything was fine. To make sure they were safe. How could he keep her safe if he didn't have her with him?

"No. This is not going to work for me. You need to

move in with me, or I need to move in with you. This has to… This has to be my choice."

"No," she said.

"I can't guarantee that I'm not going to fight you for full custody if you don't do this."

"Well, I will sic your brother on you. And I'm pretty sure I'll win that fight. Because Juniper and Chance are going to side with me."

And there was the entanglement working against him in a way he hadn't quite envisioned. His brother was accountable to her sister. And he had a whole bunch of threats inside him all bottled up. A desperate bid to control the situation, and he couldn't do it. He couldn't do it, because she wasn't wrong. His brother would tear him a new one. Or just remove the part of his anatomy that had accomplished making the baby in the first place.

"Well, I'm going to be at your house. Every morning. On your damned doorstep. Making sure you're okay."

"Why are you being a nightmare? Why don't we get to know each other?"

"Because I don't want to get to know you. You're the mother of my child."

"It is a zygote, Kit. Calm down."

"No. I will not calm down. Because you can twist and spin situations in life all you want. And you can try to avoid thinking about the logical, reasonable outcomes of things, and you can try to live in denial, but it does not change anything. Believe me. I've done that. I tried it. I tried just…being positive and happy for my sister when she was dying and…trying to be optimistic. It doesn't change a damn thing. When shit comes for you, you have to deal with it. You have to be realistic."

"I'm realistic. Don't talk to me now like I've never

lost anything. Don't talk to me like I don't understand that life is difficult. I do. I do. I know how hard things can be. You know I know it. You know I do."

"Shelby," he said, suddenly feeling like there was a boulder in his chest. "I don't see it working where the two of us are trading a kid back and forth on the weekend."

"It has to. Because that's the only thing that I can deal with. Kit, it's all there can ever be."

They sat in silence for a long time. "We'll see."

"This isn't a negotiation."

"And that's where you're wrong. Because it isn't just your life anymore. And it isn't just mine. We are going to have to figure out what's best for this kid. And I'm going to argue my position on that."

And he could see that he had stumped her there.

"So what now?" she asked.

"Let's schedule a doctor appointment."

"Okay."

"I'd like to be there."

"I can't argue with that."

"I think you could. I think for some reason, on this, you don't want to fight me."

He looked at her profile, and he saw tears welling up in her dark eyes. "Well, maybe I don't want to be alone."

"Good. I don't want to leave you alone. That's not how this should be. It's not what I want."

"I'll let you know when I schedule one."

"You going to talk to the rest of your family?"

"Yeah. I guess I have to."

"Would you like me to go with you?"

"Would you like to be a Kit-skin rug on my grand-father's floor?"

"Hey," he said. "I offered to marry you. You turned me down."

"Yes, but you did have sex with me outside the bonds of holy matrimony."

"And you had sex with me right back," he said.

"Point is, I think you should maybe not be there."

He did not like this. This woman's insistence on independence. And it wasn't because he didn't respect an independent woman. It was because it all felt… He wanted to pick her up and wrap her in a blanket and carry her around. He wanted to make sure that she was safe, that the baby was safe. It all suddenly felt so fraught and fragile he didn't know what to do.

And yeah, part of him thought… It would be easier if this wasn't happening. It would be easiest if something went wrong now.

But there was another part of him, a large part, the biggest part, in fact, that couldn't cope with the idea of something going wrong. It would be one loss too many. It would be unfair. Unendurable. He didn't want her to go through that pain. He didn't want to go through it again.

So you're gonna be a dad.

If he hadn't been sitting down, the idea would've brought him down to his knees. It was unfathomable. He had never thought about being a dad. He had shoved that thought way to the side if anything even remotely resembling it had come up. Yeah. It was not his ideal.

He didn't know what to make of it now.

"I actually need some time by myself," she said.

"Are you brushing me off?"

"Yes. I am. Because today has been a lot."

"I don't deny that. But don't you think that you and I should… Talk about this more?"

"I already told you, I don't feel secure enough in this even being a thing to worry about that just now. We don't need to be picking out preschools, or whatever you're thinking."

"I was not thinking that. But thanks."

"I assume you're going to tell your family?"

"I have to tell my family. Because of Chance."

"Fair point. I understand that."

"Right. Well. Since we're not doing it together, I expect I better drive you back to your car and let you get on with things, and then I'll get on with things." He didn't like it. He didn't like any of it. But he didn't really have a choice either.

He put the truck in Reverse, turned around and started to head back toward the barn. Started to head back toward where Shelby had left her car.

He wanted to do something. Wanted to kiss her. But they didn't do that. *You weren't going to be doing things like that. Yeah. And since when do you just take things lying down?*

He didn't. And he wouldn't. As she got into her car to drive away, he began to put a few very concrete directives in place. He was going to prove to her that it was better if they were together. That it was better if they made a family. He was never going to be her late husband. He was never going to mean that much to her. But they could have another version of a family. And he was going to prove that to her. Even if he had to seduce her around the idea.

Chapter 9

"Well. He asked me to marry him."

"Good," Juniper said. "If he had done anything else I would've hung him out to dry and…"

"I said no."

"What?" Her sister's voice was a shriek in her ear.

"I said no, Juniper. I'm not going to marry him just because I'm pregnant."

"Okay. Forgive me. But I don't understand why not. Because you want a family, Shelby…"

"No. I wanted a family with the man I was married to. We were a family. I am not in love with Kit." The words stuck something tender and hollow at the center of her chest.

She wanted to cry all of a sudden. She had made it through that whole thing with him mostly without crying. Mostly. And she just couldn't…

She couldn't. This was too hard. It was scraping

against things she didn't want to examine. It was making her... Feel things.

She hadn't even been tempted to say yes to him for a second, though. Because the idea of Kit and marriage just didn't go together. The idea of taking the thing that they were, this wild, untamed thing, the sharp edges that made her feel exhilaration and shame all at once, and pushing them into the life that she'd had before... She just couldn't imagine that. Of course, she couldn't quite imagine him being a father.

The father of her child. She had spent a lot of time imagining herself being a mother, and in that picture, she was soft. Sitting in a rocking chair, holding a baby. She was a different sort of woman.

Definitely not the woman who had climbed all over Kit Carson and encouraged him to do dirty, incendiary things to her in that bedroom.

That was not the woman bursting with maternal instinct who wanted more than anything to nurture a child.

That woman had been a moment out of time. A moment of insanity. A moment to inhabit a different reality.

That woman could not be the one who took control now.

She looked around her house. Small and humble. She tried to imagine Kit filling the space.

She couldn't. But then, she had no idea what her life was now. She had no idea what she was doing.

And she had a feeling that she wasn't going to find answers anytime soon.

But the sad thing was, there was a timer ticking on her getting things sorted out now. A timer growing in her womb.

So sort things out she was going to have to do. Starting with her family. Kit Carson was a problem for another day.

All his brothers were assembled at the Thirsty Mule. Well. All except for Buck. But that was normal. Another shitty normal in the Carson family.

This was all of them now.

It had just so happened that they were all available. He hadn't actually purposefully put the whole squad together for this announcement. And really, he probably should've first told his mother, who was going to be so thrilled about having a grandchild she wasn't going to be able to deal, but that was part of the problem. She was going to want to see Shelby. She was going to want assurances that the kid was going to be around all the time. And frankly, he had no such assurances. So, his brothers were going first.

"Surprised the old ball and chain let you out of the house," Jace said, slapping Chance on the back.

"The old ball and chain is on call, and was also exhausted after a day working the ranch. She's got too much pride to let me pay for everything, so she's just still working her ass off. But you know, I like that about her."

"That she's stubborn?"

"Yeah. Believe me. It's one of her better attributes."

And unfortunately, Kit knew exactly what his brother was getting at, since he had tasted the steely determination that family had. And found that it was very good indeed. Though, it was also a source of irritation for him right now.

"It's good," Kit said, "that all of us are together. Because I have something that I need to tell you all. So it's probably best that I only have to do it once."

And it was probably good that Chance's wife had been working, or the whole story would've been blown already.

Jace looked at him with no small amount of suspicion on his face. But then, Jace had been there when Shelby had shown up today.

"Yeah. So. There's no easy way to say it. But… I'm…" He didn't really know how you were supposed to announce this. He was having a baby? He was going to be a dad? And so probably the worst iteration of that came out of his mouth. "Shelby is pregnant."

"Dammit, Kit," Chance shouted, practically crossing three bar stools to get near him. "You knocked up my sister-in-law?"

"Yeah. I did. So… There's that."

"Juniper is going to kill you. Hell. Does she know?"

"She does know. She just wasn't allowed to tell you until I knew, and it turns out she's been working since then, obviously, or you would know."

"When did you find out?" Chance asked.

"I know when he found out," Jace said. "That'd be about three hours ago."

"Yes it would. So it's not like it's a secret that's been being sat on for a hell of a long time. Except Shelby has known for about a month. But she didn't tell anybody. But she confirmed it today."

"Right," Chance bit out. "Because of course you fucked her at my wedding."

"She fucked me back. So, maybe dial your umbrage down a little bit."

"Are you going to marry her?"

"Well, Chance, I offered. I offered like the salt-of-the-earth, code-of-the-West motherfucker that I am. And she said no."

"Of course she did," Chance said, snorting.

And he was a little bit surprised to hear his brother ruefully accept that. Except… His brother got it. That was the thing.

"You know you can't tell them anything," Kit said, meaning the Sohappy sisters in general.

"Yeah. I do."

"And because of you, I can't go hard-line on it."

Chance nodded. "I can see that."

"So unless your wife can talk some sense into her…"

"My wife is better at inciting violence than talking sense, and again, I like that about her, but I just don't know that she's going to be the one for this."

"Damn," Jace said.

Boone shook his head.

"So what are you going to do?" asked Flint.

"Well, I'm going to go on the offensive. I'm going to prove to her that she can't do this without me."

"That's what you want," Jace said.

"I'm having a kid. I wasn't going to do this. It wasn't going to be my life. It wasn't going to be what I chose to do. But it's where I'm at. You know as well as I do that sometimes shit just happens."

"Though in this case," Flint said, "shit happened because you didn't wear a condom."

"Yeah. I am aware that I have responsibility in this."

"You know we are here for you," Chance said. "No matter what."

"Thanks. Now if you'll be there to be a buffer when we tell Mom…"

"She's going to be thrilled," Flint said.

"Yep," Jace agreed.

"The real buffer you're going to need," said Chance, "is when we tell Callie. Because she's going to read you the riot act."

"I can take it."

From his perspective, right now, he could take just about anything. Except having the situation left unresolved with Shelby. That he couldn't take.

But he was going to take charge of that. Immediately.

Chapter 10

Shelby woke up, but she didn't get out of bed. She just lay there, the reality of her new life rolling over her.

She was pregnant. She was pregnant with Kit Carson's baby. There was no denying it.

And the sharp knock on her door seemed to underscore that.

Maybe it was her mom, coming to yell more.

There had been a lot of yelling last night.

It had all ended in tears. And everybody was fine now. She wasn't really surprised at the way that it had gone. They didn't want her to be a single mother. But they were reacting to stigma from a different time. And they were also acting like she was sixteen and not twenty-eight. She had the means to manage herself. She didn't care if anybody judged her. And anyway, they weren't going to. It just wasn't like that anymore. But they could not quite understand that. She understood. They were reacting not just because of the way the world was with women, but specifically because of the way the world was to Brown women. She got it. She had lived her whole life in her skin. But she was deciding to do this. And she was assured in that. She wasn't a kid. She wasn't doing this naively.

And she knew that her family would support her no matter what. They would rally around. It was just they had to air their opinions and grievances first.

And so sitting through the grievances had been a thing.

But she had endured it. And now… Someone was here for round two.

She was not quite ready for round two. Even if it involved smothering and apologies.

She rolled out of bed, and padded to the door. She pushed her hair out of her face and jerked the door open, and froze. Because there was Kit Carson. On her doorstep. Holding bags of groceries.

"What are you doing here?"

"I came to make you breakfast."

"I don't recall…" But he was sweeping past her, into the house, and she felt as if he had broken an invisible tape that had been stretched across the door. Like he had breached something. Changed it.

Because here was this man in her house. This man whom she had slept with. Who was not her husband.

And he was getting food out and setting it on the counter. And rummaging around for pots and pans.

"Coffee?"

"I'm not sure on the coffee rules with pregnancy. I think I can have one. But I might just do tea."

"Works for me. But I need some coffee. Will the smell bother you?"

"No," she said, watching, feeling dazed as he opened up a package of bacon and put a skillet on the stovetop. Her stomach growled.

He turned with his broad back to her, and she couldn't help but admire his form. His muscular shoulders, his narrow waist.

She really needed to get a grip.

But there was bacon. And Kit, and things felt very confused.

"I don't know if you like bacon. Or if you prefer sweet breakfast. But I figured I'd do up some pancakes also."

"I… I like food," she said.

And she felt grateful then that she didn't feel any sort of nausea. Because that, she was given to believe, was a hallmark of the early stages of pregnancy. And she really had felt… Mostly fine.

She had felt a grim sense of foreboding, but she hadn't been sick. Or even really fatigued.

Suddenly, she wondered if that was something she should be worried about.

Well, this was going to be a joy. Worrying about not feeling bad was certainly something she hadn't anticipated.

"What exactly are you doing, Kit?"

"I told you. I told you that I was going to try to bring you around to my way of thinking. I wasn't kidding. I also told you I was going to be involved."

"Well, I don't really think that I'm open to your way of thinking."

"I don't care. And I said this isn't going to be a one-way street. Sorry."

"I don't actually think you're sorry."

"Look," he said. "There's no point in us fighting." The bacon began to sizzle in the pan, and her stomach growled.

"I don't know about that. Maybe there is a point to us fighting. We don't agree. So… It seems to me like there might be a reason for us to fight."

"There's not. We've got some time to sort this out. But I could be here. In the morning. I could take care of things. I can take care of you."

She looked at him, and there were sharp edges to the feeling that swelled within her. How was she supposed to agree to that? To the level of domesticity that he was proposing. How was she supposed to just… Believe that it would work?

It was like agreeing to let a tiger live in your house. Reasonable. Or indeed possible. That was the thing. She looked at Kit and she just didn't see how any of this was possible. Or how it could ever be.

"I've been taking care of myself for a long time."

"I get that," he said, taking a mixing bowl out of her cupboard—how was he finding things so unerringly? She could swear that he was better at maneuvering around her kitchen than she was. "But there's more to it now. There's a baby on the way. And you don't have to do this by yourself. You don't have to do this alone. So why should you?"

"Because, Kit. Because things change. And people die. And I don't even know how all this is going to work out. And jumping into it like this… I'm sorry. But it terrifies me." Admitting that made her feel small. Weak and pale, and she didn't want to feel like any of those things. She wanted to be a brave warrior woman. Somebody who had stared one of the worst things ever in the face and come out stronger.

Right now, she just didn't know how she was going to cope with all of this. "We just… We just don't even know how all of this is going to pan out, and it scares me, frankly. It scares me. Okay? I just can't…"

"Yeah. It scares me too," he said, stopping and turning to face her. "I get it. I know how fragile things can feel."

Except she wanted to tell him it was different. It was all fine when they were talking about grief in vague terms together. He had lost his sister. She had lost her partner. The person whom she was building her whole life off of. It wasn't fair. But that was the thing about grief. It wasn't especially fair all the time. And sometimes she wanted to lash out at people when they told her they had also lost somebody. She wanted to say it wasn't the same. That they hadn't grown up with their husband. That they hadn't loved the way that she did.

Yeah. It wasn't fair. It wasn't fair at all. But sometimes she just… She just didn't want to be fair.

"Well. You're not carrying a baby. So I don't really know that you do know how fragile things can feel. Right now… It all feels precarious. It could go away. It could go away, it could just not actually be happening. And that… I can't make plans with you right now."

He turned away from her, and went back to the business of making pancakes. The bacon was still sizzling. The domesticity of it made her head hurt. Made her chest hurt.

Because this wasn't real. This was him trying to get his way. And it wasn't… It wasn't right either way.

"You're right. I'm not carrying the baby. I'm trying to help you carry a couple of things. I get it. I'm not even your plan B. I get that. But you know, I'm also not a total deadbeat. And I'm trying to prove that to you."

"I didn't say you were a deadbeat."

"I know you didn't. But I'm also not the person that you figured on doing this with. And I get the feeling that you're more comfortable with the idea of doing it by yourself because it affords you a certain level of denial."

"I did not ask for you to psychoanalyze me."

"No. It's freely offered. Lucky you."

"And what about you? Because I don't for one second think that you're doing anything in a way that isn't also just about protecting yourself. Because that's what we do. All of us people. All the time. We want to protect ourselves."

He paused again. And this time, when he turned to face her, his expression was improbably grim. "Yeah. You're not wrong about that. Here's the thing. I want to keep you safe. I want to keep the baby safe."

"You can't just do that."

"This makes me feel like I'm close to it. And I need that. Okay?"

"Do you actually…? Would it be easier for you if it all went away?"

"Maybe. Maybe, actually. But I don't want that either."

And neither did she. Because yeah. It would be easier if this particular baby went away, and if she wanted to have a baby she could just go do it with a turkey baster, and actually commit to the single-motherhood thing. But she didn't want that. Because in so many ways Kit Carson felt like her destiny, and while she couldn't explain it, standing there resisting it as hard as she was, this felt a little bit like destiny too. Or maybe she was just trying to find more excuses for the fact that he made her behave like a wanton. Either way, this was complex in a way she really didn't want. And yet, it was the reality.

"I don't either."

He nodded, his expression hard, and then he turned back to the pancakes. She was silent while he finished cooking breakfast. And she didn't have it in her to be stubborn enough to turn down the glory that was this home-cooked meal. Because it really did look good.

"So… Do I want to know why you know how to cook breakfast? Is it that guy thing? Where you have to know how to do it, because you have a lot of one-night stands?"

"No," he said, snorting. "My one-night stands never stay for breakfast, Shelby."

She scoffed. "But you do have them."

"I have, yes. And you haven't."

"Just you." Heat sizzled between them and she did her best to ignore it. "Here you are. At breakfast."

"Here you are. Having my baby."

"Here I thought I was having my baby," she said.

But the way that he looked at her, and the way that he'd said it, sent a shiver through her that had nothing to do with maternal instinct. It was that biological insanity that had brought them here in the first place.

"Mine too," he said.

"Right. Well. I guess so."

"If you enjoy the breakfast… There's plenty more where that came from."

She swallowed hard. "I think there needs to be some ground rules."

"Well. Let's go over the rules while we eat."

He dished up the breakfast for both of them, and she let him. Because it had been a long time since someone other than her mother had done anything like caring for her.

And she had to admit that she did enjoy it. A man moving around her kitchen. In her house. In her life. But the more she was trying to turn her thoughts right side up, the more she had to really think about the implications of this. He needed to be in her child's life. In their child's life. It was what he wanted. It was important to him. And that meant that they were going to have to be civil. More than civil, they were going to have to deal with each other. The passage of time. The way their lives might change. Proposing that they stay separate was safe in a lot of ways. Things would never be worse between them than they were now. They wouldn't allow for it to get sticky and toxic.

Sure, there was the unknown. Whether or not he would marry someone else.

She didn't think that she would.

But…

She ignored the cramping in her stomach that came as a direct result of that thought.

He wasn't really the marrying type. And anyway, if he ever became the marrying type, that was his business. She just felt possessive about it right now because… Well, she was pregnant with his child. That gave her the right to be possessive, didn't it?

It was just a temporary state of being. While she housed part of his genetic material. So there. That seemed like a logical place to put it.

He set the plates on the table, her mug of tea. And

she sat in front of the plate, across from him, her heart thundering harder than she would like.

"We have to keep this like this," she said emphatically.

"Excuse me?"

"We're almost friends. And I think that's probably the best place for our relationship."

"We're almost friends?"

"Yes," she said. "We had that really good conversation the night before the bachelorette party…"

"And then we had sex the night after. So why is one of those things a bigger deal than the other? Because it seems to me, the sex is actually why we're here."

"It seems to me that that is an instructive lesson in the nature of sex, and what it can do to a relationship. So I'm thinking that we don't do that again. That's what I'm thinking. I'm thinking, no sex. Because sex caused a whole lot of problems." She felt herself getting warmer and warmer each time she said the word *sex*, and she would really like to be done with that. But she had to act like it didn't matter, because she had to act like maybe they could be friends, because she needed that to be true and real and what was going to happen, because she had to get some control in the situation. She didn't have any, that was for sure.

And she needed it. That was one thing about grief. It had kept her isolated. But it was her grief to deal with and nobody else's, so while people were occasionally on hand to try and be there for her, it was essentially an all-by-yourself sort of thing.

And… She preferred that. This was joint. A partnership. With a man whom she didn't actually have a relationship with. Yes, she had long-standing avoidance of him because of her desire to see him naked, and then they'd talked, and she found that she quite liked him. And then they'd had sex, and she had found out she quite liked his body. But this was different. They had to be different. She clung to that image in her mind. The soft, sweet maternal life. Where she sat in a rocking chair and held the baby, and felt complete. Yeah. She tried to sit with that. For as long as possible.

"We're going to share custody of the child. And have to see each other. And right now, this feels good. It feels companionable."

"Companionable?" The way he asked that, low and flat and gravelly so that it echoed between her thighs, made a liar out of her, but she couldn't afford to let him know that.

"Yes," she said. "Pleasant, even. Why shouldn't we be able to share breakfast with each other? We should, right? This would be ideal. You could come over, we can have a meal. We get a family dinner sometimes. We could share custody, but also share a life."

"There's a thing for that. It's called marriage."

"No. That's disastrous. If we get married we're going to need very specific things from each other. It's going to be about us. This needs to be about our child. And so… No arguing. No sex. None of that."

"No sex."

"No."

"You're cool if I go have sex with other people?"

She ground her back molars together. "Totally fine. I have no claim on you. We are going to be a *Modern Family.*"

"What if I told you that I'm not predisposed to very modern ways of thinking?"

"Then I will tell you to go find some enlightenment. Climb to the top of the mountain or something. Commune with nature. Eat a Twinkie. Do something to reach an elevated state of being."

"What if I told you this doesn't work for me?"

"I don't want to fight with you," she said, feeling like she was tearing strips off herself even while she talked, showing the ugly wounds she carried, showing her deepest self. She hated it. "I desperately don't want to fight with you. Because my life has been a series of fights with everything that has happened to me, with everything that is going on in the world, with… My whole soul for two years now, and I am tired. I am just tired of the relentlessness of it. And I need this to not be hard."

"I hate to break it to you, sweetheart, but I think having a kid is hard. I think change on this level is hard."

"I don't want it to be," she said, the words coming out choked. She just wanted something nice. Something good. She just really wanted to be happy. "I don't want it to be. I think you're a good guy. I do."

"Why? You found me irritating all the times before, and we had one conversation and I gave you a couple of orgasms and now suddenly I'm a good guy?"

"You also cook me bacon," she said, her voice small.

"You don't really know me."

And how did she tell him that she did? She knew the particular way the sun illuminated his hair and revealed wheat and gold and glory every time it did. How did she tell him that she knew the way that his eyes lit up when he saw a woman he wanted to take home, because she'd seen that happen more than once at a bar, and she had always been held captive by the dance between him and the woman that would never be her. How did she tell him that he had caused her pain on deep, deep levels? Shame. That he had made her question whether or not she was a good person. And yet she had still found a way to live her life and stay away from him, and some of that was because… She had admiration for him.

Some of it was because of him. Just like the other feelings were about him.

How did she tell him any of that?

She didn't even like going over it to herself. Because the more she sat with it, the more she dwelled on it—which she had never done when she was married—the more she had to acknowledge that he had been a thing always.

"I've seen you around. For a lot of years. I just think that you are a decent guy. If I didn't think that I would've handled all of this very differently. That's the truth of it. But I think that we can do this, and I think that we can be happy and… I just really want that."

She was begging him now. Pleading with him. "I really need to be happy."

"Then I'm going to do what I can to make you happy."

"Oh, don't get mixed up in that. You can't make me happy. But you can contribute to my happiness, or make things more difficult. I would like it if you were trying to contribute good things."

"What's the difference?"

"There's too many things that have happened to me that you didn't have anything to do with that have made things hard. So it can't be up to you to fix them."

"Yeah. Again, I don't see why."

"Because it isn't like that. Okay?"

He shrugged. And she had the feeling that wasn't an

agreement. She had a feeling she hadn't one. She had a feeling that he was going to be a lot more difficult than she anticipated.

But if he would just shrug and make pancakes, then that was fine.

"Do you want to know the first time I thought you were beautiful?"

She lifted her face, her eyes clashing with his, horror hitting her square in the stomach. "I'm not sure that I do."

But part of her, this desperate, fluttering part of her, did want to know. Why wasn't that part of her dead? Why had not that part of her died with Chuck? This part of her that acted like a teenage girl, and wanted... To have her crush tell her that she was pretty. That's what he was. Her crush.

Her crush she was having a baby with. Her crush she'd slept with. But a crush nonetheless.

"Yeah. Well. Let's just get it out in the open. You think that the way that we are is the way that it's going to be. So I think that we need to get some stuff out there. Don't you?"

"I don't know."

"Yeah. Well. I'm a decisive kind of guy. It's a risky proposition though it may be... I remember seeing you when you first got engaged to him. And you were hanging out down in front of the bar. I think you and your friends were angling to get some beers bought for you. But you were too young. And you were laughing. And I remember the way the sun kind of hit you from behind. And you were just lit up. And it wasn't just the sun. It was your joy. And I just remember your hair was so shiny and perfect, and your skin was brown all lit up in gold. And I wanted to touch you. And there was a ring shining on your finger, and I knew that I never would. And it's a funny thing. Because I have a level of deep acceptance about that which I can't change or have in this life. Which I'm not in charge of. That comes from loss. Maybe *acceptance* is a strong word, I don't know. But I get it. I'm not in charge of everything. But it just felt… It really felt like a kick in the face. In that moment. That I could want you like I did, but never have you."

The words took the breath out of her lungs, and like all other beautiful things in her life… They were a complication. She wanted to feel flattered, but that wasn't enough. It was too easy of a response. Too shallow.

"I didn't know," she whispered.

"Why should you? It wasn't a thing that could happen. It wasn't a thing."

Did she tell him? It felt risky. It felt like standing on the edge of a cliff. But if this really was about honesty… Could she actually let the unspoken hang between them? Or did she need to say something?

"The first time I noticed you I was in middle school. You were playing football. And I thought that you were… Like a movie star."

"Is that so?"

"Yeah. Unfortunately."

"So we just kept missing each other."

"Yeah. We just kept missing each other."

"Well, we managed to make it stick when we didn't miss, didn't we?"

"I am deeply uncomfortable with all of this," she said, putting her face in her hands.

"Life's uncomfortable."

"So are you… You're going to stay here? You're not going to go back out to the circuit?"

"Yeah. I expect that's what I'll do. I was looking for confirmation. On what I should do. And this pretty much decides it for me. I have something to stay for."

"Yeah."

And there was something about that that settled her. He had something to stay for. And she had something new to live for. This child.

And she was filled with terror about it all going away, but this felt good. It felt right.

They could do this. They could do this and it would be okay. It had to be.

"Shared custody." He was mumbling and muttering while he used a pickax to get granite up out of the ground to clear out the field, and finally, Jace acknowledged the muttering.

"What's going on?"

"She thinks that we're going to have a platonic relationship wherein we share custody of the child."

"Sounds mature," Jace said.

He looked at Jace. Hard. "And you would be fine with that?"

"I didn't say I would be *fine* with that. I said it sounded mature."

"Well. I'm not fine. And maybe I'm not mature."

"And what are you going to do about it?"

"I brought her breakfast this morning. And I aim to keep doing that."

"Keep bringing her breakfast?"

"Yeah. And dinner. I want her to see that she can't do

this without me. Hell, I want to make it so she doesn't want to do this without me."

"And what do you want exactly?"

He thought of the way they'd been this morning, sitting at the kitchen table, that low-level hum of need between them.

"I want her," he said. And suddenly, it was like the sky had broken open and rained down to hallelujah. Like God had slapped him across the face and said: finally, dumbass.

"I want her," he said again. Emphatically. "I don't want to be friends. I don't want to share custody. If we are going to have a baby, we need to be a family. And hell, how else am I supposed to keep her safe?"

"Fine. But what does that have to do with her?"

And he realized that was the thing. She had said that this needed to be about the baby. But for him it would never just be about the baby. He had wanted her, and they'd slept together because of that long-held desire between them. Longer than he'd ever even realized. At least on her end. And he couldn't separate the things. The pregnancy was a direct result of that desire. It wasn't on its own. It wasn't he could never be neutral about her. He never had been. He wanted her. In his bed every night and damn everything else. He wanted to keep her safe. And that meant keeping her with him. He wanted... He wanted to take care of her.

"Are you in love with her?"

Everything in him shied away from that. That felt like a bridge too far. That felt like the kind of wound you didn't come back from. And anyway, she might be attracted to him, but she was in love with a dead man.

"I want her. Functionally, for me, it's all the same."

"Well. Let's hope your plan to bait her with food works."

"I have some other things to fall back on if it doesn't."

"And that is?"

"She didn't get pregnant for just playing checkers."

"Yes. I guess not."

"How about you?" he asked. "You ever…"

He shot Kit a look. "Don't go there."

"I haven't gone anywhere. You don't even know what I was about to ask you."

"Was it about Cara?"

"Actually no. But way to go. You just shone a big ole spotlight on yourself."

"Well, no. Generically and to Cara. Cara needs to be protected at all costs. She's been through enough. She's a strong woman, and I care about her. But it isn't like that. Protecting her means… Never… Ever."

"What's so wrong with you?"

"I could ask you the same question, Kit."

"It's not about me," Kit said. "About love in general. It's a lot of work. I love you. I love everyone in this family. I'm going to have a kid. I… I don't need more. I don't need heavier. I know that Shelby feels the same way. Life has taken it out on her pretty hard too."

"Well, Godspeed. Make sure you include dessert with dinner."

"Good idea," he said.

He wasn't happy with any of this, but he had a plan. And that was the kind of man Kit was. If it was broken, he'd do his best to fix it. He may not have wanted to take on something like this, but he was now. And he would do the absolute best with it that anybody ever could.

Chapter 11

He went to her house every day for the next couple of weeks. He made breakfast, and three times a week, he made dinner.

They sat together and they ate it. And they talked about their childhoods—it was interesting to hear her side of the family dispute, which, of course, involved his ancestor cheating in a poker game and stealing the land from her family, and though he had already accepted that version of events after Chance and Juniper had gotten together, it was important that he heard it from Shelby herself—but they also found out they weren't all that different. They had been raised on the backs of horses. Raised to love this place. Generations of blood were soaked into the dirt. And they could respect that in each other.

He loved hearing about how her grandmother had taught her to be. How she'd learn to cook traditional recipes, and how her family tried to hang on to their traditions, their ways, as much as they could, while her parents also worked to give them all the advantages of the current culture right along with it. As someone who hadn't grown up with cultural tension, it was interesting to hear about it. And he found it meant something that she trusted him with the stories. They didn't talk about her marriage. They didn't talk about grief again. And they didn't really talk about the future.

But knowing about Shelby's foundation mattered.

He was supposed to be making her realize that she needed him. But all this was growing an attachment that he hadn't quite counted on. One that he hadn't anticipated.

But he had to wonder if Shelby just felt like they were growing that friendship she wanted. For him, it was something more. Something deeper.

He had her doctor appointment marked on his calendar, and when the day arrived, he got up early to make her breakfast like he always did, then he went to the bathroom and threw up. Though he didn't let her know about the throwing up.

He realized that he was… He was not handling this well. Because he knew as well as anyone that life just didn't always hand you good things. What if they went and there was no baby? What if all of this was gone before they got to have it? He wasn't sure that he could handle that. He wasn't sure… Yes. He wasn't sure about any of it. He knocked on the door, and she answered, looking tired. And maybe a little bit sick herself.

"You okay?"

"Yeah," she said. Then she groaned. "No. I'm nervous. Because if not for the positive pregnancy test, and the missed periods, I don't know that I would even know I was pregnant. And I did some online research…"

"Damnation, woman. Don't you know better than that?"

"It can indicate that you have a low level of hCG. Which could mean that something is wrong."

"Well, that's a fucked-up mess. Feeling worse when you're pregnant is better?"

"It's just what I read. I don't know… I don't know. I'm almost twelve weeks. So it's like… If everything is okay today, then maybe everything is okay. But what if it's not okay? What if we just spent all this time… For nothing?"

"Let me make you some breakfast."

"I don't think I can eat."

"Well, let's do our best."

He didn't tell her that he'd thrown his guts up forty-five minutes earlier. Because what was the point in letting her know that he wasn't any better off than she was? He wanted to spare her that. He didn't want to validate any of her worries.

He made a scaled-back breakfast, and they both did the best they could to eat. Maybe she was trying to be brave for him too. The thought made him smile a little bit.

"Let me drive," he said, opening up the passenger-side door of his truck and guiding her into it.

"Thank you," she said. "For being with me. It actually does mean a lot, and you know that I hate to admit that."

"I do know that, Shelby. I know you don't like to admit to needing anyone."

"I don't need you," she said, in defiance, and it made him laugh. In spite of it.

"Of course not," he said.

"I don't," she said. "I can't afford to need anybody. Not ever again. Needing people just… It just hurts in the end. It just hurts and hurts, and what's the point? You can't control whether or not you get to keep a person, so you can't really ever let yourself need someone."

"You know, I get that." Except he hadn't needed his sister. It wasn't that. But he understood how fragile everything was. "But I'm not sure that cutting yourself off from those kinds of connections is a good thing either."

"I didn't ask."

"I guess you didn't."

The little clinic that they went to just outside town was old and quaint and had definitely seen better days. And he didn't know what to expect from any of it. He'd never done anything like this before. Never been to a place like this.

"I come here for my yearly," she said. "So. You didn't need to know that." She was scribbling on paperwork and sitting deeply in one of the vinyl chairs.

"Why don't I need to know that?"

"It's not the kind of thing that we really need to share."

"I'm about to go into a doctor appointment with you. I can certainly handle mentions of your yearly."

And yet, it was notable in difference, because he had certainly never been in a relationship with a woman that was this intimate. And they'd only slept together one time. It was weird as hell.

But it also didn't feel… Bad. Not at all.

They got called into the room, and she sent him out while she got dressed in a hospital gown. He thought it was a little bit silly, all things considered. But when he came back in, she was lying on the table, covered by a blanket.

"So what exactly are they going to do?"

"I think they… Check for a heartbeat? And maybe do an ultrasound. To check how far along and all that."

"Well. We already know that," he said.

"True. I guess a lot of people can't be sure. But we're sure."

"Yeah. Pretty damn sure."

The door opened and an older, short man came in, and began to speak in a soothing voice, explaining exactly what he was going to do. Which was essentially what Shelby had said she thought would happen.

There was a small portable ultrasound machine and the doctor brought it up to the side of the bed. Kit suddenly felt frozen. He hadn't been prepared for this. He didn't know what the hell he'd been prepared for. But not this. Not the knowledge that they were going to see the child now. She looked similarly distressed, and reached out and took hold of his hand. He squeezed it tightly.

The doctor lifted up her gown and pushed the sheet low, before squirting a gel over Shelby's stomach, and putting the wand there. The sound was instantaneous. A strange pumping, whooshing sound that filled up the room. And then they saw movement. "Holy shit," he said, leaning into the screen. "Is that it?"

The doctor looked at him in a vaguely scolding manner, but Kit didn't care. "Yes. That's the baby." He wiggled the wand, and then moved it down lower. "And feet."

"And the heartbeat?" Kit asked.

The doctor moved the wand again, and he could see

a fluttering gray thing, surrounded by black. "There it is. I'm just going to take some measurements."

Shelby squeezed his hand, and when he looked at her, he saw that her lips were pale. "Are you okay?"

She nodded, but didn't say anything.

"Based on what I'm seeing here, and on the dates you gave me… I'm going to put the date at March 1."

It seemed like both an eternity and a blink away. And he couldn't quite process the entire situation.

"Everything looks normal?" Shelby asked.

"Everything looks on track," the doctor said. "Exactly what I would expect to see."

"So I just… What do I do?"

"You come back in a month," the doctor said. "We should be able to do an ultrasound to establish the gender then if you'd like."

"Yeah," Shelby said, her eyes suddenly bright. "Okay."

The doctor left them, and Kit prepared to go too.

"It's okay," she said. "You can stay."

Without being asked, he turned to face the wall as she got up. He listened to the sound of her putting her clothes on. Fabric against skin.

Normally, he would be turning this into something a little bit more sensual. But for now… All he could think about was what he had just seen on the screen. All he could think about was the reality crashing in on him.

It looked so small and helpless. It was contained inside her body. There was nothing he could do. Nothing he could do to make sure that this went well. For him or for her.

"Are you okay?" he asked.

"Yeah," she said. "You can turn around now."

She was dressed again. And she looked so vulnerable. He wanted...

He wanted to protect her from everything. And what an uncomfortable feeling that was.

Because he knew that he couldn't. Because he knew that the world was cruel. Because he...

"Why don't we go home," he said. "You can take a rest. I'll be back by tonight for dinner."

And he realized that he'd said *home*, like it was theirs. But she didn't correct him, so he didn't bother to walk it back.

He didn't want to. And when he dropped her back at her house and said goodbye to her, he marveled at the fact that his relationships usually centered on sex. This one... Well, sex had certainly played a part in it, but there was all this other stuff, and it made it so singular. Different. Unlike anything he had ever even imagined.

In that sense, he was almost glad that she put a moratorium on the physical. Because it had forced them to get to know one another. It had forced them to build this other thing.

And he wanted to keep on building it.

He didn't know what that meant, or where it was headed.

But there was something about his plan that seemed unfocused now. It wasn't about him anymore. It was about her.

And that was the strangest realization of all.

Chapter 12

She woke up crying. She was glad she had the nap after the doctor appointment, but she had a dream... This dream where Kit was sitting in a rocking chair, shirtless, holding a tiny baby, somehow the epitome of her fantasies, both sexual and domestic all at once, and seeing him there with that familiar wood paneling behind him, seeing him enmeshed in her life, had made her cry in that dream. And when she'd woken up, the crying hadn't been only in the dream.

She tried to get herself together. She went to sit and work on a bracelet that she'd been beading for a few days now, but she couldn't focus.

She was pregnant. Really pregnant, and there was nothing wrong.

Kit had been there for her exhaustively... And she was... She was having a really hard time. With everything. She didn't understand how her life had gone from stagnant and stuck to this. She had wanted something different, but this was decidedly more different than she had been anticipating.

He was coming for dinner. He was cooking for her again. He did it for her all the time, and she just…

She was beginning to feel helpless. Like all these changes were spinning out of her control. It certainly wasn't the sweet, easier life that she had planned for.

That she had thought she would maybe begin to pursue.

Maybe the problem is you don't know what you want.

She did. She wanted the baby. She wanted everything to go smoothly with Kit.

She was not ready for him to show up, and when he did, she felt pretty raw still from everything.

"How are you?" And it was the concern that got her. The concern that made her want to run and hide from this. From him. But she didn't have the luxury of doing that. It was all supposed to be easy, right? Because they were friends?

Except when he breezed past her and went into her kitchen, grocery bags in hand, she had the sudden realization of why it wasn't easy.

They were having a marriage. All this intimacy, emotional and deep. Sex had at least been a distraction after their conversation about grief at the ranch, but… This was just all the emotional stuff. Nothing else.

He threw a dish towel over his broad shoulder and started to take ingredients out of the bag in front of him. She didn't know that was such a sexy thing to do, but it was. That sort of determined and focused competence. More than competence. The thing about Kit was that he was great at everything he did.

Get it together.

He got out a cutting board, and some vegetables, and began to slice through them with ruthless efficiency. And she was enthralled.

Trying to wrap her head around this moment. This life. And suddenly, it was like all the feelings were just too big for her. All of this. Because how was he here in her kitchen. And how was she here, pregnant with his baby? And what was her life? Was she still herself even?

It had seemed simpler when it was sex.

Because the sex wasn't like anything else. It was like a fantasy. It wasn't like her marriage. It wasn't like building a life. It was like burning everything to the ground. In an incendiary flame. It wasn't thinking or talking. It let her make him into something less complicated. Muscle and rough hands and a hard body.

That's what it let her have. And so she did what her body was begging her to do. What her senses demanded. She moved up behind him, and pressed her breasts to his back. She felt him go still. Completely and utterly still. He set the knife down flat on the counter, and then he growled, turning around and cupping her face, her chin held tightly in his palm. "What exactly are you offering me?"

And suddenly, this was dangerous Kit. The one who had put everything she knew in jeopardy every time she saw his face. The one who made her question everything.

It was that Kit. Yeah. That one.

"I would think that was pretty obvious," she said, sucking a sharp breath as she moved her hands to the front of his jeans. Her knees buckled. But thankfully, he was holding so tightly to her that she didn't fall. Because there he was. Hard and rigid already beneath her hand. Big and heavy and she could remember what it had been like to have him inside her.

Yeah. She could well remember.

Her breath hissed through her teeth as she let her fingers skim his hardened length. "I want you," she said.

"Do you?"

"Yes," she said. "I want you, now. In me."

"Me? Or are you thinking about someone else?"

"I have never thought about someone else when I wanted you."

And that was when he growled, feral and rough, and walked her back so that she was pressed flat against the kitchen wall. Her shirt was tugged up violently over her head, cast onto the floor. Her bra followed, and he kissed his way down her neck, her collarbone, took one of her sensitive nipples between his lips and sucked.

"Shit," he breathed. "You're more beautiful than I remembered."

He moved his hand with carnal reverence over her breasts, down her stomach, where he flicked open the button on her jeans and lowered the zipper.

Then he pushed his hand down beneath the waistband of her underwear, and found her wet with need for him. Because it only took a second.

She gasped, her head falling back against the wall as he began to stroke her. This was… This was that wild sex. That wild desire. Wild desire that she thought wasn't real.

It was so starkly different from what she'd had before. What she had before had been nice. What she had before had been manageable. And there was nothing manageable about Kit. He was too big. Too wild.

Too much. He was something she couldn't control, and she'd been foolish just now thinking that she could. That this was her game. That she could take him and make him into something that she could dominate. It wasn't possible.

Because here in her house where she had built a life before, he was breaking her into small little pieces. Something she was afraid she would never be able to put back together. But her life was broken, so why shouldn't she be?

Is it broken, or are you just afraid of what's been built?

She shoved that thought aside, because she didn't want to think. She wanted pleasure. She wanted sex. She wanted Kit and his cock and nothing else. She didn't want anything more than this gloried, heady desire that was unlike anything she had ever experienced. And before she knew it, she was naked, with him fully clothed before her. He knelt down, lifted her leg up over his shoulder and parted her wide as his mouth made contact with the heart of her, already slick with her need as he began to lick her, deeper and deeper until she was shaking. Until she was clinging to his shoulders and crying out with unfulfilled desire.

Damn him. It was a blessing. A curse. Everything, all rolled into one.

It was light and shadow and impossibly out of reach.

And yet there she was, clinging to him for all she was worth, her fingers speared into his hair as she held his head right there. Just there. She rocked her hips, lost in the pagan rhythm that he set with his wicked tongue. And then she burst. Broke open. Shattered. Gasping and crying out his name.

And she knew that this was just another game that she had lost.

But before she could protest, he straightened, lifted her up, flipped that dish towel off his shoulder, set it on the counter and then set her bare ass right on top of that. "Didn't want you to be cold," he said against her mouth.

"Oh," she said, her brain a fog.

Then he stripped his shirt off and her mouth went dry. And her brain went blank.

He was the most beautiful man she'd ever seen.

And her need was a desperate thing. Clawing at her. And there was no biological excuse for it. She was already pregnant. She was already pregnant, and so there was nothing to hide behind. This was just need. Pure, filthy need. She'd already had an orgasm, but it wasn't enough. Because she wanted to feel his possession. She wanted his cock buried deep inside her. When she cried out his name.

She wanted him. All of him. She wanted to lose herself and find herself all at once. And she knew that the only way to do that was...

He undid the buckle on his jeans and tugged the zipper down roughly. She pushed his jeans down his lean hips, and he freed his arousal, drawing her close to him as he pressed slowly into her heat.

"Kit," she shouted, almost embarrassed by the intensity of the demand wound around his name.

She couldn't. She could not. And yet she was. They were. Because it was all the things and everything, and it was him and her together. Like nothing and no one had ever been.

Did everybody feel like this? Except, dimly, she knew that not everybody had this. So no. Not everybody felt like this. Because she'd never felt like this before. Like sex was a wonderful mystery that they alone had unlocked. That only they could ever figure the combination that would make this particular pleasure click.

He was so big and hard inside her, like he was made to fit her. Just a bit too much, but in the very best way.

She didn't want her sex comfortable. She didn't want it easy. She wanted hard and rough with a slight bite of pain. And he delivered. Cupping her ass as he pulled her against him, thrusting hard inside her and leaving her breathless each and every time.

His strokes were deep, and she lost herself in it. In this. In him.

She looked into his eyes, and she felt what burned there resonated in her soul.

And it terrified her. Made her tremble. Made her want to look away. Made her want to escape, but he held her face still as he drove into her again, and again. As her own desire wound around her like a golden thread, making her shiver.

Making her come apart at the seams.

And then she broke. Crying out his name just a moment before he shouted hers, spilling deep inside her, his hardness pulsing deep within her.

"Kit," she whispered. And he kissed her. Her mouth, her forehead, her cheeks. He kissed her and kissed her like there was nothing else he wanted to do in the whole world.

Like he was shocked and unmade by this thing she was.

In her house. In her little house that she had shared with Chuck for all those years.

And suddenly, she couldn't picture Chuck in it. And

sadness closed her throat. Made her gasp. Made it hard to breathe.

"We'll have dinner later," he said, scooping her up and carrying her from the kitchen into the bathroom. As if he had been here a hundred times. As if he lived here. He turned the water on, and she waited, shivering as he undressed all the way. And when the water was warm, he put her in the shower and moved his hands over her body, gently, with great care. The warm water washed over her. And it did something to her. She didn't know if it was healing or hurting. She honestly couldn't tell.

"I…"

"Hey," he said. "You are okay. You're okay."

And she didn't know how he could say that. Because he didn't know. He didn't know. He wrapped his arms around her and pulled her naked body flush against his. He moved his hands over her curves, and he kissed her. Kissed her until she couldn't think.

Then he turned the shower off, dried her off and carried her to the bed, where he left her for a full forty-five minutes. And she just lay there. Feeling shell-shocked. Afraid that he would join her. Afraid that he wouldn't. And then he appeared wearing only a pair of jeans, holding two plates of food. He handed her one, and she took it, curled up beneath the blankets still. Then he got into the space beside her, on top of the blankets, his own plate on his lap. "How you doing?"

"Hungry," she said, drawing the plate up to her face.

"Good. Eat."

But how did she tell him? How did she explain the strange, fractured feeling blooming in her chest? Like a chip had been put into a windowpane long ago, and now the pressure, the cold, the heat, something, was making that crack expand. Spider outward.

"I think we should get married, don't you?"

And she didn't know how to say no. Not this time. Because what leg did she have to stand on? It had made sense to kiss him an hour ago. It had seemed like the best idea in the world. Like it would wrench some control back. Like finding that sexual connection again would somehow erase the tenderness that they'd found. But it hadn't. Here he was, in bed with her, eating dinner.

"I don't… I don't…"

"I want to take care of you," he said, and she was so grateful he'd said that. Because that wasn't marriage as she knew it. And somehow, that made it feel safer. "When my sister was sick, my brother and I made her a little wagon. And we decorated it. I spent hours taking her around in that thing. Like she was a little princess. And I loved it. I think I believed in things still. Different than I do now. Like I believed that there was some kind of healing power in love. I couldn't fix her. And if love could've healed her, then she would've been here. Believe me."

And oh, she knew that. She felt it. Deep in her soul, and it just hurt. It hurt so much to hear him say this, she wanted him to stop. It wrapped itself around her own grief and regret and pain. Around the futility of loss, and the merciless movement of the world as it kept on spinning even after your heart had been crushed.

She knew what it was like to wish love could save someone.

To be devastated that it couldn't.

Even as his words hurt, she felt closer to him. Felt like she understood him.

"And I'm… I spent a lot of years afraid," he said. "Afraid that I'd lose her. And then I did. And then I was afraid when my mom got pregnant with Callie. That something would happen to her. That something would happen to the baby. And it's like I've spent my whole life on this hypervigilant watch. Thinking that somehow… My love was gonna stop something from happening. My… My will for everything to be okay was going to fix something, and I always thought that caring was just so exhausting I never wanted to care for another person as long as I lived. Not an extra one. But I care for you. I'll even give you a ride in a wagon if you want."

And her heart just felt like it cracked in two. Because she was tired. She was tired and he wanted to carry this. She was tired and he wanted to carry her. In a wagon. It wasn't some empty gesture from some guy who didn't know the weight of loss. He knew. And he still wanted this. And she could have it. Because it was different. Because… Because she was just so damned tired of being by herself. Because she wanted him to touch her every night. Because she wanted her baby to have a father. And maybe because she was scared and didn't want stigma.

"I'll marry you," she said. "I'll… Yeah."

"We don't have to have a wedding."

She nodded, tears filling her eyes. "Good. Good. I don't want to have another one."

"We just need to go sign the paperwork and do the thing. You don't even have to really formalize all that. We can have a court witness if you want."

"I would like that. Thank you. We can just tell everybody that we eloped. I think that would be for the best."

"Do you want me to move in with you or do you want to move in with me?"

And she realized she hadn't even been to his house. And she was torn. So torn, because having him here in this place, in her bed was… Unfathomable. But she had imagined raising the baby here.

"I don't know yet," she said.

"That's okay. We don't even have to move in together right away. We've got time."

"I hear a *but*."

"Yeah. But, I think we should get married. As quickly as possible."

"Are you afraid I'll change my mind?"

"Yes," he said. And she had to laugh. Because she sort of was too. And she couldn't really put her finger on why. No. She really couldn't.

"You want to go get a marriage license tomorrow?"

"Sure," she said.

"Do you want me to leave you alone tonight?"

She shoveled in the last bite of her dinner. "I don't know."

"I tell you what. I'm gonna stay."

And he stayed on top of the covers, with her naked beneath them, and pulled her to him, holding her close. And that was how they stayed all night.

Chapter 13

Kit felt like he should feel a little more about getting Shelby to agree to marry him. Like he should feel triumphant or something. But he didn't. Instead, he felt a vague sense of disquiet that he couldn't quite put his finger on. Because he didn't feel... Like you did when you accomplished something. At least, not what he really wanted. But he couldn't quite figure out what he wanted. He couldn't really say either what had possessed him to tell her the story about Sophie. But nonetheless, the next day, they went to town with the appropriate documentation and went to the courthouse to file for a marriage license.

"Getting married again," the older woman in the register's office said, smiling at Shelby. "I'm so happy for you, honey."

"Thank you," Shelby said, her cheeks going dark pink.

"We'll want to come back and do the thing in three days," Kit said.

"Not a problem," the woman said. "There are plenty of spots available. Just call ahead, and Sherm will be happy to do the ceremony."

"Great," he said.

"Boy, your families really did get rid of that feud, didn't they?"

"Yeah," Shelby said. "I guess you could say we did, Rose. Thank you."

When they walked back out of the courthouse, onto the main street of Lone Rock, which didn't hold a whole lot, Shelby looked tired. "I need to make a stop by Carefree Buffalo. They have some money for me. Because they sold a few of my pieces."

"Yeah," he said.

He walked down the street with her, and into a little shop that sold handmade knives, jewelry and leather goods.

There was a little corner with a variety of beaded items. Bracelets, earrings, barrettes.

"You did all these?" he asked, pointing to the display.

"Yeah," she said, looking embarrassed.

The owner of the store came out, and Shelby greeted him, and what they were saying kind of faded into the background.

He watched her, and he watched her in a different way than he ever had. He knew her now. The rhythm of her. The way that she smiled, the way she laughed. The way she breathed. He had shared a bed with her last night, and he had never shared a bed with a woman all night. They hadn't had sex in that bed, and it had felt as astonishingly intimate as what had taken place in the kitchen. If not more so. He just… When she turned to look at him, a lingering smile from her conversation with the shopkeeper on her face, his heart stopped. Everything stopped. He was in love with her. He was in love with her, and that was why he wanted to marry her. He'd never been in love. He'd never wanted to be. He thought it sounded like work, and heavy work at that. But it didn't seem heavy, loving her. It was all in the showing up, every day. And it wasn't carrying the weight of the world on his shoulders. It was… Feeling like the weight of her and all her concerns wasn't all that heavy. And like maybe his life wouldn't matter if he was walking around carefree, with empty arms.

Maybe that was it. He just… He just wanted her. Her. And all of the baggage that came with it. And he didn't think she loved him. She loved Chuck. And that was fair. Maybe he was way too tied up in some things that made her feel guilty for her to ever have feelings for him. Or maybe she would just never be in love again. But that didn't change the way he felt. It didn't mean he didn't want her. Because he did. Dammit all, he did. But he knew he couldn't tell her. Not now. Because she just agreed to marry him, and he didn't want to rock that boat. So Kit Carson kept the truth of it to himself.

And it struck him, when he dropped her back off at her house, that he had probably loved her for a long time. And it had all just been about waiting for the right time. So he was still waiting for the right time. That was all.

Shelby didn't tell anyone in her family that she was getting married today. They had taken the first available spot with the judge that morning.

Kit had not spent the night. He hadn't the last two nights. They'd had dinner. They'd had sex. Because she couldn't keep her hands off him. And there was a wild determination in her need for him. But now that she'd given in to it, she didn't want to control herself at all. Was angry that she ever had. Now that she had given in, she wanted to do it over and over again. Because somehow it made… Somehow it made the fact that she was marrying him seem more distant.

But then he picked her up, and he was wearing a black button-down shirt, a black hat and a pair of dark jeans. And he was holding a beautiful bouquet of flowers, and suddenly everything seemed just a little bit too real.

"Hi," she said.

"You look beautiful."

But she'd worn jeans. And a tank top. And she suddenly felt like there was something wrong with her. But he said she was beautiful, and it made everything inside her hurt.

She didn't wear her wedding ring anymore. But suddenly the idea of wearing a different one…

But maybe he didn't have one. They hadn't talked about rings. But he had brought flowers.

They got into the truck, and he put it in Reverse. "Did you get rings?"

"I did," he said.

"Could we… Could we put them on now? Or after? But not during?"

"Whatever you need," he said.

"We can just put them on now," she said, starting to rummage through the bags that were in the truck.

And suddenly, he pulled over to the side of the dirt

road they were still on, and took out the boxes with the rings. Then he took her left hand in his, and opened up the velvet box. Inside was the most stunning diamond she'd ever seen. "Kit…"

"I hope you like it. I got a carefree buffalo."

"It's beautiful."

His eyes met hers, there in the truck. And suddenly… Her stomach dropped. Because she thought that maybe if they put them on now it wouldn't feel the same. It wouldn't feel like marriage. It wouldn't feel like a promise. But as he slipped that band on her finger, she knew that she was an idiot. Because this felt so real. She had gotten a marriage license, and he was putting a ring on her finger, and it was real. "Shelby…" She went to pull away, but he put his hand on her cheek and held her fast, and then he was kissing her. Deep and hard.

"Kit…"

And then she couldn't speak, because it was them. Him. And she just always wanted him. No matter what.

And when they parted, he was breathing heavily. Then he opened up the next box. And inside it was a gold band. For him.

And she looked up at him, fear and regret coiling through her. "I can't."

And there was a grim sort of determined look on his face. "Well, I won't wear it until you can."

Then he steered the truck back onto the road, and they kept on going into town. It was a pretty short drive, and they got there and were able to park out front.

They went inside, and waited to be called into the judge's chambers.

"Good to see you," the judge said to Shelby.

"You too," she said.

Rose was their witness. And Shelby held the bouquet that Kit had brought in sweaty hands.

"None of your family come?" Rose asked.

"Well, I... No," Shelby said. "We didn't exactly tell them."

"You're eloping," said Rose. "So romantic."

Her hands trembled as Kit took them in his.

"We won't be exchanging rings," Kit said.

"All right," the judge said, clearly not put off by it at all. But she imagined that in the world of courthouse weddings, that wasn't all that uncommon. But then it came to vows. And she could feel tears pushing against her eyes. Feel herself breathing far too hard. "Do you, Shelby Sohappy, take this man to be your lawfully wedded husband? In sickness and in health, for richer or poorer, as long as you both shall live?"

As long as they lived. That was it. As long as you lived. That was all.

It ended after that. Her first marriage had ended. And here she was, on the verge of another life.

She was terrified.

"I do," she said before she could lose her nerve.

"And do you, Kittredge Carson, take this woman to be your lawfully wedded wife? To have and to hold, in sickness and in health, as long as you both shall live?"

And it was like the world stopped. The whole world. "I do," said Kit.

"And now, by the authority given to me by the state of Oregon, I pronounce you husband and wife."

And without being told that they could kiss, Kit pulled her into his arms, and kissed her. And she clung to him, kissing him back, because he was the lifeline in the moment, even as he was the thing that made her tremble.

And when they parted, it was over. She had a husband. Another husband. But Kit wasn't another of anything. He was… Somehow she had married Kit Carson.

And she didn't know how she was ever going to get her head around that. She expected him to drive her back home. But he didn't.

"Kit…"

"I decided we ought to have a honeymoon."

"A honeymoon?"

"Yeah. Just…figured we'd stay at a nice place on the Deschutes River. Enjoy the view. Some good food."

And she found that she didn't have words. She didn't even know what to think. He turned on the radio, and there was a Jimmie Allen song on, and she tried to focus on the lyrics, and not on her confusion as they drove on the highway, headed north.

"Where exactly are we going?"

"Bend," he said.

"Oh. I didn't know you were wanting to go into the city."

He chuckled. "I just thought it might be nice to go somewhere a little… You know. Nice."

It took two hours to get there. They pulled into a hotel that she'd never been to before. Right there on the Deschutes River.

"I packed an overnight bag for us," he said as he reached into the back of the truck and produced it, before getting out and heading into the lobby.

And she just sat there. Feeling stupid.

Then she got it together, unbuckling and scrambling out behind him, walking into what was a beautiful, woodsy room with high ceilings and metal art all over the place. Fish and elk wrought from iron standing proud over stone tiles.

"This is beautiful," she said.

"I just wanted… I wanted something to mark the day."

And suddenly, she just wanted him. She wanted him, because it might do something to blot out the feelings that were rioting through her. The things that felt sharp and jagged and a little bit broken.

It took a moment for them to get all checked in, and then they went upstairs, to the suite down at the end of the hall.

"Kit," she breathed. "This is too much."

And she hadn't fully appreciated until just then that she had married a man with money. She just hadn't thought about it at all. Well. That was… Handy. She supposed. Except she didn't really want for much of anything in her life. Except she…

And then she couldn't think, because Kit was kissing her.

And at least when Kit was kissing her, she could blot out all her doubts and just feel.

Chapter 14

He kissed her like he was starving, because he was. Like he was gasping for air and she was the only source.

He should've told her his plans. He could see that she was a little bit shell-shocked. The rings, the vows, everything, that it had all been a little bit much for her. And it was tearing him apart. Breaking him open. Because he needed her. He needed this. He wanted... He wanted her to feel like his wife. Because she damn well felt like it to him. He wanted this to matter. He wanted it to be everything.

Maybe he wanted too much.

But life had knocked him down and kneed him in the groin enough times for him to know that things weren't magic. For him to know that this might be hard. For him to know that he might always be competing with a love that had been thwarted before its time had come to an end. And maybe there was no competing with that. Not ever. But he didn't want to compete anyway. Not really. He wanted to be different. He wanted to be singular. He wanted to be new. He wanted to be Shelby and Kit, nothing that had come before. And nothing that could ever come after. He wanted to be everything.

And so he kissed her, walking her back to the bed as he stripped the tank top, the jeans, the determined non-wedding outfit from her body. Whatever she needed to do. But he wanted her to be his.

If this was the only way to do it, if this was the only way to reach her, then he damn well would. So he stripped her naked, the sight of her bronze curves filling him with awe, filling him with need. He wanted this woman. He wanted her more than he wanted his next breath.

"Lie down," he ordered. "I want to look at you."

"Kit…"

"You're my wife," he said. "You're mine."

And suddenly, a deep feeling of possession burst inside him. He could scarcely breathe around it. Couldn't think. All he could do was feel.

"Damn, you're so pretty. So damned pretty."

The words came out rough, almost violent. But it was a violence in him. Tearing through him, rioting through his chest, making him feel like a stranger to himself.

And there was a glint of something, something like fear in her dark eyes, and he wanted to make it go away. But he also wanted to push. To push past it.

Because every time they came to this point, and it felt like an important thing, they didn't get further. Something stopped them. There was a barrier that went up, and he didn't know what that was. Didn't know how to fight it. And he wanted to. Because he wanted… He wanted everything.

He stood at the foot of the bed and began to take his clothes off slowly.

He looked at her, and he knew that she wanted him. He knew that she wanted this, this thing that burned between them hotter and brighter than anything.

He slowly undid the buckle on his jeans, undressed and moved to the edge of the bed. "Get on your knees," he commanded. She obeyed, and it was a strange and beautiful thing to see her, still filled with fire, but not fighting against him at all.

"Take me in your mouth, Shelby."

And he made sure to keep his gaze locked with hers, to hold her captive with his eyes as she moved forward, curling her fingers around his aching cock as she lowered her head to take him into her mouth.

The soft sound she made vibrated through his body, and he thought his soul had exited the building.

Kit was pretty sure he was deceased. A ghost. Just from that soft, slick contact from her lips. Her tongue. She lowered her head and took him in deep, pulling back slightly when it was clear it was a little too much for her. And there was something about it that thrilled him. Something about it that made him feel like a god. And maybe that was wrong. Maybe it was messed up. But he didn't care. Because… How could it be? How could it be when he just loved her? When he wanted to possess her in every way. That was the thing. When he wanted all of it, every last thing. Her and nothing more. And he wanted… He wanted her to prove to him right now, beyond a shadow of a doubt, that it was more than just desire. Because while it was desire on a level he had never known, it was something more.

She'd been under his skin for a long damned time. And he knew what it was now. That thing that he was so afraid of. That thing he could never name. And why would he? She'd been off-limits to him. In love with someone else. And it was entirely possible she still was. Entirely possible that he was competing against her love for a dead man. And he was alive. So he would make mistakes. He would frustrate her. They were going to have a child together. They were going to be under different stress. And she hadn't chosen him. Maybe it would be easy for her to resent him. Maybe he would never be able to live up to all that. But they had this. They had this, and she was sucking him like he was her favorite damn thing. And that was real.

Maybe for her it wasn't love. But he would take emphatic, absolute need. He would take desire that was undeniable. Desire that transcended common sense. Desire that was more, shot higher, farther into the stratosphere than anything else either of them had ever experienced. And for him, it would be love. Always.

And it was like some truths broke open inside him. All around him. All that stress, all that care. It was love. Always. And the grief that he felt over the loss of his sister was all that love with no one left to care for. But it was still there. Love was something that couldn't be taken away. And somehow, during a blow job, he was having the single greatest moment of clarity in his life. Maybe because he had never loved anyone or anything more than Shelby. Maybe because he loved the vision of the life they could have. Enough to risk everything. But even if that vision didn't come out perfect. Even if it was never everything, he would love her. Because love was a sacred space, one he could choose to dedicate his whole soul to. One that could live on, no matter what was given in return. No matter what.

He felt himself reaching the end of his control, and he gripped her hair tight, guiding her head back up. "I want to be inside you."

Her lips curved up into a coy smile. "I mean. Technically you were."

"You know what I mean."

"Yeah," she said, but the word was heavy, and it was like she knew. Heavy with need. Heavy with the intensity of all that they were. And he was on fire with it.

On fire with all of it.

He kissed her. Drowning in her. If he never had anything but her, it would be okay. He wasn't marrying her for the baby. He'd married her for her. And she was his wife.

His wife.

His knees nearly buckled with the wonder of it. He kissed her, laying her flat on the bed, her legs parting for him. And he entered her in one smooth thrust. The feeling of her body holding him like this, of being in her, overwhelmed him, no matter how many times it happened.

He knew she'd only had one lover other than him. And he had a fair few. But none of it mattered. Not now. Because this wasn't like anything. She wasn't like anything. They were altogether new and glorious. They were the stars.

He could remember well that night, before the first time he'd ever touched her, when he looked up at the sky and noticed those stars.

Like he was seeing them for the first time. She made him see things. She made him feel things. She took him from the gray haze of grief, and she painted his world all different colors.

And he never wanted to go back. And he didn't have to. He lost himself in her. Over and over again. And when she trembled beneath him, crying out his name, he released hold on all of his control. All of it. He kissed her, his mouth against hers as he said the only thing that existed inside him. The only truth. The only thing that mattered. "I love you."

She was lying there, awash in sensation and pleasure after the intensity of their coming together, and his words were rolling over her like a tsunami. And she couldn't find anything to grab on to. She didn't know what to do. She was drowning. In sorrow, and guilt. And regret. He loved her? He loved her.

That wasn't possible. Not Kit Carson. Kit Carson, that object of her desire. Whom she had considered dangerous and something else altogether. Because he had been part of the Carson family.

Because she was supposed to love someone else. She did love someone else. She did.

She did.

And she couldn't betray him. Not like this. Not like that. When she had… She had wanted Kit. She had wanted Kit while she was married, and if she loved him now too, and she was having a baby with him, then what had she kept for the man she'd made vows to?

You made vows to Kit too.

She couldn't breathe. She was panicking.

"You don't need to say anything," he said. "But I

wanted you to know. I didn't marry you because of the baby. I married you because I wanted to be your husband. Because I fell in love with you, Shelby. I don't know when. It seems silly to say years ago, but maybe it was then. But for sure in these last weeks. It was like all that electricity between us came together and started to make sense. Maybe it was just waiting for the right time. Hell, I don't know. But I love you. I love talking to you. I love being with you. I love being in you. And I don't ever want to be with anyone else. Not ever again. I just… I just love you. And when I say that, it's from a position of having worked really hard to climb that mountain. But I realized something. I love my sister, even though she's gone. But I love her still. I don't know. I guess I felt like I lost that. But I didn't. I still get to have it. I still get to have love. It's a miracle."

He was being so raw. So honest.

It was Kit and she couldn't handle it.

It was so deep and she didn't want to go that far.

She couldn't.

"I don't feel that way," she said. "Because it isn't the same. I had a husband. And I loved him."

She felt sick. She felt like she was going to throw up. Or maybe die.

"I had a husband and I loved him. And I can't…"

"What?"

"I just feel so guilty. I feel like I'm betraying him. And myself. I feel like… I don't want this. I don't want to love you. I can't love you."

"Shelby. I'll wait. I don't need you to do a damn thing. We can go on like we have. Like we always have. We can go on like this."

"Maybe you can," she said. "But I can't. I just don't think I can. I think… I think it was a mistake."

"It wasn't a mistake."

"All of it was," she said. "How can I… How can I think that this would work? I just… It isn't going to. It can't."

"Shelby, my love isn't dependent on you giving it back. All I know is that the first time I noticed you, it changed something for me. And it took all these years for it to lead here. I can wait more years. I can wait more."

And she didn't know why that infuriated her. Why he was acting like this was okay. Like maybe it was a good thing. When that word, when the idea of him…

"This isn't love. Not as I understand it. This… This is something else. It's chemistry. It's desire. I want you. I want to be with you. I like you to do things to me that I've never liked before. I like doing things to you that I've never liked before. I always knew I wanted your body, Kit. But that's the kind of man you are. You're a really great body."

Guilt lashed at her.

"Is that all?"

"It's all you can be for me."

"Well, I'm the body that married you. I'm the body that helped to make this baby. I'm the body that loves you. But I'm gonna prove to you that there's not a time frame on this. I want you to take my truck, and go home. Take all the time you need."

"This is our honeymoon."

"You just said you didn't want all that."

She felt like her pain was pushing her into the ground. Like she was being driven farther and farther into a hole.

"I just want to leave you with one thing."

"What's that?"

He turned around and took something out of his overnight bag. The box that had his ring in it.

"Now what I want you to do is keep this. And when you're ready, you put it on my finger."

"I won't… I can't…"

"Then you give it back to me."

She couldn't, though. She couldn't make her hand release it. She wanted to be able to have him in her life. She wanted to keep sleeping with him. She wanted him to be a father to her child. She wanted… She wanted all of that without any risk. And it was a misery. Standing there frozen. Not being able to take either thing that she wanted. Not being able to be… As strong as she wanted to be. As good as she wanted to be. As brave.

"That's what I thought. Hang on to it."

"How are you going to get home?" she said.

"Don't worry about me, Shelby. I'll figure it out. I've got family. I've got time."

She took the truck keys, and she took the ring. And she started to collect her clothes. Then she walked out of her honeymoon suite like she hadn't just entered an hour before. She walked out with her heart on the ground, or maybe it was just back in the room with him. All she knew was that she needed to protect something. Except right now… She felt like she didn't have anything.

You have his truck keys, and his wedding ring.

Yeah. She had those two things. And what the hell was she supposed to do with them?

Chapter 15

Well. That had not gone well. He sat down, bare-ass naked on the end of the bed in his honeymoon suite. And he did something he really didn't want to do. He called his brother.

"Hey, Chance," he said. "You up for driving to Bend?"

"When?"

"You know. Now, maybe?"

"Why?"

"Well, I'm in Bend. Because I got married and my wife just left me and took my truck."

"What the fuck did you do?" asked Chance.

"I didn't do anything, actually. But thank you. I just told her that I loved her."

"Oh. Well. I'll be there in a minute."

It didn't feel like a minute. And really, it wasn't. It was a hell of a long time before his brother managed to get there, and by the time he did, Kit was a little bit drunk.

"Oh, boy," said Chance. "So she rejected your ass?"

"Yeah. I... I'm in love with her, Chance. I'm in love with her... And... She's not in love with me."

"I think that's bullshit. I think you know that too."

"Do I?"

"Yeah. I think so. I think she's scared."

"Yeah. I get that."

"And why exactly aren't you scared anymore?" Chance asked.

"I don't know. The same reason you aren't. Love is just more important."

"It is."

"I'll wait for her."

"That's how you know it's real. It feels urgent. But if you can be patient... If you could be patient, then... It's the real thing."

"I've been patient."

"Yeah, I know."

"It's all right with me if she still loves him. Maybe for her, that's how it will always be. But for me... It's fate. There's nobody else but her."

"I don't see why you can't be her fate too."

"Well, I respect what she had."

"You're here. And you're together. I suspect that her real problem is that she's a little bit afraid that you and her might have been inevitable."

Well. That made sense. But it was a damned optimistic view.

"And how is it that you have so much faith in that?"

"Because it took amnesia, a very strange lie and a whole lot of letting go for me to find love, but I did it anyway. I believe you'll have the same. So… That's it. I just believe in it."

He was going to cling to that. And he did. The whole ride back to Lone Rock. That was what he clung to.

Chapter 16

She should go talk to Juniper. She should go talk to somebody. Anybody. But instead she found herself driving to the graveyard. It made her feel grim and sad, and she didn't go there all that often, because there was something so definitive about it that she just hated.

But that plot had been meant for the both of them. And there was just something… There was just something… She parked in the cemetery parking lot and lowered her head over the steering wheel and started to cry. Deep, wrenching sobs. And somehow, she couldn't make herself get out.

Finally, she did. Finally, she caught her breath enough to do that.

She got out of the truck and walked down the familiar path to where Chuck's gravestone was.

"This is weird," she said. "I'm not given to talking

to you. I guess you know that. Or you don't. I... I don't know how I feel about it."

But the stone was unresponsive. And the ring was heavy in her pocket.

Real.

The weight of it was real.

Present.

Here.

Now.

And suddenly, she felt so stark and clear what Juniper had said to her when she'd first confessed that she was pregnant, and the guilt that she felt. That Chuck would never be a father, that he would never have had that dream, but she was moving on and living. Because she was alive.

She didn't know if she believed in the idea that a person had a set number of days. In the idea that when it was your time it was your time. In fact, she had resisted that hard, because it had felt like in no way could it be her twenty-six-year-old husband's time.

But she supposed in the end it didn't matter. He had the years and the life he'd been given. And they'd been happy.

Her heart had been his, because she'd given it to him, and even with her attraction to Kit, she had devoted her love and her body to the man she'd made her vows to.

Till death do us part.

And it had parted them. So much earlier than she'd anticipated. But it had.

And she was holding herself back. Holding herself back with a foot in her old life. No. Worse. With her heart in her old life.

What if she let go? What if she listened to Kit?

Listened to what he'd said. That love wouldn't go away. It wasn't gone. It was different. But it lived in her. What if she trusted that? And what if she quit feeling so damned guilty that she had fantasies about Kit?

She wanted to cry. Wanted to weep at the injustice of everything.

But not at the life she was living now. For the first time in a very long time. She was angry that the world was cruel and Chuck had died too young. But she wasn't angry that she was here with Kit. She wasn't angry that she was having his baby.

"I'm happy."

And she had to put her hand over her mouth to stifle a sob.

She was happy. She loved Kit.

And the sound that tore from her body was half exultation, half despair.

She loved Kit Carson. And it wasn't like anything else. They were everything. They were obsession and heat and fire and love. They were a previously undiscovered passion that she hadn't known existed. They were connected. And they always had been. And if fate was real, then maybe she had to accept that she'd been walking toward him all this time.

Maybe she had to accept that she had been Chuck's fate. And they'd had love. And it had been real. But where his road ended, hers kept going. He had been love. And it had been real. But her fate went on. It went forward.

She felt…giddy and guilty and afraid, because how could it be this easy? How could it be this clear? Was it okay that Kit felt like fate? Was it okay if he might be the love of her life?

And on the heels of that came desperation. Fear. And it all became clear. It wasn't the guilt. It was that what she felt for Kit was so big… That if she loved again, and she lost again… She had survived Chuck. But she couldn't survive losing Kit.

She couldn't survive it.

She loved him. In a deep, all-consuming way. As a woman who had known loss. As a woman who had known risk. As a woman who had been married before, and knew what things she would do differently now. Yeah. Because she knew a good marriage. But she also just knew marriage. And the truth was, if she could start from scratch… Kit would be whom she chose. Because they had something more complete. They had a chemistry that you couldn't deny.

And that didn't mean she regretted what she had before. She didn't. It didn't mean it didn't matter. But she was older, and had more perspective. And she knew… She knew the hardship that life could bring your way. She knew the cost of love.

But oh, admitting that Kit was more… That was… She felt like her soul had been bruised. There was the pain of what was behind her, and the fear of what was before her, and she just… She didn't know quite how she was going to go on. Except she could. Because she was here. And it was a gift.

And she remembered the wonder on Kit's face when he'd said that he loved her. When he'd shared with her his realization about love.

There was still more to learn. For him. For her. They were having a baby. And they were married.

She knew why she was here. She had to leave the idea of no one but Chuck as her husband behind her.

She had to put away the visions of the life she thought she would have. Because when she put Kit's ring on his finger, he was the one and only. He was the love of her life. Because her life stretched out before her. Her fate, because how could he be anything else?

"You were a good husband," she said. "And I loved our life. It ended too soon. And now I have to keep living. Now I get to keep living." And it was like a weight had been lifted from her shoulders. This revelation that made her feel bruised also made her lit up.

Because she could be happy. There was no limit to that happiness. There was no limit to the love. If only she was willing to stop standing in the past. She had already experienced the loss. And no amount of clinging to it would change it.

No amount of clinging to it would keep her safe.

It would just keep her living a half life, and she needed to want better for herself. She really and truly did.

She walked back to the car, tears still on her cheeks. And she took her phone out of her pocket and dialed her sister. "Juniper... Do you by any chance know where Kit is?"

"As a matter fact I do. But... After you find him... You and I need to talk. Just about everything that's happened."

"Yeah. We do. But after I find Kit."

Kit was sitting at his house, on the front porch. And he knew that waiting out here today was probably pretty foolish. But... He couldn't bring himself to stop waiting. Couldn't bring himself to stop looking.

And then, his own truck came driving up the road. It was his wife.

His heart leaped up into his throat.

She parked in front of the porch, and got out, scrambling toward him, and his initial response was to feel worried. Seeing those tears on her face.

"Are you okay?"

She started to cry. Deep, wrenching sobs that shook her shoulders. "How can you ask that? After what I did to you. How can you still care?" she sobbed. "How can that be the first thing that you ask?"

"Because I love you. Because I've decided to care no matter what."

"I'm okay," she said. "I'm just… I love you," she said.

And he knew they needed to talk. He knew they did. But right now all he wanted to do was kiss her. Kiss those words right from her lips. "I love you," he growled, and he carried her up the steps into the house. They were a fever. She tore his clothes from his body, and he tore hers from hers. This was theirs. It had been theirs for all these years, and they hadn't been able to do anything about it, and now they could do whatever they wanted.

So he stripped her bare, and laid her down on the floor, made her cry out her love for him at least ten more times before he satisfied them both, shaking as he found his pleasure inside her.

"I love you."

And then he picked her up, ready to carry her to the bed.

"Wait," she said.

"What?"

"I just have to get…" She scrambled down from his

arms, and grabbed her pants, then she took the ring box out of the pocket.

"I have this for you."

"Damn, sweetie."

They were naked, in his living room, and she was standing in front of him like she had at their wedding.

"I just wanted... I just needed... I want to make vows just for you. For us. Vows that are like the stars we looked at together. Because I thought a lot about what I want. I thought a lot about marriage. About what it is. And about what I want us to have." She brushed a tear away from her face. And he knew right then that no bride could ever have been more beautiful than his. Naked in front of him. Honest and open and not hiding at all.

"Kit Carson," she said, "I think you might be my fate." He'd never cared much for that word. Because he hadn't had a lot of good things in life that could be attributed to fate. But he wanted to believe she was fate. That they were.

So he chose to believe it.

She drew in a jagged breath. "And I have spent a long time trying to avoid that thought. I felt guilty that I was attracted to you. It felt like a sin. And I wanted to make it something less than it was. But my road was always going to lead to you, whether I knew it or not. I can tell you honestly that I made vows to another man, and I kept them. But he's not my husband anymore. I just say that, because I want you to know that these vows that I'm making to you I'm going to keep. I'm gonna keep them with everything I am."

A tear trailed down her cheek and he reached up and wiped it away. He wanted to make all of her pain easier.

Always. He knew too much about life to think he could keep her from it entirely, but he could carry some of it.

"I'm not married to you because of the baby," she said. "I know that marriage is more than that. Deeper than that. I love you, and I want to share a life with you. House with you. A bed with you. I love you because you make me feel things I didn't know were possible. I love you, because… Even just talking to you… It made me feel like I could shake myself out of this hole that I was standing in. That place where I was stuck. You made me feel that way. And I really wanted that. But then we… We became more. We became what I think we were meant to be."

"Shelby… I love you. And I know for a fact that I was meant to be with you. And there were all these things, all these terrible things that made me feel like I couldn't be with anyone, but when I sat back, and I honored what I lost instead of just being angry about it… That was when it made sense. That was when I could love you. And I really do love you."

"I love you too," she said. "So much. I love you so much and it was all just fear. I'm not gonna say I don't… That I don't feel any now. I do. It's scary. Feeling all of this. It's terrifying. Because, Kit… You're everything in a way no one else has ever been. The way that we talk. The way that we are. And I resisted… The image of you in my house, the image of you in my life, because… It's just so much. It's everything. I was never afraid that I couldn't care about you enough. I was always afraid that if I admitted it, it would be too much. And I promise you… If it ever feels like too much, I'm not going to pull away again. I'm going to lean right in."

And then she took the ring out of the box, and took

his hand in hers. And she slipped that band onto his finger. "For better or worse. In sickness and in health. Till forever."

"Till forever," he agreed.

"Also...six inches is patently not enough."

He chuckled. "Glad you came around to seeing things that way.

"I love you."

"It was always you," she said. "It's always you."

Epilogue

Their daughter might not be able to walk yet, but she made a beautiful flower girl.

And when Shelby Carson married her husband for the second time, with a wedding dress and both families in attendance, and no tiara, it was one of the happiest days of her life. She had wanted to have a wedding, a real one, because she wanted everybody to share this with them. But the happiest day of her life was the day she had chosen him for real. For always.

She looked at the head of the aisle, and she saw him standing there. Her gaze had always found him. Always, for all these years.

And she knew that it always would.

* * * * *

WANT ME, COWBOY

Chapter 1

November 1, 2018
Location: Copper Ridge, Oregon

WIFE WANTED—

Rich rancher, not given to socializing. Wants a wife who will not try to change me. Must be tolerant of moods, reported lack of sensitivity and the tendency to take off for a few days' time in the mountains. Will expect meals cooked. Also, probably a kid or two. Exact number to be negotiated. Beard is nonnegotiable.

November 5, 2018
Revised draft for approval by 11/6

WIFE WANTED—

~~Rich rancher, not given to socializing.~~ Successful
rancher searching for a wife who enjoys rural living. ~~Wants a wife who will not try to change me.~~
~~Must be tolerant of moods, reported lack of sensi-~~
~~tivity, and the tendency to take off for a few days'~~
~~time in the mountains.~~ Though happy with my
life, it has begun to feel lonely, and I would like
someone to enhance my satisfaction with what I
have already. I enjoy extended camping trips and
prefer the mountains to a night on the town. ~~Will~~
~~expect meals cooked. Also, probably a kid or two.~~
~~Exact number to be negotiated. Beard is nonnego-~~
~~tiable. I~~ I'm looking for a traditional family life,
and a wife and children to share it with.

"This is awful."

Poppy Sinclair looked up from her desk, her eyes
colliding with her boss's angry gray stare. He was holding a printout of the personal ad she'd revised for him
and shaking it at her like she was a dog and it was a
newspaper.

"The *original* was awful," she responded curtly,
turning her focus back to her computer.

"But it was all true."

"Lead with being less of an asshole."

"I *am* an asshole," Isaiah said, clearly unconcerned
with that fact.

He was at peace with himself. Which she admired
on some level. Isaiah was Isaiah, and he made no apologies for that fact. But his attitude would be a problem if

the man wanted to find a wife. Because very few other people were at peace with him just as he was.

"I would never say I want to—" he frowned "'—enhance my enjoyment.' What the hell, Poppy?"

Poppy had known Isaiah since she was eighteen years old. She was used to his moods. His complete lack of subtlety. His gruffness.

But somehow, she'd never managed to get used to *him*. As a man.

This grumpy, rough, bearded man who was like a brick wall. Or like one of those mountains he'd disappear into for days at a time.

Every time she saw him, it felt as if he'd stolen the air right from her lungs. It was more than just being handsome—though he was. A lot of men were handsome. His brother Joshua was handsome, and a whole lot easier to get along with.

Isaiah was… Well, he was her very particular brand of catnip. He made everything in her sit up, purr…and want to be stroked.

Even when he was in full hermit mode.

People—and interacting with them—were decidedly not his thing. It was one reason Poppy had always been an asset to him in his work life. It was her job to sit and take notes during meetings…and report her read on the room to him after. He was a brilliant businessman, and fantastic with numbers. But people…not so much.

As evidenced by the ad. Of course, the very fact that he was placing an ad to find a wife was both contradicting to that point—suddenly, he wanted a wife!—and also, somehow, firmly in affirmation of it. He was placing an ad to find her.

The whole situation was Joshua's fault. Well, probably Devlin and Joshua combined, in fairness.

Isaiah's brothers had been happy bachelors until a couple of years ago when Devlin had married their sister Faith's best friend, Mia.

Then, Joshua had been the next to succumb to matrimony, a victim of their father's harebrained scheme. The patriarch of the Grayson family had put an ad in a national newspaper looking for a wife for his son. In retaliation, Joshua had placed an ad of his own, looking for an unsuitable wife that would teach his father not to meddle.

It all backfired. Or…front fired. Either way, Joshua had ended up married to Danielle, and was now happily settled with her and her infant half brother who both of them were raising as their son.

It was after their wedding that Isaiah had formed his plan.

The wedding had—he had explained to Poppy at work one morning—clarified a few things for him. He believed in marriage as a valuable institution, one that he wanted to be part of. He wanted stability. He wanted children. But he didn't have any inclination toward love.

He didn't have to tell her why.

She *knew* why.

Rosalind.

But she wouldn't speak her foster sister's name out loud, and neither would he. But she remembered. The awful, awful fallout of Rosalind's betrayal.

His pain. Poppy's own conflicted feelings.

It was easy to remember her conflicted feelings, since she still had them.

He was staring at her now, those slate eyes hard and

glinting with an energy she couldn't quite pin down. And with coldness, a coldness that hadn't been there before Rosalind. A coldness that told her and any other woman—loud and clear—that his heart was unavailable.

That didn't mean her own heart didn't twist every time he walked into the room. Every time he leaned closer to her—like he was doing now—and she got a hint of the scent of him. Rugged and pine-laden and basically lumberjack porn for her senses.

He was a contradiction, from his cowboy hat down to his boots. A numbers guy who loved the outdoors and was built like he belonged outside doing hard labor.

Dear God, he was problematic.

He made her dizzy. Those broad shoulders, shoulders she wanted to grab on to. Lean waist and hips—hips she wanted to wrap her legs around. And his forearms…all hard muscle. She wanted to lick them.

He turned her into a being made of sensual frustration, and no one else did that. Ever. Sadly, she seemed to have no effect on him at all.

"I'm not trying to mislead anyone," he said.

"Right. But you *are* trying to entice someone." The very thought made her stomach twist into a knot. But jealousy was pointless. If Isaiah wanted her…well, he would have wanted her by now.

He straightened, moving away from her and walking across the office. She nearly sagged with relief. "My money should do that." As if that solved every potential issue.

She bit back a weary sigh. "Would you like someone who was maybe…interested in who you are as a person?"

She knew that was a stupid question to ask of Isaiah Grayson. But she was his friend, as well as his employee. So it was kind of…her duty to work through this with him. Even if she didn't want him to do this at all.

And she didn't want him to find anyone.

Wow. Some friend she was.

But then, having…complex feelings for one's friend made emotional altruism tricky.

"As you pointed out," he said, his tone dry, "I'm an asshole."

"You were actually the one who said that. I said you *sounded* like one."

He waved his hand. "Either way, I'm not going to win Miss Congeniality in the pageant, and we both know that. Fine with me if somebody wants to get hitched and spend my money."

She sighed heavily, ignoring the fact that her heart felt an awful lot like paper that had been crumpled up into a tight, mutilated ball. "Why do you even *want* a wife, Isaiah?"

"I explained that to you already. Joshua is settled. Devlin is settled."

"Yes, they are. So why now?"

"I always imagined I would get married," he said simply. "I never intended to spend my whole life single."

"Is your biological clock ticking?" she asked drily.

"In a way," he said. "Again, it all comes back to logic. I'm close to my family, to my brothers. They'll have children sooner rather than later. Joshua and Danielle already have a son. Cousins should be close in age. It just makes sense."

She bit the inside of her cheek. "So you…just think you can decide it's time and then make it happen?"

"Yes. And I think Joshua's experience proves you can make anything work as long as you have a common goal. It *can* be like math."

She graduated from biting her cheek to her tongue. Isaiah was a numbers guy unto his soul. "Uh-huh."

She refused to offer even a pat agreement because she just thought he was wrong. Not that she knew much of anything about relationships of…any kind really.

She'd been shuffled around so many foster homes as a child, and it wasn't until she was in high school that she'd had a couple years of stability with one family. Which was where she'd met Rosalind, the one foster sibling Poppy was still in touch with. They'd shared a room and talked about a future where they were more than wards of the state.

In the years since, Poppy felt like she'd carved out a decent life for herself. But still, it wasn't like she'd ever had any romantic relationships to speak of.

Pining after your boss didn't count.

"The only aspect of going out and hooking up I like is the hooking up," he said.

She wanted to punch him for that unnecessary addition to the conversation. She sucked her cheek in and bit the inside of it too. "Great."

"When you think about it, making a relationship a transaction is smart. Marriage is a legal agreement. But you don't just get sex. You get the benefit of having your household kept, children…"

"Right. Children." She'd ignored his first mention of them, but… She pressed her hands to her stomach unconsciously. Then, she dropped them quickly.

She should not be thinking about Isaiah and chil-

dren or the fact that he intended to have them with another woman.

Confused feelings was a cop-out. And it was hard
to deny the truth when she was steeped in this kind of
reaction to him, to his presence, to his plan, to his talk
about children.

The fact of the matter was, she was tragically in
love with him. And he'd never once seen her the way
she saw him.

She'd met him through Rosalind. When Poppy had
turned eighteen, she'd found herself released from her
foster home with nowhere to go. Everything she owned
was in an old canvas tote that a foster mom had given
her years ago.

Rosalind had been the only person Poppy could think
to call. The foster sister she'd bonded with in her last
few years in care. She'd always kept in touch with Rosalind, even when Rosalind had moved to Seattle and
got work.

Even when she'd started dating a wonderful man she
couldn't say enough good things about.

She was the only lifeline Poppy had, and she'd
reached for her. And Rosalind had come through. She'd
had Poppy come to Rosalind's apartment, and then she'd
arranged for a job interview with her boyfriend, who
needed an assistant for a construction firm he was with.

In one afternoon, Poppy had found a place to live,
gotten a job and lost her heart.

Of course, she had lost it, immediately and—in the
fullness of time it had become clear—irrevocably, to
the one man who was off-limits.

Her boss. Her foster sister's boyfriend. Isaiah Grayson.
Though his status as her boss had lasted longer than

his status as Rosalind's boyfriend. He'd become her fiancé. And then after, her ex.

Poppy had lived with a divided heart for so long. Even after Isaiah and Rosalind's split, Poppy was able to care for them both. Though she never, ever spoke to Rosalind in Isaiah's presence, or even mentioned her.

Rosalind didn't have the same embargo on mentions of Isaiah. But in fairness, Rosalind was the one who had cheated on him, cost him a major business deal and nearly ruined his start-up company and—by extension—nearly ruined his relationship with his business partner, who was also his brother.

So.

Poppy had loved him while he'd dated another woman. Loved him while he nursed a broken heart because of said other woman. Loved him when he disavowed love completely. And now she would have to love him while she interviewed potential candidates to be his wife.

She was wretched.

He had said the word *sex* in front of her like it wouldn't do anything to her body. Had talked about children like it wouldn't make her…yearn.

Men were idiots. But this one might well be their king.

"Put the unrevised ad in the paper."

She shook her head. "I'm not doing that."

"I could fire you." He leaned in closer and her breath caught. "For insubordination."

Her heart tumbled around erratically, and she wished she could blame it on anger. Annoyance. But she knew that wasn't it.

She forced herself to rally. "If you haven't fired me

yet, you're never going to. And anyway," she said, narrowing her tone so that the words would hit him with a point, "I'm the one who has to interview your prospective brides. Which makes this my endeavor in many ways. I'm the one who's going to have to weed through your choices. So I would like the ad to go out that I think has the best chance of giving me less crap to sort through."

He looked up at her, and much to her surprise seemed to be considering what she said. "That is true. You will be doing the interviews."

She felt like she'd been stabbed. She was going to be interviewing Isaiah's potential wife. The man she had been in love with since she was a teenage idiot, and was still in love with now that she was an idiot in her late twenties.

There were a whole host of reasons she'd never, ever let on about her feelings for him, Rosalind and his feelings on love aside.

She loved her job. She loved Isaiah's family, who she'd gotten to know well over the past decade, and who were the closest thing she had to a family of her own.

Plus, loving him was just…easy to dismiss. She wasn't the type of girl who could have something like that. Not Poppy Sinclair whose mother had disappeared when she was two years old and left her with a father who forgot to feed her.

Her life was changing though, slowly.

She was living well beyond what she had ever imagined would be possible for her. Gray Bear Construction was thriving; the merger between Jonathan Bear and the Graysons' company a couple of years ago was more successful than they'd imagined it could be.

And every employee on every level had reaped the benefits.

She was also living in the small town of Copper Ridge, Oregon, which was a bit strange for a girl from Seattle, but she did like it. It had a different pace. But that meant there was less opportunity for a social life. There were fewer people to interact with. By default she, and the other folks in town, ended up spending a lot of their free time with the people they worked with every day. There was nothing wrong with that. She loved Faith, and she had begun getting close to Joshua's wife recently. But it was just… Mostly there wasn't enough of a break from Isaiah on any given day.

But then, she also didn't enforce one. Didn't take one. She supposed she couldn't really blame the small-town location when the likely culprit of the entire situation was *her*.

"Place whatever ad you need to," he said, his tone abrupt. "When you meet the right woman, you'll know."

"I'll know," she echoed lamely.

"Yes. Nobody knows me better than you do, Poppy. I have faith that you'll pick the right wife for me."

With those awful words still ringing in the room, Isaiah left her there, sitting at her desk, feeling numb and ill used.

The fact of the matter was, she probably *could* pick him a perfect wife. Someone who would facilitate his life, and give him space when he needed it. Someone who was beautiful and fabulous in bed.

Yes, she knew exactly what Isaiah Grayson would think made a woman the perfect wife for him.

The sad thing was, Poppy didn't possess very many of those qualities herself.

And what she so desperately wanted was for Isaiah's perfect wife to be *her*.

But dreams were for other women. They always had been. Which meant some other woman was going to end up with Poppy's dream.

While she played matchmaker to the whole affair.

Chapter 2

"I put an ad in the paper."

"For?" Isaiah's brother Joshua looked up from his computer and stared at him like he was waiting to hear the answers to the mystery of the universe.

Joshua, Isaiah and their younger sister, Faith, were sitting in the waiting area of their office, enjoying their early-morning coffee. Or maybe enjoying was overstating it. The three of them were trying to find a state of consciousness.

"A wife."

Faith spat her coffee back into her cup. "What?"

"I placed an ad in the paper to help me find a wife," he repeated.

Honestly, he couldn't understand why she was having such a large reaction to the news. After all, that was how Joshua had found his wife, Danielle.

"You can't be serious," Joshua said.

"I expected you of all people to be supportive."

"Why *me*?"

"Because that's how you met Danielle. Or you have you forgotten?"

"I have not forgotten how I met my wife. However, I didn't put an ad out there seriously thinking I was going to find someone to marry. I was trying to prove to dad that *his* ad was a stupid idea."

"But it turned out it wasn't a stupid idea," Isaiah said. "I want to get married. I figured this was a hassle-free way of finding a wife."

Faith stared at him, dumbfounded. "You can't be serious."

"I'm serious."

The door to the office opened, and Poppy walked in wearing a cheerful, polka-dotted dress, her dark hair swept back into a bun, a few curls around her face.

"Please tell me my brother is joking," Faith said. "And that he didn't actually put an ad in the paper to find a wife."

Poppy looked from him back to Faith. "He doesn't joke, you know that."

"And you know that he put an ad in the paper for a wife?" Joshua asked.

"Of course I know," Poppy responded. "Who do you think is doing the interviews?"

That earned him two slack-jawed looks.

"Who else is going to do it?" Isaiah asked.

"You're not even doing the interview for your own wife?" Faith asked.

"I trust Poppy implicitly. If I didn't, she wouldn't be my assistant."

"Of all the… You are insane." Faith stormed out of the room. Joshua continued to sit and sip his coffee.

"No comment?" Isaiah asked.

"Oh, I have plenty. But I know you well enough to know that making them won't change a damn thing. So I'm keeping my thoughts to myself. However," he said, collecting his computer and his coffee, "I do have to go to work now."

That left both Isaiah and Poppy standing in the room by themselves. She wasn't looking at him; she was staring off down the hall, her expression unreadable. She had a delicate profile, dark, sweeping eyelashes and a fascinating curve to her lips. Her neck was long and elegant, and the way her dress shaped around her full breasts was definitely a pleasing sight.

He clenched his teeth. He didn't make a habit of looking at Poppy that way. But she was pretty. He had always thought so.

Even back when he'd been with Rosalind he'd thought there was something…indefinable about Poppy. Special.

She made him feel… He didn't know. A little more grounded. Or maybe it was just because she treated him differently than most people did.

Either way, she was irreplaceable to him. In the running of his business, Poppy was his barometer. The way he got the best read on a situation. She did his detail work flawlessly. Handled everything he didn't like so he could focus on what he was good at.

She was absolutely, 100 percent, the most important asset to him at the company.

He would have to tell her that sometime. Maybe buy her another pearl necklace. Though, last time he'd done that she had gotten angry at him. But she wore it. She was wearing it today, in fact.

"They're right," she said finally.

"About?"

"The fact that you're insane."

"I think I'm sane enough."

"Of course you do. Actually—" she let out a long, slow breath "—I don't think you're insane. But, I don't think this is a good idea."

"Why?"

"This is really how you want to find a wife? In a way that's this…impersonal?"

"What are my other options? I have to meet someone new, go through the process of dating… She'll expect a courtship of some kind. We'll have to figure out what we have in common, what we don't have in common. This way, it's all out in the open. That's more straightforward."

"Maybe you deserve better than that," she said, her tone uncharacteristically gentle.

"Maybe this is better for *me*."

She shook her head. "I don't know about that."

"When it comes to matters of business, there's no one I trust more than you. But you're going to have to trust that I know what will work best in my own life."

"It's not what I want for you."

A strange current arced between them when she spoke those words, a spark in her brown eyes catching on something inside him.

"I appreciate your concern."

"Yes," she echoed. "My concern."

"We have work to do. And you have wife applications to sort through."

"Right," she said.

"Preference will be given to blondes," he said.

Poppy blinked and then reached up slowly, touching her own dark hair. "Of course."

And then she turned and walked out of the room.

Isaiah hadn't expected to receive quite so many responses to his ad. Perhaps, in the end, Poppy had been right about her particular tactic with the wording. It had certainly netted what felt to him to be a record number of responses.

Though he didn't actually know how many women had responded to his brother's personal ad.

He felt only slightly competitive about it, seeing as it would be almost impossible to do a direct comparison between his and Joshua's efforts. Their father had placed an ad first, making Joshua sound undoubtedly even nicer than Poppy had made Isaiah sound.

Thereafter, Joshua had placed his own ad, which had offered a fake marriage and hefty compensation.

Isaiah imagined that a great many more women would respond to that.

But he didn't need quantity. He just needed quality. And he believed that existed.

It had occurred to him at Joshua and Danielle's wedding that there was no reason a match couldn't be like math. He believed in marriage; it was romance he had gone off of.

Or rather, the kind of romance he had experience with.

Obviously, he couldn't dispute the existence of love. His parents were in love, after all. Forty years of marriage hadn't seemed to do anything to dampen that. But then, he was not like his mother. And he wasn't like his father. Both of them were warm people. *Compassionate*. And those things seemed to come easily to them.

Isaiah was a black-and-white man living in a world filled with shades of gray. He didn't care for those shades, and he didn't like to acknowledge them.

But he wasn't an irrational man. Not at all.

Yet he'd been irrational once. Five years with Rosalind and they had been the best of his life. At least, he had thought so at the time.

Then she had betrayed him, and nearly destroyed everything.

Or rather, he had.

Which was all he had needed to learn about what happened to him and his instincts under the influence of love.

He'd been in his twenties then, and it had been easy to ignore the idea that his particular set of practices when it came to relationships meant he would be spending his life without a partner. But now he was in his thirties, and that reality was much more difficult to ignore. When he'd had to think about the future, he hadn't liked the idea of what he was signing himself up for.

So, he had decided to change it. That was the logical thing to do when you found yourself unhappy with where you were, after all. A change of circumstances was not beyond his reach. And so, he was reaching out to grab it.

Which was why Poppy was currently on interview number three with one of the respondents to his ad. Isaiah had insisted that anyone responding to the ad come directly to Copper Ridge to be interviewed. Anyone who didn't take the ad seriously enough to put in a personal appearance was not worthy of consideration, in his opinion.

He leaned back in his chair, looking at the neat expanse of desk in front of him. Everything was in its place in his office, as it always was. As it should be. And soon, everything in his personal life would be in place too.

Across the hall, the door to Poppy's office opened and a tall, willowy blonde walked out. She was definitely his type in the physical sense, and the physical mattered quite a bit. Emotionally, he might be a bit detached, but physically, everything was functioning. Quite well, thank you.

In his marriage-math equation, sex was an important factor.

He intended to be faithful to his wife. There was really no point in making a lifelong commitment without fidelity.

Because of that, it stood to reason that he should make sure he chose in accordance with his typical physical type.

By the time he finished that thought process the woman was gone, and Poppy appeared a moment later. She was glaring down the hall, looking both disheveled and generally irritated. He had learned to recognize her moods with unerring accuracy. Mostly because it was often a matter of survival. Poppy was one of the few people on earth who wasn't intimidated by him. He should be annoyed by that. She was his employee, and ought to be a bit more deferential than she was.

He didn't want her to be, though. He liked Poppy. And that was a rarity in his world. He didn't like very many people. Because most people were idiots.

But not her.

Though, she looked a little bit like she wanted to kill him at the moment. When her stormy, dark eyes connected with his across the space, he had the fleeting thought that a lesser man would jump up and run away, leaving his boots behind.

Isaiah was not that man.

He was happy to meet her. Steel-capped toe to pointy-toed stiletto.

"She was stupid," Poppy pronounced.

He lifted a brow. "Did you give her an IQ test?"

"I'm not talking about her intelligence," Poppy said, looking fierce. "Though, the argument could be made that any woman responding to this ad…"

"Are you about to cast aspersions on my desirability?"

"No," she said. "I cast those last week, if you recall. It would just be tiresome to cast them again."

"Why is she stupid?" he pressed.

"Because she has no real concept of what you need. You're a busy man, and you live in a rural…area. You're not going to be taking her out to galas every night. And I know she thought that because you're a rich man galas were going to be part of the deal. But I explained to her that you only go to a certain number of business-oriented events a year, and that you do so grudgingly. That anyone hanging on your arm at such a thing would need to be polished, smiling, and, in general, making up for you."

He spent a moment deciding if he should be offended by that or not. He decided not to be. Because she was right. He knew his strengths and his limitations.

"She didn't seem very happy about those details. And that is why I'm saying she's stupid. She wants to take this…job, essentially. A job that is a life sentence. And she wants it to be about her."

He frowned. "Obviously, this marriage is not going to be completely about me. I am talking about a *marriage* and not a position at the company." Though, he supposed he could see why she would be thinking in those terms. He had placed an ad with strict requirements. And he supposed, as a starting point, it *was* about him.

"Is that true, Isaiah? Because I kind of doubt it. You don't want a woman who's going to inconvenience you."

"I'm not buying a car," he said.

"Aren't you?" She narrowed her eyes, her expression mean.

"No. I realize that."

"You're basically making an arranged marriage for yourself."

"Consider it advanced online dating," he said. "With a more direct goal."

"You're having your assistant choose a wife for you." She enunciated each word as if he didn't understand what he'd asked of her.

Her delicate brows locked together, and her mouth pulled into a pout. Though, she would undoubtedly punch him if he called it a pout.

In a physical sense, Poppy was not his type at all. She was not tall, or particularly leggy, though she did often wear high heels with her 1950s housewife dresses. She was petite, but still curvy, her hair dark and curly, and usually pulled back in a loose, artfully pinned bun that allowed tendrils to slowly make their escape over the course of the day.

She was pretty, in spite of the fact that she wasn't the type of woman he would normally gravitate toward.

He wasn't sure why he was just now noticing that. Perhaps it was the way the light was filtering through the window now. Falling across her delicately curved face. Her mahogany skin with a bit of rose color bleeding across her cheeks. In this instance, he had a feeling the color was because she was angry. But, it was lovely nonetheless.

Her lips were full—pouty or not—and the same rose color as her cheeks.

"I don't understand your point," he said, stopping his visual perusal of her.

"I'm just saying you're taking about as much of a personal interest in finding a wife as someone who was buying a car."

He did not point out that if he were buying a car, he would take it for a test drive, and that he had not suggested doing anything half so crass with any of the women who'd come to be interviewed.

"How many more women are you seeing today?" he asked, deciding to bypass her little show of indignation.

"Three more," she said.

There was something in the set of her jaw, in the rather stubborn, mulish look on her face that almost made him want to ask a question about what was bothering her.

But only almost.

"Has my sister sent through cost estimates for her latest design?" he asked.

Poppy blinked. "What?"

"Faith. Has she sent through her cost estimates? I'm

going to end up correcting them anyway, but I like to see what she starts with."

"I'm well aware of the process, Isaiah," Poppy said. "I'm just surprised that you moved on from wife interviews to your sister's next design."

"Why would you be surprised by that? The designs are important. They are, in fact, why I am a billionaire."

"Yes. I know," Poppy said. "Faith's talent is a big reason why we're all doing well. Believe me, I respect the work. However, the subject change seems a bit abrupt."

"It *is* a workday."

Deep brown eyes narrowed in his direction. "You're really something else, do you know that?"

He did. He always had. The fact that she felt the need to question him on it didn't make much sense to him.

"Yes," he responded.

Poppy stamped.

She stamped her high-heel-clad foot like they were in a black-and-white movie.

"No, she hasn't sent it through," Poppy said.

"You just stomped your foot at me."

She flung her arms wide. "Because you were just being an idiot at me."

"I don't understand you," he said.

"I don't need you to understand me." Her brow furrowed.

"But you *do* need me to sign your paychecks," he pointed out. "I'm your boss."

Then, all the color drained from her cheeks. "Right. Of course. I do need that. Because you're my boss."

"I am."

"Just my boss."

"I've been your boss for the past decade," he pointed out, not quite sure why she was being so spiky.

"Yes," she said. "You have been my boss for the past decade."

Then, she turned on her heel and walked back into her office, shutting the door firmly behind her.

And Isaiah went back to his desk.

He had work to do. Which was why he had given Poppy the task of picking him a wife. But before he chased Faith down for those estimates, he was going to need some caffeine. He sent a quick text to that effect to Poppy.

There was a quick flash of three dots at the bottom of the message box, then they disappeared.

It popped up again, and disappeared again. Then finally there was a simple: of course.

He could only hope that when he got his coffee it wasn't poisoned.

Three hours and three women later, Poppy was wishing she had gone with her original instinct and sent the middle finger emoji to Isaiah in response to his request for coffee.

This was too much. It would be crazy for anyone to have their assistant pick their wife—a harebrained scheme that no self-respecting personal assistant should have to cope with. But for her especially, it was a strange kind of emotional torture. She had to ask each woman questions about their compatibility with Isaiah. And then, she had to talk to them about Isaiah. Who she knew better than she knew any other man on the face of the earth. Who she knew possibly better than she knew anyone else. And all the while his words rang in her ears.

I'm your boss.

She was his *employee.*

And that was how he saw her. It shouldn't surprise her that no-nonsense, rigid Isaiah thought of her primarily as his employee. She thought of him as her friend.

Her best friend. Practically family.

Except for the part of her that was in love with him and had sex dreams about him sometimes.

Though, were she to take an afternoon nap today, her only dreams about Isaiah would involve her sticking a pen through his chest.

Well, maybe not his chest. That would be fatal. Maybe his arm. But then, that would get ink and blood on his shirt. She would have to unbutton it and take it off him…

Okay. Maybe she was capable of having both dreams at the same time.

"Kittens are my hard line," the sixth blonde of the day was saying to her. All the blondes were starting to run together like boxes of dye in the hair care aisle.

"I…" Poppy blinked, trying to get a handle on what that meant. "Like… Sexually… Or?"

The woman wrinkled her nose. "I mean, I need to be able to have a kitten. That's nonnegotiable."

Poppy was trying to imagine Isaiah Grayson with a kitten living in his house. He had barn cats. And he had myriad horses and animals at his ranch, but he did not have a kitten. Though, because he already had so many animals, it was likely that he would be okay with one more.

"I will… Make a note of that."

"Oh," the woman continued. "I can also tie a cherry stem into a knot with my tongue."

Poppy closed her eyes and prayed for the strength to not run out of the room and hit Isaiah over the head with a wastebasket. "I assume I should mark that down under special skills."

"Men like that," the woman said.

Well, maybe that was why Poppy had such bad luck with men. She couldn't do party tricks with her tongue. In fairness, she'd never tried.

"Good to know," Poppy continued.

Poppy curled her hands into fists and tried to keep herself from… She didn't even know what. Screaming. Running from the room.

One of these women who she interviewed today might very well be the woman Isaiah Grayson slept with for the rest of his life. The last woman he ever slept with. The one who made him completely and totally unavailable to Poppy forever.

The one who finally killed her fantasy stone-cold.

She had known that going in. She had. But suddenly it hit her with more vivid force.

I am your boss.

Her boss. Her boss. He was her boss. Not her friend. Not her lover. Never her lover.

Maybe he didn't see his future wife as a new car he was buying. But he basically saw Poppy as a stapler. Efficient and useful only when needed.

"Well, I will be in touch," Poppy stated crisply.

"Why are *you* interviewing all the women? Is this like a sister wives thing?"

Poppy almost choked. "No. I am Mr. Grayson's assistant. Not his wife."

"I wouldn't mind that," Lola continued. "It's always seemed efficient to me. Somebody to share the workload of kids and housework. Well, and sex."

"Not. His. Wife." Poppy said that through clenched teeth.

"He should consider that."

She tightened her hold on her pen, and was surprised she didn't end up snapping it in half. "Me as his wife?"

"Sister wives."

"I'll make a note," Poppy said drily.

Her breath exited her body in a rush when Lola finally left, and Poppy's head was swimming with rage.

She had thought she could do this. She had been wrong. She had been an idiot.

I am your boss.

He was her boss. Because she worked for him. Because she had worked for him for ten years. Ten years.

Why had she kept this job for so long? She had job experience. She also had a nest egg. The money was good, she couldn't argue that, but she could also go get comparable pay at a large company in a city, and she now had the experience to do that. She didn't have to stay isolated here in Copper Ridge. She didn't have to stay with a man who didn't appreciate her.

She didn't have to stay trapped in this endless hell of wanting something she was never going to have.

No one was keeping her here. Nothing was keeping her here.

Nothing except the ridiculous idea that Isaiah had feelings for her that went beyond that of his assistant.

Friends could be friends in different cities. They didn't have to live in each other's pockets. Even if he had misspoken and he did see them as friends—and really, now that she was taking some breaths, she imagined that was closer to the truth—it was no excuse to continue to expose herself to him for twelve hours a day.

He was her business life. He was her social life. He was her fantasy life. That was too much for one man. Too much.

She walked into his office, breathing hard, and he looked up from his computer screen, his gray eyes assessing. He made her blood run hotter. Made her hands shake and her stomach turn over. She wanted him. Even now. She wanted to launch herself across the empty space and fling herself into his arms.

No. It had to stop.

"I quit," she said, the words tumbling out of her mouth in a glorious triumph.

But then they hit.

Hit him, hit her. And she knew she could take them back. Maybe she should.

No. She shouldn't.

"You *quit*?"

"It should not be in my job description to find you a wife. This is ludicrous. I just spent the last twenty minutes talking to a woman who was trying to get me to add the fact that she could tie a cherry stem into a knot with her tongue onto that ridiculous, awful form of yours underneath her '*skills*.'"

He frowned. "Well, that is a skill that might have interesting applications..."

"I know that," she said. "But why am I sitting around having a discussion with a woman that is obviously about your penis?"

Her cheeks heated, and her hands shook. She could

not believe she had just… Talked about his penis. In front of him.

"I didn't realize that would be a problem."

"Of course you didn't. Because you don't realize *anything*. You don't care about anything except the bottom line. That's all you ever see. You want a wife to help run your home. To help organize your life. By those standards *I* have been your damned wife for the past ten years, Isaiah Grayson. Isn't that what you're after? A personal assistant for your house. A *me* clone who can cook your dinner and…and…do wife things."

He frowned, leaning back in his chair.

He didn't speak, so she just kept going. "I quit," she repeated. "And you have to find your own wife. I'm not working with you anymore. I'm not dealing with you anymore. You said you were my boss. Well, you're not now. Not anymore."

"Poppy," he said, his large, masculine hands pressing flat on his desk as he pushed himself into a standing position. She looked away from his hands. They were as problematic as the rest of him. "Be reasonable."

"No! I'm not going to be reasonable. This situation is so unreasonable it isn't remotely fair of you to ask me to be reasonable within it."

They just stayed there for a moment, regarding each other, and then she slowly turned away, her breath coming in slow, harsh bursts.

"Wait," he said.

She stopped, but she didn't turn. She could feel his stare, resting right between her shoulder blades, digging in between them. "You're right. What I am looking for is a personal version of you. I hadn't thought about it that way until just now. But I am looking for a PA. In all areas of my life."

An odd sensation crept up the back of her neck, goose bumps breaking out over her arms. Still, she fought the urge to turn.

"Poppy," he said slowly. "I think you should marry me."

Chapter 3

When Poppy turned around to face him, her expression was still. Placid. He wasn't good at reading most people, but he knew Poppy. She was expressive. She had a bright smile and a stormy frown, and the absence of either was…concerning.

"Excuse me?"

"You said yourself that what I need is someone like you. I agree. I've never been a man who aims for second best. So why would I aim for second best in this instance? You're the best personal assistant I've ever had."

"I doubt you had a personal assistant before you had me," she said.

"That's irrelevant," he said, waving a hand. "I like the way we work together. I don't see why we couldn't make it something more. We're good partners, Poppy."

Finally, her face moved. But only just the slightest bit. "We're good partners," she echoed, the words hollow.

"Yes," he confirmed. "We are. We always have been. You've managed to make seamless transitions at every turn. From when we worked at a larger construction firm, to when we were starting our own. When we expanded, to when we merged with Jonathan Bear. You've followed me every step of the way, and I've been successful in part because of the confidence I have that you're handling all the details that I need you to."

"And you think I could just… Do that at your house too?"

"Yes," he said simply.

"There's one little problem," Poppy said, her cheeks suddenly turning a dark pink. She stood there just staring for a moment, and the color in her face deepened. It took her a long while to speak. "The problem being that a wife doesn't just manage your kitchen. *That* is a housekeeper."

"I'm aware of that."

"A wife is supposed to…" She looked down, a pink blush continuing to bleed over her dark skin. "You don't feel that way about me."

"Feel what way? You know my desire to get married has nothing to do with love and romance."

"Sex." The word was like a mini explosion in the room. "Being a wife does have something to do with sex."

She was right about that, and when he had made his impromptu proposal a moment earlier, he hadn't been thinking of that. But now that he was…

He took a leisurely visual tour of her, similar to the one he had taken earlier. But this time, he didn't just appreciate her beauty in an abstract sense. This time, he allowed it to be a slightly more heated exploration.

Her skin looked smooth. He had noticed how lovely it was earlier. But there was more than that. Her breasts looked about the right size to fit neatly into his hands, and she had an extremely enticing curve to her hips. Her skirts were never short enough to show very much of her leg, but she had nice ankles.

He could easily imagine getting down on his knees and taking those high heels off her feet. And biting one of her ankles.

That worked for him.

"I don't think that's going to be a problem," he said.

Poppy's mouth dropped open and then snapped shut. "We've never even… We've never even kissed, Isaiah. We've never even almost kissed."

"Yes. Because you're my assistant."

"Your assistant. And you're my foster sister's ex-fiancé."

Isaiah gritted his teeth, an involuntary spike of anger elevating his blood pressure. Poppy knew better than to talk about Rosalind. And hell, she had nothing to do with Poppy. Not in his mind, not anymore.

Yes, she was the reason Poppy had come to work for him in the first place, but Poppy had been with him for so long her presence wasn't connected with the other woman in any way.

He wasn't heartbroken. He never had been, not really. He was angry. She'd made a fool of him. She'd caused him to take his focus off his business. She'd nearly destroyed not only his work, but his brother's. And what would eventually be their sister's too.

All of it, all the success they had now had nearly

been taken out by his own idiocy. By the single time he'd allowed his heart to control him.

He would never do that again.

"Rosalind doesn't have anything to do with this," he said.

"She's in my life," Poppy pointed out.

"That's a detail we can discuss later." Or not at all. He didn't see why they were coming close to discussing it now.

"You don't want to marry me," Poppy said.

"Are you questioning my decision-making, Poppy? How long have you known me? If there's one thing I'm not, it's an indecisive man. And I think you know that."

"You're a dick," Poppy said in exasperation. "How dare you… Have me interviewing these women all day… And then… Is this some kind of sick test?"

"You threatened to quit. I don't *want* you to quit. I would rather have you in all of my life than in none of my life."

"I didn't threaten to quit our friendship."

"I mostly see you at work," he said.

"And you value what I do at work more than what you get out of our friendship, is that it?"

That was another question he didn't know how to answer. Because he had a feeling the honest answer would earn him a spiked heel to the forehead. "I'm not sure how the two are separate," he said, thinking he was being quite diplomatic. "Considering we spend most of our time together at work, and my enjoyment of your company often dovetails with the fact that you're so efficient."

Poppy let out a howl that would not have been out of

place coming from an enraged chipmunk. "You are...
You are..."

Well, if her objection to the marriage was that they
had never kissed, and never almost kissed, and he didn't
want to hear her talk anymore—and all those things
were true—he could only see one solution to the entire situation.

He made his way over to where Poppy was standing like a brittle rose and wrapped his arms around her
waist. He dragged her to him, holding her in place as
he stared down at her.

"Consider this your almost-kiss," he said.

Her brown eyes went wide, and she stared up at him,
her soft lips falling open.

And then his heart was suddenly beating faster, the
unsettled feeling in his gut transforming into something else. Heat. Desire. He had never looked at Poppy
this way, ever.

And now he wondered if that had been deliberate.
Now he wondered if he had been purposefully ignoring
how beautiful she was because of all the reasons she
had just mentioned for why they shouldn't get married.

The fact she was his assistant. The fact that she was
Rosalind's foster sister.

"Isaiah..."

He moved one hand up to cup her cheek and brought
his face down closer to hers. She smelled delicate, like
flowers and uncertainty. And he found himself drawn
to her even more.

"And this will be your kiss."

He brought his lips down onto hers, expecting... He
didn't know what.

Usually, sexual attraction was a straightforward

thing for him. That was one of the many things he liked about sex. There was no guesswork. It was honest. There was never anything shocking about it. If he saw a woman he thought was beautiful, he approached her. He never wondered if he would enjoy kissing her. Because he always wanted to kiss her before he did. But Poppy…

In the split second before their mouths touched, he wondered. Wondered what it would be like to kiss this woman he had known for so long. Who he had seen as essential to his life, but never as a sexual person.

And then, all his thoughts burned away. Because she tasted better than anything he could remember and her lips just felt right.

It felt equally right to slide his fingertips along the edge of her soft jawline and tilt her face up farther so he could angle his head in deep and gain access. It felt equally right to wrap both arms around her waist and press her body as tightly to his as he possibly could. To feel the soft swell of her breasts against his chest.

And he waited, for a moment, to see if she was going to stick her claws into him. To see if she was going to pull away or resist.

She did neither. Instead, she sighed, slowly, softly. Sweetly. She opened her mouth to his.

He took advantage of that, sliding his tongue between her lips and taking a taste.

He felt it, straight down to his cock, a lightning bolt of pleasure he'd had no idea was coming.

Suddenly, he was in the middle of a violent storm when only a moment ago the sky had been clear.

He had never experienced anything like it. The idea that Poppy—this woman who had been a constant in his world—was a hidden temptress rocked him down to his soul. He had no idea such a thing was possible.

In his world, chemistry had always been both straightforward and instant. That it could simply exist beneath the surface like this seemed impossible.

And yet, it appeared there was chemistry between himself and Poppy that had been dormant all this time.

Her soft hands were suddenly pressed against his face, holding on to him as she returned his kiss with surprising enthusiasm.

Her enthusiasm might be surprising, but he was damn well going to take advantage of it.

Because if chemistry was her concern, then he was more than happy to demolish her worry here and now.

He reversed their positions, turning so her back was to his desk, and then he walked her backward before sliding one arm beneath her ass and picking her up, depositing her on top of the desk. He bent down to continue kissing her, taking advantage of her shock to step between her legs.

Or maybe he wasn't taking advantage of anything. Maybe none of this was calculated as he would like to pretend that it was. Maybe it was just necessary. Maybe now that their lips had touched there was just no going back.

And hell, why should they? If she couldn't deny the chemistry between them… If it went to its natural conclusion…she had no reason to refuse his proposal.

He slid one hand down her thigh, toward her knee, and then lifted that leg, hooking it over his hip as he drew her forward and pressed himself against her.

Thank God for the fullness of her skirt, because it

was easy to make a space for himself right there between her legs. He was so hard it hurt.

He was a thirty-six-year-old man who had a hell of a lot more self-control now than he'd ever had, and yet, he felt more out of control than he could ever remember being before.

That did not add up. It was bad math.

And right now, he didn't care.

Slowly, he slid his other hand up and cupped her breast. He had been right. It was exactly the right size to fill his palm. He squeezed her gently, and Poppy let out a hoarse groan, then wrenched her mouth away from his.

Her eyes were full of hurt. Full of tears.

"Don't," she said, wiggling away from him.

"What?" he asked, drawing a deep breath and trying to gain control over himself.

Stopping was the last thing he wanted to do. He wanted to strip that dress off her, marvel at every inch of uncovered skin. Kiss every inch of it. He wanted her twisting and begging underneath him. He wanted to sink into her and lose himself. Wanted to make her lose herself too.

Poppy.

His friend. His assistant.

"How dare you?" she asked. "How dare you try to manipulate me with… wth *sex*. You're my friend, Isaiah. I trusted you. You're just…trying to control me the way you control everything in your life."

"That isn't true," he said. It wasn't. It might have started out as…not a manipulation, but an attempt to prove something to both of them.

But eventually, he had just been swept up in all this. In her. In the heat between them.

"I think it is. You… I quit."

And then she turned and walked out of the room, leaving him standing there, rejected for the first time in a good long while.

And it bothered him more than he would have ever imagined.

Poppy was steeped in misery by the time she crawled onto the couch in her pajamas that evening.

Her little house down by the ocean was usually a great comfort to her. A representation of security that she had never imagined someone like her could possess.

Now, nothing felt like a refuge. Nothing at all. This whole town felt like a prison.

Her bars were Isaiah Grayson.

That had to stop.

She really was going to quit.

She swallowed, feeling sick to her stomach. She was going to quit and sell this house and move away. She would talk to him sometimes, but mostly she had to let the connection go.

She didn't mean to him what he did to her. Not just in a romantic way. Isaiah didn't… He didn't understand. He didn't feel for people the way that other people felt.

And he had used the attraction she felt for him against her. Her deepest, darkest secret.

There was no way a woman without a strong, pre-existing attraction would have ever responded to him the way she had.

It had been revealing. Though, now she wondered

if it had actually been revealing at all, or if he had just always known.

Had he known—all this time—how much she wanted him? And had he been…laughing at her?

No. Not laughing. He wouldn't do that. He wasn't cruel, not at all. But had he been waiting until it was of some use to him? Maybe.

She wailed and dragged a blanket down from the back of the couch, pulling it over herself and curling into a ball.

She had kissed Isaiah Grayson today.

More than kissed. He had… He had touched her.

He had *proposed* to her.

And, whether it was a manipulation or not, she had felt…

He had been hard. Right there between her legs, he had been turned on.

But then, he was a man, and there were a great many men who could get hard for blowup dolls. So. It wasn't like it was that amazing.

Except, something about it felt kind of amazing.

She closed her eyes. Isaiah. He was… He was absolutely everything to her.

She could marry him. She could keep another woman from marrying him.

Great. And then you can be married to somebody who doesn't love you at all. Who sees you as a convenience.

She laughed aloud at that thought. Yes. Some of that sounded terrible. But… She had spent most of her life in foster care. She had lived with a whole lot of people who didn't love her. And some of them had found her to be inconvenient. So that would put marrying Isaiah several steps above some of the living situations she'd had as a kid.

Then there was Rosalind. Tall, blond Rosalind who was very clearly Isaiah's type. While Poppy was...not.

How would she ever...cope with that? With the inevitable comparisons?

He hates her. He doesn't hate you.

Well. That was true. Rosalind had always gone after what she wanted. She had devastated Isaiah in the process. So much so that it had even hurt Poppy at the time. Because as much as she wanted to be with Isaiah, she didn't want him to be hurt.

And then, Rosalind had gone on to her billionaire. The man she was still with. She traveled around the world and hosted dinner parties and did all these things that had been beyond their wildest fantasies when they were growing up.

Rosalind wasn't afraid of taking something just for herself. And she didn't worry at all about someone else's feelings.

Sometimes, that was a negative. But right about now... Poppy was tempted—more than a little bit tempted—to be like Rosalind.

To go after her fantasy and damn the feelings and the consequences. She could have him. As her husband. She could have him...kissing her. She could have him naked.

She could be *his*.

She had been his friend and his assistant for ten years. But she'd never been his in the way she wanted to be.

He'd been her friend and her boss.

He'd never been hers.

Had anyone ever been hers?

Rosalind certainly cared about Poppy, in her own way. If she didn't, she wouldn't have bailed Poppy out when she was in need. But Rosalind's life was very much about her. She and Poppy kept in touch, but that communication was largely driven by Poppy.

That was…it for her as far as family went. Except for the Graysons.

And if she married Isaiah…they really would be her family.

There was a firm, steady knock on her door. Three times. She knew exactly who it was.

It was like thinking about him had conjured him up.

She wasn't sure she was ready to face him.

She looked down. She was wearing a T-shirt and no bra. She was definitely not ready to face him. Still, she got up off the couch and padded over to the door. Because she couldn't *not*…

She couldn't not see him. Not right now. Not when all her thoughts and feelings were jumbled up like this. Maybe she would look at him and get a clear answer. Maybe she would look at him and think, *No, I still need to quit*.

Or maybe…

She knew she was tempting herself. Tempting him.

She hoped she was tempting him.

She scowled and grabbed hold of her blanket, wrapping it tightly around her shoulders before she made her way to the door. She wrenched it open. "What are you doing here?"

"I came to talk sense into you."

"You can't," she said, knowing she sounded like a bratty kid and not caring at all.

"Why not?"

"Because I am an insensible female." She whirled around and walked back into her small kitchen, and Isaiah followed her, closing the front door behind him.

She turned to face him again, and her heart caught in her throat. He was gorgeous. Those cold, clear gray eyes, his sculpted cheekbones, the beard that made him more approachable. Because without it, she had a feeling he would be too pretty. And his lips...

She had kissed those lips.

He was just staring at her.

"I'm emotional."

He said nothing to that.

"I might actually throw myself onto the ground at any moment in a serious display of said emotion, and you won't like it at all. So you should probably leave."

Those gray eyes were level with hers, sparking heat within her, stoking a deep ache of desire inside her stomach.

"Reconsider." His voice was low and enticing, and made her want to agree to whatever commandment he issued.

"Quitting or marrying you?" She took a step back from him. She couldn't be trusted to be too close to him. Couldn't be trusted to keep her hands to herself. To keep from flinging herself at him—either to beat him or kiss him she didn't know.

"Both. Either."

Just when she thought he couldn't make it worse.

"That's not exactly the world's most compelling proposal."

"I already know that my proposal wasn't all that compelling. You made it clear."

"I mean, I've heard of bosses offering to give a raise to keep an employee from leaving. But offering marriage…"

"That's not the only reason I asked you to marry me," he said.

She made a scoffing sound. "You could've fooled me."

"I'm not trying to fool you," he said.

Her heart twisted. This was one of the things she liked about Isaiah. It was tempting to focus on his rather grumpy exterior, and when she did that, the question of why she loved him became a lot more muddled. Because he was hot? A lot of men were hot. That wasn't it. There was something incredibly endearing about the fact that he said what he meant. He didn't play games. It simply wasn't in him. He was a man who didn't manipulate. And that made her accusation from earlier feel…wrong.

Manipulation wasn't really the right way to look at it. But he was used to being in charge. Unquestioned.

And he would do whatever he needed to do to get his way, that much she knew.

"Did you take the kiss as far as you did because you wanted to prove something to me?"

"No," he said. "I kissed you to try and prove something to *me*. Because you're right. If we were going to get married, then an attraction would have to be there."

"Yes," she said, her throat dry.

"I can honestly say that I never thought about you that way."

She felt like she'd just been stabbed through the chest with a kitchen knife. "Right," she said, instead of letting out the groan of pain that she was tempted to issue.

"We definitely have chemistry," he said. "I was genuinely caught off guard by it. I assume it was the same for you."

She blinked. He really had no idea? Did he really not know that her response to him wasn't sudden or random?

No. She could see that he didn't.

Isaiah often seemed insensitive because he simply didn't bother to blunt his statements to make them palatable for other people. Because he either didn't understand or care what people found offensive. Which meant, if backed into a corner about whether or not he had been using the kiss against her, he would have told her.

"I'm sorry," she said.

Now he looked genuinely confused. "You're apologizing to me. Why?"

"I'm apologizing to you because I assumed the worst about you. And that wasn't fair. You're not underhanded. You're not always sweet or cuddly or sensitive. But you're not underhanded."

"You like me," he pointed out.

He looked smug about that.

"Obviously. I wouldn't have put up with you for the past ten years. Good paying job or not. But then, I assume you like me too. At least to a degree."

"We're a smart match," he said. "I don't think you can deny that."

"Just a few hours ago you were thinking that one of those bottle blondes was your smart match. You can see why I'm not exactly thrilled by your sudden proposal to me."

"Are you in love with someone else?"

The idea was laughable. She hadn't even been on a date in…

She wasn't counting. It was too depressing.

"No," she said, her throat tightening. "But is it so wrong to want the possibility of love?"

"I think love is good for the right kind of people. Though my observation is that people mostly settle into a partnership anyway. The healthiest marriage is a partnership."

"Love is also kind of a thing."

He waved a hand. "Passion fades. But the way you support one another… That's what matters. That's what I've seen with my parents."

She stared at him for a long moment. He was right in front of her, asking for marriage, and she still felt like he was standing on the other side of a wall. Like she couldn't quite reach him. "And you're just…never going to love anyone."

"I *have* loved someone," he said simply.

There was something so incredibly painful about that truth. That he had loved someone. And she had used the one shot he was willing to give. It wasn't fair. That Rosalind had gotten his love. If Poppy would have had it, she would have preserved it. Held it close. Done anything to keep it for always.

But she would never get that chance. Because her vivacious older foster sister had gotten it first. And Rosalind hadn't appreciated what she'd had in him.

It was difficult to be angry at Rosalind over what had happened. Particularly when her and Isaiah being together had been painful for Poppy anyway. But right now… Right now, she was angry.

Because whole parts of Isaiah were closed off to Poppy because of the heartbreak he'd endured.

Or maybe that was silly. Maybe it was just going to take a very special woman to make him fall in love. And she wasn't that woman.

Well, on the plus side, if you don't marry him, you'll give him a chance to find that woman.

She clenched her teeth, closing her eyes against the pain. She didn't think she could handle that. It was one terrible thing to think about watching him marry another woman. But it was another, even worse thing to think about him falling in love with someone else. If she were good and selfless, pure and true, she supposed that's what she would want for him.

But she wasn't, and she didn't. Because if he fell in love, that would mean she wasn't going to get what she wanted. She would lose her chance at love. At least, the love she wanted.

How did it benefit her to be that selfless? It just didn't.

"I'll think about it," she said.

Chapter 4

"I'm not leaving here until I close this deal," he said.

"I'm not a business deal waiting to happen, Isaiah."

He took a step toward her, and she felt her resolve begin to weaken. And then, she questioned why she was even fighting this at all.

He was the one driving this train. He always was.

Because she loved him.

Because he was her boss.

Because he possessed the ability to remain somewhat detached, and she absolutely did not.

She could watch him trying to calculate his next move. She could see that it was difficult for him to think of this as something other than a business deal.

No, she supposed that what Isaiah was proposing *was* a business deal. With sex.

"You can't actually be serious," she said.

"I'm always serious."

"I get that you think you can get married and make it not about...*feelings*. But it's... I can't get over the sex thing, Isaiah. I can't."

There were many reasons for that, not the least of which being her own inexperience. But she was not going to have that discussion with him.

"The kiss was good." He said it like that solved everything. Like it should somehow deal with all of her concerns.

"A kiss isn't sex," she said lamely. As if pointing out one of the most obvious things in the world would fix this situation.

"Do you think it's going to be a problem?"

"I think it's going to be weird."

Weird was maybe the wrong word. Terrifying.

Able to rip her entire heart straight out of her chest.

"You're fixating," he said simply. "Let's put a pin in the sex."

"You can't put a pin in the sex," she protested.

"Why can't I put a pin in the sex?"

"Because," she said, waving her hand in a broad gesture. "The sex is like the eight-hundred-pound gorilla in the room. In lingerie. It will not be ignored. It will not be...pinned."

"Put a pin in it," he reiterated. "Let's talk about everything else that a marriage between the two of us could offer you."

She sputtered. "Could offer *me*?"

"Yes. Of course, I don't expect you to enter into an arrangement that benefits only me. So far, I haven't presented you with one compelling reason why marriage between the two of us would be beneficial to you."

"And you think that's my issue?"

"I think it's one issue. My family loves you. I appreciate that. Because I'm very close to my family. Anyone I marry will have to get along with my family. You already do. I feel like you love my family…"

She closed her eyes. Yes. She did love the Grayson family. She loved them so much. They were the only real, functional family she had ever seen in existence. They were the reason she believed that kind of thing existed outside the land of sitcoms. If it weren't for them, she would have no frame of reference for that kind of normalcy. A couple who had been together all those years. Adult children that loved their parents enough to try to please them. To come back home and visit. Siblings who worked together to build a business. Who cared for each other.

Loud, boisterous holiday celebrations that were warm and inviting. That included her.

Yes, the Grayson family was a big, fat carrot in all of this.

But what Isaiah didn't seem to understand was that he was the biggest carrot of all.

An inescapably sexual thought, and she had been asked to put a pin in the sex. But with Isaiah she could never just set the sex aside.

"You love my ranch," he said. "You love to come out and ride the horses. Imagine. You would already be sleeping there on weekends. It would be easy to get up and go for a ride."

"I love my house," she protested.

"My ranch is better," he said.

She wanted to punch him for that. Except, it was true.

His gorgeous modern ranch house with both rustic and modern details, flawlessly designed by his sister, was a feat of architectural engineering and design. There was not a single negative thing she could say about the place.

Set up in the mountains, with a gorgeous barn and horses and all kinds of things that young, daydreamer Poppy would have given her right arm to visit, much less inhabit.

He had horses. And he'd taught her to ride a year earlier.

"And I assume you want children."

She felt like the wind had been knocked out of her. "I thought we weren't going to talk about sex."

"We're not talking about sex. We're talking about children."

"Didn't your parents tell you where babies come from?"

His mouth flattened into a grim line. "I will admit there was something I missed when I was thinking of finding a wife through an ad."

She rolled her eyes. "Really?"

"Yes. I thought about myself. I thought about the fact that I wanted children in the abstract. But I did not think about what kind of mother I wanted my children to have. You would be a wonderful mother."

She blinked rapidly, fighting against the sting of sudden tears. "Why would you think that?"

"I know you. I've watched the way you took care of me and my business for the last ten years. The way you handle everything. The details in my professional life, Joshua and Faith's, as well. I've seen you with Joshua's son."

"I was basically raised by wolves," she pointed out. "I don't know anything about families."

"I think that will make you an even better mother. You know exactly what not to do."

She huffed out a laugh. "Disappearing into a heroin haze is a good thing to avoid. That much I know."

"You know more than that," he said. "You're good with people. You're good at anticipating what they want, what they need. You're organized. You're efficient."

"You make me sound like an app, Isaiah."

"You're warm and...and sometimes sweet. Though, not to me."

"You wouldn't like me if I were sweet," she pointed out.

"No. I wouldn't. But that's the other thing. You know how to stand up to me." The sincerity on his face nearly killed her. "We would be good together."

He sounded so certain. And she felt on the opposite side of the world from certain.

This was too much. It really was. Too close to everything she had ever dreamed about—without one essential ingredient. Except... When had she really ever been allowed to dream?

She had watched so many other people achieve their dreams. While she'd barely allowed herself to imagine...

A life with Isaiah.

Children.

A family of her own.

Isaiah had simply been off-limits in her head all this time. It had made working with him easier. It had made being his friend less risky.

But he was offering her fantasy.

How could she refuse?

"Your parents can't know it's fake," she said.

"Are you agreeing?"

She blinked rapidly, trying to keep her tears back. "They can't know," she repeated.

"It's not fake," he said simply. "We'll have a real marriage."

"They can't know about the ad. They can't know that you just… Are hiring me for a new position. Okay?"

"Poppy…"

"They can't know you're not in love with me."

She would die. She would die of shame. If his wonderful, amazing parents who only ever wanted the best for their children, who most certainly wanted deep abiding love for Isaiah, were to know this marriage was an arrangement.

"It's not going to come up," he said.

"Good. It can't." Desperation clawed at her, and she wasn't really sure what she was desperate for. For him to agree. For him to say he had feelings for her. For him to kiss her. "Or it's off."

"Agreed."

"Agreed."

For a moment she thought he *was* going to kiss her again. She wasn't sure she could handle that. So instead, she stuck her hand out and stood there, staring at him. He frowned but took her offered hand, shaking it slowly.

Getting engaged in her pajamas and ending it with a handshake was not the romantic story she would need to tell his family.

He released his hold on her hand, and she thought he was going to walk away. But instead, he reached out and pulled her forward, capturing her mouth with his after all, a flood of sensation washing over her.

And then, as quickly as it began, the kiss ended.

"No. It's not going to be a problem," he said.

She expected him to leave then. He was supposed to leave. But instead, he dipped his head and kissed her again.

She felt dizzy. And she wanted to keep on kissing him. This couldn't be happening. It shouldn't be happening.

But they were engaged. So maybe this had to happen.

She didn't know this man, she realized as he let out a feral growl and backed her up against her wall. This was not the cool, logical friend she had spent all these years getting to know. This was…

Well, this was Isaiah as a man.

She had always known he was a man. Of course she had. If she hadn't, she wouldn't have been in love with him. Wouldn't have had so many fantasies about him. But she hadn't *really* known. Not like this. She hadn't known what it would be like to be the woman he wanted. Hadn't had any idea just how hot-blooded a man as detached and cool as he was on a day-to-day basis could be when sex was involved.

Sex.

She supposed now was the time to bring up her little secret.

But maybe this was just a kiss, maybe they weren't going to have sex.

He angled his head then, taking the kiss deeper. Making it more intense. And then he reached down and gripped the hem of her T-shirt, pulling it up over her head.

She didn't have a bra on underneath, and she was left completely exposed. Her nipples went tight as he looked at her, as those familiar gray eyes, so cold and rational most of the time, went hot.

He stared at her, his eyes glittering. "How did I not know?"

"How did you not know what?" Her teeth chattered when she asked the question.

Only then did she realize she was afraid this would expose her. Because while she could handle keeping her love for Isaiah in a little corner of her heart while she had access to his body—while she claimed ownership of him, rather than allowing some other woman to have him—she could not handle him knowing how she felt.

She'd had her love rejected too many times in her life. She would never subject herself to that again. Ever.

"How did I not know how beautiful you were?" He was absolutely serious, his sculpted face looking as if it was carved from rock.

She reached out, dragged her fingertips over his face. Over the coarse hair of his beard.

She could touch him now. Like this.

The kiss in his office had been so abrupt, so shocking, that while she had enjoyed it, she hadn't fully been able to process all that it meant. All the changes that came with it.

She didn't touch Isaiah like this. She didn't touch him ever.

And now… She finally could.

She frowned and leaned forward, pressing her lips slowly against his. They were warm, and firm, and she couldn't remember anything in the world feeling this wonderful.

Slowly, ever so slowly, she traced the outline of his bottom lip with her tongue.

She was tasting him.

Ten years of fantasies, vague and half-realized, and they had led here. To this. To him.

She slid her hands back, pushing them through his hair as she moved forward, pressing her bare breasts to his chest, still covered by the T-shirt he was wearing.

She didn't want anything between them. Nothing at all.

Suddenly, pride didn't matter.

She pulled away from him for a moment, and his eyes went straight down to her breasts again.

That would be her salvation. The fact that he was a man. That he was more invested in breasts than in feelings.

He was never going to see how she felt. Never going to see the love shining from her eyes, as long as he was looking at her body. And in this, in sex, she had the freedom to express everything she felt.

She was going to.

Oh, she was going to.

She wrapped her arms around his neck and pushed forward again, claiming his mouth, pouring everything, every fantasy, into that moment.

He growled, his arm wrapping around her waist like a steel band, the other one going down to her thighs as he lifted her up off the ground, pulling her against him. She wrapped her legs around his waist and didn't protest at all when he carried them both from the kitchen back toward her bedroom.

She knew exactly where this was going.

But it was time.

If she were totally, completely honest with herself, she knew why she hadn't done this before.

She was waiting for him.

She always had been.

A foolish, humiliating truth that she had never allowed herself to face until now. But it made pausing for consideration pointless.

She was going to marry him.

She was going to be with him.

There was nothing to think about.

There was a small, fragile bubble of joy in her chest, something she had never allowed herself to feel before. And it was growing inside her now.

She could have this. She could have him.

She squeaked when he dropped her down onto the bed and wrenched his shirt up over his head. She lay back, looking at him, taking in the fine, sculpted angles of his body. His chest was covered with just the right amount of dark hair, extending in a line down the center of his abs, disappearing beneath the waistband of his jeans.

She was exceptionally interested in that. And, for the first time, she hoped she was going to have those questions answered. That her curiosity would be satisfied.

He moved his hands to his belt buckle and reality began to whisper in her ear as he worked through the loops.

She didn't know why reality had showed up. It was her knee-jerk reaction to good things, she supposed.

In her life, nothing stayed good for long. Not for her. Only other girls got what they wanted.

The fact of the matter was, she wasn't his second choice after her much more beautiful foster sister.

She wasn't even his tenth choice.

She had come somewhere down the line of she-didn't-even-want-to-know-how-many bar hookups and the women who had been in her office earlier today.

On the list of women he might marry, Poppy was below placing an ad as a solution.

That was how much of a last resort she was.

At least this time you're a resort at all. Does it really matter if you're the last one?

In many ways, it didn't. Not at all.

Because she wanted to be chosen, even if she was chosen last.

He slowly lowered the zipper on his jeans and all of her thoughts evaporated.

Saved by the slow tug of his underwear, revealing a line of muscle that was almost obscene and a shadow of dark hair before he drew the fabric down farther and exposed himself completely, pushing his pants and underwear all the way to the floor.

She tried not to stare openmouthed. She had never seen a naked man in person before. And she had never counted on seeing Isaiah naked. Had dreamed about it, yes. Had fantasized about it, sure. But, she had never really imagined that it might happen.

"Now it's your turn," he said, his voice husky. Affected.

"I…"

She was too nervous. She couldn't make her hands move. Couldn't find the dexterity to pull her pajama pants down. And, as skills went, taking off pajama pants was a pretty easy one.

He took pity on her. He leaned forward, cupping her chin and kissing her, bringing himself down onto the bed beside her and pressing his large, warm palm between her shoulder blades, sliding his hand down the line of her back, just beneath the waistband of those pajamas. His hand was hot and enticing on her ass, and she arched her hips forward, his erection brushing against the apex of her thighs.

She gasped, and he kissed her, delving deep as he did, bringing his other hand around to cup her breast, his thumb sliding over her nipple, drawing it into an impossibly tight bud.

She pressed her hands against his chest, and just stared at them for a moment. Then she looked up at his face and back down at her hands.

She was touching his bare chest.

Isaiah.

It was undeniable.

He was looking down at her, his dark brows locked together, his expression as serious as it ever was, and it was just…*him*.

She slid her hands downward, watching as they traveled. Her mouth went dry when she touched those ab muscles, when her hands went down farther. She paused, holding out her index finger and tracing the indention that ran diagonally across his body, straight toward that place where he was most male.

She avoided touching him there.

She didn't know *how*.

But then, he took hold of her hand, curved his fingers around it and guided her right toward his erection.

She held back a gasp as he encouraged her to curl her fingers around his thick length.

He was so hot. Hot and soft and hard all at once. Then she looked back up, meeting his eyes, and suddenly, it wasn't so scary. Because Isaiah—a man who was not terribly affected by anything at all in the world, who seemed so confident in his ability to control everything around him—looked absolutely at a loss.

His forehead had relaxed, his eyes fluttering closed, his lips going slack. His head fell back. She squeezed him, and a groan rumbled in his chest.

Right now, she had the control, the power.

Probably for the first and only time in their entire relationship.

She had never felt anything like this before. Not ever.

A pulse began to beat between her legs, need swamping her. She felt hollow there, the slickness a telltale sign of just how much she wanted him too. But she didn't feel embarrassed about it. It didn't make her feel vulnerable. They were equals in this. It felt…exhilarating. Exciting. Right here in her little bed, it felt safe. To want him as much as she did.

How could it not, when he wanted her too?

Experimentally, she pumped her hand along his length, and he growled.

He was beautiful.

Everything she'd ever wanted. She knew he'd been made for her. This man who had captured her heart, her fantasies, from the moment she'd first met him.

But she didn't have time to think about all of that, because she found herself flipped onto her back, with Isaiah looming over her. In an easy movement, he reached between them and yanked off her pants and underwear.

He made space for himself between her legs, gripping his arousal and pressing it through her slick folds, the intimacy of the action taking her breath away, and then the intense, white-hot pleasure that assaulted her when he hit that perfect spot cleared her mind of anything and everything.

He did it again, and then released his hold on himself, flexing his hips against her. She gasped, grabbing his shoulders and digging her fingers into his skin.

His face was a study in concentration, and he cupped her breast, teasing her nipple as he continued to flex his hips back and forth across that sensitive bundle of nerves.

Something gathered low in her stomach, that hollow sensation between her legs growing keener…

And he didn't stop. He kept at it, teasing her nipple, and moving his hips in a maddening rhythm.

The tension within her increased, further and further until it suddenly snapped. She gasped as her climax overtook her, and he captured that sound of pleasure with his mouth, before drawing back and pressing the himself into the entrance of her body. And then, before she had a chance to tense up, he pressed forward.

The shocking, tearing sensation made her cry out in pain.

Isaiah's eyes clashed with hers.

"What the hell?"

Chapter 5

Isaiah was trying to form words, but he was completely overtaken by the feel of her around his body. She was so tight. So wet. And he couldn't do anything but press his hips forward and sink even deeper into her in spite of the fact that she had cried out with obvious pain only a second before.

He should stop. But she was kissing him again. She was holding him against her as she moved her hips in invitation. As her movements physically begged him to stay with her.

Poppy was a virgin.

He should stop.

He *couldn't* stop.

He couldn't remember when that had ever happened to him before. He didn't know if it ever had. He was all about control. It was necessary for a man like him. He had to override his emotions, his needs.

Right now.

But she was holding him so tight. She felt…so good. He had only intended to give her a kiss before he left. And he *had* intended to go. But he'd been caught up…in her. Not in triumph over the fact that he had convinced her to marry him.

No, he had been caught up in *her*.

In the wonder of kissing her. Uncovering her. Exploring her in a way he had never imagined he might.

But he'd had no idea—none at all—that she was this inexperienced.

Poppy was brash. She gave as good as she got. She didn't shy away from anything. And she hadn't shied away from this either.

She still wasn't.

Her hands traveled down to cup his ass, and she tugged at him, as if urging him on.

"Isaiah," she whispered. "Isaiah, please."

And he had no choice but to oblige.

He moved inside her, slowly at first, torturing them both, and trying to make things more comfortable for her.

He had no idea how he was supposed to have sex with a damned virgin. He never had before.

He had a type. And Poppy was against that type in every single way.

But it seemed to be working just fine for him now.

She pressed her fingertips to his cheek, then pulled him down toward her mouth. She kissed him. Slow and sweet, and he forgot to have control.

He would apologize later. For going too fast. Too hard. But she kept making these sounds. Like she wanted it. Like she liked it. She wrapped her legs around his hips and urged him on, like she needed it. And he couldn't slow down. Couldn't stop. Couldn't make it better, even if he should.

He should make her come at least three more times before he took his own pleasure, but he didn't have the willpower. Not at all.

His pleasure overtook him, squeezing down on his windpipe, feeling like jaws to his throat, and he couldn't pull back. Not now. When his orgasm overtook him, all he could hear was the roar of his own blood in his ears, the pounding of his heartbeat. And then Poppy arched beneath him, her nails in his shoulders probably near to drawing blood as she let out a deep, intense cry, her internal muscles flexing around him.

He jerked forward, spilling inside her before he withdrew and rolled over onto his back. He was breathing hard, unable to speak. Unable to think.

"Poppy..."

"I don't want to talk about it," she said, crawling beneath a blanket beside him, covering herself up. She suddenly looked very small, and he was forced to sit there and do the math on their age difference. It wasn't that big. Well, eight years. But he had never thought about what that might mean.

Of course, he had never known her to have a serious relationship. But then, he had only had the one, and he had certainly been having sex.

"We should talk about it."

"Why?" Her eyes were large and full of an emotion he couldn't grab hold of. But it echoed in him, and it felt a lot like pain. "There's really nothing to talk about. You know that my... My childhood was terrible. And

I don't see why we have to go over all the different issues *that* might've given me."

"So you've been avoiding this."

It suddenly made sense why she had been so fixated on the sex aspect of his proposal. He'd been with a lot of women. So he had taken for granted that sex would be sex.

Of course, he had been wrong. He looked down at her, all vulnerable and curled into a ball. He kissed her forehead.

It hadn't just been sex. And of course poor Poppy had no reference at all for what sex would be like anyway.

"I'm sorry," he said.

"Don't be sorry. But I… I need to be alone."

That didn't sit well with him. The idea of leaving her like this.

"Please," she said.

He had no idea how to handle a woman in this state. Didn't know how to…

He usually wasn't frustrated by his difficulty connecting with people. He had a life that suited him. Family and friends who understood him. Who he knew well enough to understand.

Usually, he understood Poppy. But this was uncharted territory for the two of them, and he was at a loss for the right thing to do.

"If you really need that."

She nodded. "I do."

He got up, slowly gathering his clothes and walking out of the bedroom. He paused in her living room, holding those clothes in his hands. Then he dropped them. He lay down on her couch, which he was far too tall for, and pulled a blanket over himself.

There. She could be alone. In her room. And tomorrow they would talk. And put together details for their upcoming wedding.

He closed his eyes, and he tried not to think about what it had felt like to slide inside her.

But that was all he thought about.

Over and over again, until he finally fell asleep.

Poppy's eyes opened wide at three in the morning. She padded out into the hall, feeling disoriented. She was naked. Because she'd had sex with Isaiah last night.

And then she had sent him away.

Because… She didn't know why. She hated herself? She hated him? And everything good that could possibly happen to her?

She'd panicked. That was the only real explanation for her reaction.

She had felt stripped and vulnerable. She had wanted—needed—time to get a hold of herself.

Though, considering how she felt this morning, there probably wasn't enough time in the entire world for her to collect herself.

She had asked him to leave. And he'd left.

Of course he had.

She cared for that man with a passion, but he was not sensitive. Not in the least. Not even a little bit.

You asked him to go. What do you want from him?

It was silly to want anything but exactly what she had asked for. She knew it.

She padded out toward the living room. She needed something. A mindless TV show. A stiff drink. But she wasn't going to be able to go back to sleep.

When she walked into the living room, her heart

jumped into her throat. Because there was a man-shaped something lying on her couch.

Well, it wasn't just man-shaped. It *was* a man.

Isaiah. Who had never left.

Who was defying her expectations again.

He'd been covered by a blanket, she was pretty sure, considering the fact that there was a blanket on the floor bunched up next to him. But he was still naked, sprawled out on her couch and now uncovered. He was...

Even in the dim light she could see just how incredible he was. Long limbs, strong muscles. So hard. Like he was carved from granite.

He was in many ways a mystery to her, even though she knew him as well as she knew anyone. If not better.

He was brilliant with numbers. His investments, his money management, was a huge part of what made Gray Bear Construction a success. He wasn't charismatic Joshua with an easy grin, good with PR and an expert way with people. He wasn't the fresh-faced wunderkind like Faith, taking the architecture world by storm with designs that outstripped her age and experience. Faith was a rare and unique talent. And Jonathan Bear was the hardest worker she had ever met.

And yet, Isaiah's work was what kept the company moving. He was the reason they stayed solvent. The reason that everything he had ever been involved with had been a success in one way or another.

But he was no pale, soft, indoor man. No. He was rugged. He loved spending time outdoors. Seemed to thrive on it. The moment work was through, Isaiah was out on his ranch. It amazed her that he had ever managed to live in Seattle. Though, even then, he had been hiking on the weekends, mountain biking and staying in cabins outside the city whenever he got the chance.

She supposed in many ways that was consistent enough. The one thing he didn't seem to have a perfect handle on was people. Otherwise, he was a genius.

But he had stayed with her.

In spite of the fact that she had asked him not to. She wasn't sure if that was an incredible amount of intuition on his part or if it was simply him being a stubborn ass.

"Are you just going to stand there staring at me?"

She jumped. "I didn't know you were awake."

"I wasn't."

"You knew I was looking at you," she said, shrinking in on herself slightly, wishing she had something to cover up her body.

Isaiah, for his part, looked completely unconcerned. He lifted his arms and clasped his hands, putting them behind his head. "Are you ready to talk?"

"I thought it was the woman who was supposed to be all needy and wanting to talk."

"Traditionally. Maybe. But this isn't normal for me. And I'm damn sure this isn't normal for you. You know, on account of the fact that you've never done this before."

"I said I didn't want to talk about my hymenal status."

"Okay."

He didn't say anything. The silence between them seemed to balloon, expand, becoming very, very uncomfortable.

"It wasn't a big deal," she said. "I mean, in that I wasn't waiting for anything in particular. I was always waiting for somebody to care about me. Always. But then, when I left home… When I got my job with you…" She artfully left out any mention of Rosalind. "That was when I finally felt like I fit. And there just wasn't room for anything else. I didn't want there to be. I didn't need there to be."

"But now, with me, you suddenly changed your mind?"

She shifted, covering herself with her hand as she clenched her thighs more tightly together. "It's not that I changed my mind. I didn't have a specific No Sex Rule. I just hadn't met a man I trust, and I trust you and…and I got carried away."

"And that's never happened to you before," he said, keeping his tone measured and even. The way he handled people when he was irritated but trying not to show it. She knew him well enough to be familiar with that reaction.

"No," she admitted. Because there was no point in not telling him.

"You wanted this," he said, pushing into a sitting position. "You wanted it, didn't you?"

"Yes," she said. "I don't know how you could doubt that."

"Because you've never wanted to do this before. And then suddenly… You did. Poppy, I knew I was coercing you into marriage, but I didn't want to coerce you into bed."

"You didn't. We're engaged now anyway and… It was always going to be you," she blurted out and then quickly tried to backtrack. "Maybe it was never going to happen for me if I didn't trust and know the person. But I've never had an easy time with trusting. With you, it just kind of…happened."

"Sex?"

"Trust."

"Come here."

"There?"

He reached out and took hold of her wrist, and then he tugged her forward, bringing her down onto his lap in an elegant tumble. "Yes."

He was naked. She was naked. She was sitting on his lap. It should feel ridiculous. Or wrong somehow. This sudden change.

But it didn't feel strange. It felt good.

He felt good.

"I'm staying," he said.

"I asked you to leave," she pointed out.

"You didn't really want me to."

"You can't know that," she said, feeling stubborn.

It really wasn't fair. Because she *had* wanted him to stay.

"Normally, I would say that's true. But I know you. And I knew that you didn't really want me to leave you alone *alone*."

"You knew that?"

"Yes, even I knew that," he said.

She lifted her hand, let it hover over his chest. Then he took hold of it and pressed it down, over his heart. She could feel it thundering beneath her palm.

"I guess you can stay," she whispered.

"I'm too tall for this couch," he pointed out.

"Well, you can sleep on the floor."

That was when she found herself being lifted into the air as Isaiah stood. "I think I'll go back to your bed."

She swallowed, her heart in her throat, her body trembling. Were they really going to… Again?

"It's not a very comfortable bed," she said weakly.

"I think I can handle it."

Then he kissed her, and he kept on kissing her until they were back in her room.

Whatever desire she had to protect herself, to withdraw from him, was gone completely.

For the first time in her life, she was living her dream in Isaiah's arms. She wasn't going to keep herself from it.

Chapter 6

Poppy was not happy when he insisted they drive to work together the next day.

But it was foolish for them to go separately. He was already at her house. She was clearly resisting him taking over every aspect of the situation, and he could understand that. But it didn't mean he could allow for impracticality.

Still, she threw him out of the bedroom, closed herself in and didn't emerge until it was about five minutes to the time they were meant to be there.

She was back in her uniform. A bright red skirt that fell down to her knees and a crisp, white top that she had tucked in. Matching red earrings and shoes added to the very Poppy look.

"Faith and Joshua are going to have questions," she said, her tone brittle as she got into the passenger seat of his sports car.

"So what? We're engaged."

"We're going to have to figure out a story. And… We're going to have to tell your parents. Your parents are not going to be happy if they're the last to know."

"We don't have to tell my siblings we're engaged."

"Oh, you just figure we can tell them we knocked boots and leave it at that?" Her tone told him she didn't actually think that was a good idea.

"Or not tell them anything. It's not like either of them keep me apprised of their sexual exploits."

"Well, Joshua is married and Faith is your little sister."

"And?"

"You are an endless frustration."

So was she, but he had a feeling if he pointed that out at the moment it wouldn't end well for him.

This wasn't a real argument. He'd already won. She was here with him, regardless of her protestations. He'd risk her wrath when it was actually necessary.

"Jonathan will not be in today, if that helps. At least, he's not planning on it as far as I know."

She made a noise halfway between a snort and clearing her throat. "The idea of dealing with Jonathan bothers me a lot less than dealing with your siblings."

"Well. We have to deal with them eventually. There's no reason to wait. It's not going to get less uncomfortable. I could probably make an argument for the fact that the longer we wait the more uncomfortable we'll get."

"You know. If you could be just slightly less practical sometimes, it would make us mere mortals feel a whole lot better."

"What do you mean?"

"Everything is black-and-white to you. Everything is…easy." She looked like she actually meant that.

"That isn't true," he said. "Things are easy for me when I can line them out. When I can make categories and columns, so whenever I can do that, I do it. Life has variables. Too many. If you turn it into math, there's one answer. If the answer makes sense, go with that."

"But life *isn't* math," she said. "There's not one answer. We could hide this from everyone until we feel like not hiding it. We could have driven separate cars."

"Hiding it is illogical."

"Not when you're a woman who just lost her virginity and you're a little embarrassed and don't necessarily want everyone to know."

"You know," he said, his tone dry, "you don't have to walk in and announce that you just lost your virginity."

"I am aware of that," she snapped. She tapped her fingernails on the armrest of the passenger door. "You know. You're a pretty terrible cowboy. What with the sports car."

"I have a truck for the ranch. But I also have money. So driving multiple cars is my prerogative."

She made a scoffing sound. And she didn't speak to him for the rest of the drive over.

For his part, Isaiah wasn't bothered by her mood. After she had come to speak to him in the early hours of the morning, he had taken her back to bed where he had kept her up for the rest of the night. She had responded to every touch, every kiss.

She might be angry at him, but she wanted him. And that would sustain them when nothing else would.

The whole plan was genius, really.

Now that they'd discovered this attraction between them, she really was the perfect wife for him. He liked her. She would be a fantastic mother. She was an amazing partner, and he already knew it. And then there was this…this heat.

It was more than he'd imagined getting out of a relationship.

So he could handle moments of spikiness in the name of all they had going for them.

They drove through the main street of town in silence, and Isaiah took stock of how the place looked, altered for Christmas. All the little shops adorned with strings of white lights and evergreen boughs.

It made him wonder about Poppy's life growing up. About the Christmases she might have had.

"Did you celebrate Christmas when you were a child?" he asked.

"What?"

"The Christmas decorations made me wonder. We did. Just…very normal Christmases. Like movies. A tree, family. Gifts and a dry turkey."

She laughed. "I have a hard time believing your mother ever made a dry turkey."

"My grandma made dry turkey," he said. "She died when I was in high school. But before then…"

"It sounds lovely," Poppy said. "Down to the dry turkey. I had some very nice Christmases. But there was never a routine. I also had years where there was no celebration. I don't have…very strong feelings about Christmas, actually. I don't have years of tradition to make into something special."

When they pulled into the office just outside of town, he parked, and Poppy wasted no time in getting out of the car and striding toward the building. Like she was trying to outrun appearing with him.

He shook his head and got out of the car, following behind her. Not rushing.

If she wanted to play a game, she was welcome to it. But she was the one who was bothered. Not him.

He walked into the craftsman-style building behind her, and directly into the front seating area, where his sister, Faith, was curled on a chair with her feet underneath her and a cup of coffee beside her.

Joshua was sitting in a chair across from her, his legs propped up on the coffee table.

"Are you having car trouble?" Faith directed that question at Poppy.

Poppy looked from Isaiah to Joshua and then to Faith. And he could sense when she'd made a decision. Her shoulders squared, her whole body became as stiff as a board, as if she were bracing herself.

She took a deep breath.

"No," she said. "I drove over with your brother because I had sex with him last night."

Then she swept out of the room and stomped down the hall toward her office. He heard the door slam decisively behind her.

Two heads swiveled toward him, wide eyes on his face.

"What?" his sister asked.

"I don't think she could have made it any clearer," he said, walking over to the coffeepot and pouring himself a cup.

"You had sex with Poppy," Joshua confirmed.

"Yes," Isaiah responded, not bothering to look at his brother.

"You… *You*. And Poppy."

"Yes," he said again.

"Why do I know this?" Faith asked, covering her ears.

"I didn't know she was going to make a pronouncement," Isaiah said. He felt a smile tug at his lips. "Though, she was kind of mad at me. So. I feel like this is her way of getting back at me for saying the change in our relationship was simple."

Faith's eyes bugged out. "You told her that it was simple. The whole thing. The two of you...*friends*... *Poppy*, an employee of the past ten years... *Sleeping together.*" Faith was sputtering.

"It was good sex, Faith," he commented.

Faith's look contorted into one of abject horror, and she withdrew into her chair.

"There's more," Isaiah said. "I'm getting married to her."

"You are...*marrying Poppy*?" Now Faith was just getting shrill.

"Yes."

"You don't have to marry someone just because you have sex with them," Joshua pointed out.

"I'm aware of that, but you know I want to get married. And considering she and I have chemistry, I figured we might as well get married."

"But... Poppy?" Joshua asked.

"Why *not* Poppy?"

"Are you in love with her?" Faith asked.

"I care about her more than I care about almost anyone."

"You didn't answer my question," Faith said.

"Did no one respond to your ad?" Joshua was clearly happy to skip over questions about feelings.

Isaiah nodded. "Several women did. Poppy interviewed six of them yesterday."

Joshua looked like he wanted to say something that he bit back. "And you didn't like any of them?"

"I didn't meet any of them."

"So," Faith said slowly, "yesterday you had her interviewing women to marry you. And then last night you…hooked up with her."

"You're skipping a step. Yesterday afternoon she accused me of looking for a wife who was basically an assistant. For my life. And that was when I realized… She's actually the one I'm looking for."

"That is… The least romantic thing I've ever heard," Faith said.

"Romance is not a requirement for me."

"What about Poppy?"

He lifted a shoulder. "She could have said no."

"Could she have?" Faith asked. "I mean, no offense, Isaiah, but it's difficult to say no to you when you get something in your head."

"You don't want to hear this," Isaiah said, "but particularly after last night, I can say confidently that Poppy and I suit each other just fine."

"You're right," Faith said, "I don't want to hear it." She stood up, grabbing her coffee and heading back toward her office.

"I hope you know what you're doing," Joshua said slowly.

Isaiah looked over at his brother. "What about any of this doesn't look like I know what I'm doing?"

"Getting engaged to Poppy?" Joshua asked.

"You like Poppy," Isaiah pointed out.

"I do," Joshua said. "That's my concern. She's not like you. Your feelings are on a pretty deep freeze, Isaiah. I shouldn't have to tell you that."

"I don't know that I agree with you," he said.

"What's your stance on falling in love?"

"I've done it, and I'm not interested in doing it again."

"Has Poppy ever been in love before?" Joshua pressed.

Isaiah absolutely knew the answer to this question, not that it was any of his brother's business how he knew it. "No."

"Maybe she wants to be. And I imagine she wants her husband to love her."

"Poppy wants to be able to trust someone. She knows she can trust me. I know I can trust her. You can't get much better than that."

"I know you're anti-love... But what Danielle and I have..."

"What you and Danielle have is statistically improbable. There's no way you should have been able to place an ad in the paper for someone who is the antithesis of everything you should need in your life and fall madly in love with her. Additionally, I don't want that. I want stability."

"And my life looks terribly unstable to you?" Joshua asked.

"No. It doesn't. You forget, I was in a relationship for five years with a woman who turned out to be nothing like what I thought she was."

"You're still hung up on Rosalind?"

Isaiah shook his head. "Not at all. But I learned from my mistakes, Joshua. And the lesson there is that you can't actually trust those kinds of feelings. They blind you to reality."

"So you think I'm blind to reality?"

"And I hope it never bites your ass."

"What about Mom and Dad?"

"It's different," he said.

"How?"

"It's different for you too," Isaiah said. "I don't read people like you do. You know how to charm people. You know how to sense what they're feeling. How to turn the emotional tide of a room. I don't know how to do that. I have to trust my head because my heart doesn't give me a whole lot. What works for you isn't going to work for me."

"Just don't hurt her."

"I won't."

But then, Isaiah suddenly wasn't so sure. She was already hurt. Or at least, annoyed with him. And he wasn't quite sure what he was supposed to do about it.

He walked back toward Poppy's office and opened the door without knocking. She was sitting in her chair at her desk, not looking at anything in particular, and most definitely fuming.

"That was an unexpected little stunt," he said.

"You're not in charge of this," she pointed out. "If we are going to get married, it's a partnership. You don't get to manipulate me. You're not my boss in our marriage."

His lips twitched. "I could be your boss in the bedroom."

The color in her cheeks darkened. "I will allow that. However, in real life…"

"I get it."

He walked toward her and lowered himself to his knees in front of her, taking her chin in his hand. "I promise, I'm not trying to be a dick."

"Really?" He felt her tremble slightly beneath his touch.

He frowned. "I never try to be. I just am sometimes."

"Right."

"Joshua and Faith know. I mean, they already knew about the ad, and there was no way I was getting it by them that this wasn't related to that in some way."

"What did they say?"

"Joshua wants to make sure I don't hurt you."

She huffed a laugh. "Well. I'm team Joshua on that one."

"When do you want to tell my parents?" he asked. "We have our monthly dinner in three weeks."

"Let's…wait until then," she said.

"You want to wait that long?"

"Yes," she said. "I'm not…ready."

He would give her that. He knew that sometimes Poppy found interactions with family difficult. He'd always attributed that to her upbringing. "I understand. In the meantime, I want you to move your things into my house."

"But what about *my* house?" she asked.

"Obviously, you're coming to live on my ranch."

"No sex until we get married." The words came out fast and desperate.

He frowned. "We've already had sex. Several times."

"And that was…good. To establish our connection. It's established. And I want to wait now."

"Okay," he said.

She blinked. "Good."

He didn't think she'd hold to that. But Poppy was obviously trying to gain a sense of power here, and he was happy to give it to her.

Of course, that didn't mean he wouldn't try to seduce her.

Chapter 7

Poppy didn't have time to think much about her decision over the next few days. Isaiah had a moving company take all of her things to his house, and before she knew it, she was settling into a routine that was different from anything she had ever imagined she'd be part of.

They went to work together. They spent all day on the job, being very much the same Poppy and Isaiah they'd always been. But then they went home together.

And sexual tension seemed to light their every interaction on fire. She swore she could feel his body heat from across the room.

He had given her a room, her own space. But she could tell he was confused by her abstinence edict.

Even she was wondering why she was torturing herself.

Being with him physically was wonderful. But she felt completely overwhelmed by him.

She'd spent ten years secretly pining for him. Then in one moment, he'd decided he wanted something different, something more, and they'd been on their way to it. Isaiah had snapped his fingers and changed her world, and she didn't recognize even one part of it anymore.

Not even the ceiling she saw every morning when she opened her eyes.

She had to figure out a way to have power in this relationship. She was the one who was in love, and that meant she was at a disadvantage already. He was the one who got to keep his house. He was the one with the family she would become a part of.

She had to do something to hold on to her sanity.

It was hard to resist him though. So terribly hard.

When she felt lonely and scared at night, worrying for the future in a bedroom that was just down the hall from his, she wished—like that first night—that he would do a little less respecting of her commandments. That he would at least try to tempt her away from her resolve. Because if he did, she was sure it would fail.

But he didn't. So it was up to her to hang on to that edict.

No matter what.

Even when they had to behave like a normal couple for his parents' sakes.

And she was dreading the dinner at his parents' house tonight. With all of her soul.

Dreading having to tell a vague story about how they had suddenly realized their feelings for each other and were now making it official.

The fact that it was a farce hurt too badly.

But tonight they would actually discuss setting a wedding date.

A wedding date.

She squeezed her eyes shut for a moment, and then looked up at the gorgeous, custom-made cabinets in Isaiah's expansive kitchen. Maybe she should have a glass of wine before dinner. Or four. To calm her nerves.

She was already dressed and ready to go, but Isaiah had been out taking care of his horses, and she was still waiting for him to finish showering.

Part of her wished she could have simply joined him. But she'd made an edict and she should be able to stick to it.

She wondered if there was any point in preserving a sanity that was so frazzled as it was. Probably not.

Isaiah appeared a moment later, barefoot, in a pair of dark jeans with a button-up shirt. He was wearing his cowboy hat, looking sexy and disreputable, and exactly like the kind of guy who had been tailor-made for her from her deepest fantasies.

Or, maybe it was just that *he* was her fantasy.

Then he reached into his pocket and pulled out a black velvet box.

"No," she said.

He held it up. "No?"

"I didn't… I didn't know you were going to…"

"You have to have a ring before we see my parents."

"But then I'm going to walk in with a ring and they're going to know." As excuses went, it was a weak one. They were going to inform his parents of their engagement anyway.

They were engaged.

It was so strange. She didn't feel engaged to him. *Maybe because you won't sleep with him?* *No. Because he doesn't love me.*

She had a snotty response at the ready for her internal critic. Because really.

"They won't know you're engaged to me. And even so, were not trying to make it a surprise. We're just telling them in person."

The ring inside the box was stunning. Ornately designed, rather than a simple solitaire.

"It's vintage," he said. "It was part of a museum collection, on display in Washington, DC. I saw it online and I contacted the owner."

"You bought a vintage ring out of a museum." It wasn't a question so much as a recitation of what he'd just said.

"It was a privately owned collection." As if that explained it. "What?" he asked, frowning after she hadn't spoken for a few moments. "You don't look happy."

She didn't know how to describe what she was feeling. It was the strangest little dream come true. Something she would never have even given a thought to. Ever. She never thought about what kind of engagement ring she might want. And if she had, she would have asked for something small, and from the mall. Not from…*a museum collection.*

"I know how much you like vintage. And I know you don't like some of the issues surrounding the diamond trade."

She had gone on a small tirade in the office after seeing the movie *Blood Diamond* a few years ago. Just once. It wasn't like it was a cause she talked about regularly. "You…listened to that?"

"Yes," he responded.

Sometimes she wondered if everybody misunderstood him, including her. If no one knew just how deeply he held on to each moment. To people. Remembering a detail like that wasn't the mark of an unemotional man. It seemed…remarkably sentimental for him to remember such a small thing about her. Especially something that—at the time—wouldn't have been relevant to him.

She saw Isaiah as such a stark guy. A man who didn't engage in anything unnecessary. Or hold on to anything he didn't need to hold on to.

But that was obviously just what he showed the world. What he showed her.

It wasn't all of him.

It was so easy to think of him as cold, emotionless. He would be the first person to say a relationship could be a math equation for him, after all.

But remembering her feelings on diamonds wasn't math. It was personal.

There was no other man on earth—no other person on earth—who understood her the way Isaiah Grayson did.

She hadn't realized it until this moment. She'd made a lot of accusations about him being oblivious, but she was just as guilty.

And now…

She wanted to wear his ring. The ring he'd chosen for her with such thought and…well, extravagance. Because who had ever given her that kind of thought before? No one.

And certainly no one had ever been so extravagant for her.

Only him.

Only ever him.

He walked over to where she was sitting and took the

ring out of the box, sliding it onto her finger. He didn't get down on one knee. But then, that didn't surprise her.

More to the point, it didn't matter.

The ring itself didn't even matter. It was the thought. It was the man.

Her man.

It was how much she wanted it that scared her. That was the real problem. She wanted to wear his ring more than she wanted anything in the world.

And she was going to take it.

"Are you ready to go to dinner?"

She swallowed hard, looking down at the perfect, sparkly rock on her finger.

"Yes," she said. "I'm ready."

Isaiah felt a sense of calm and completion when they pulled into his parents' house that night. The small, modest farmhouse looked the same as it ever did, the yellow porch light cheery in the dim evening. It was always funny to him that no matter how successful Devlin, Joshua, Faith or Isaiah became, his parents refused to allow their children to buy them a new house. Or even to upgrade the old one at all.

They were perfectly happy with what they had.

He envied that feeling of being content. Being so certain what home was.

He liked his house, but he didn't yet feel the need to stop changing his circumstances. He wasn't settled.

He imagined that this new step forward with Poppy would change that. Though, he would like it if she dropped the sex embargo.

He wasn't quite sure why she was so bound by it, though she had said something about white weddings and how she was a traditional girl at heart, even though he didn't believe any of it since she had happily jumped into bed with him a few weeks earlier.

It was strange. He'd spent ten years not having sex with Poppy. But now that they'd done it a few times, it was damn near impossible to wait ten days, much less however long it was going to be until their wedding. He was fairly confident she wouldn't stick to her proclamation that whole time, though. At least, he had been confident until nearly three weeks had passed without her knocking on his bedroom door.

But then, Poppy had been a twenty-eight-year-old virgin. Her commitment to celibacy was much greater than his own. He might have spent years abstaining from relationships, but he had not abstained from sex.

They got out of the car, and she started to charge ahead of him, as she had done on the way into the office that first morning after they'd made love. He was not going to allow that this time.

He caught up with her, wrapping his arm around her waist. "If you walk into my parents' living room and announce that we had sex I may have to punish you."

She turned her head sharply, her eyes wide. "Punish me? What sort of caveman proclamation is that?"

"Exactly the kind a bratty girl like you needs if you're plotting evil."

"I'm *not* plotting evil," she said, her cheeks turning pink.

He examined her expression closely. Knowing Poppy like he did, he could read her better than he could read just about anyone else. She was annoyed with him. They certainly weren't back on the same footing they had been.

But she wanted him. She couldn't hide that, even now, standing in front of his parents' home.

"But you're a little bit intrigued about what I might do," he whispered.

She wiggled against him, and he could tell she absolutely, grudgingly was intrigued. "Not at all."

"You're a liar."

"You have a bad habit of pointing that out." She sounded crabby about that.

"I don't see the point of lies. In the end, they don't make anything less uncomfortable."

"Most people find small lies á great comfort," she disagreed.

"I don't," he said, a hot rock lodging itself in his chest. "I don't allow lies on any level, Poppy. That, you do have to know about me."

He'd already been in a relationship with a woman who had lied to him. And he hadn't questioned it. Because he'd imagined that love was somehow the same as having two-way trust.

"I won't lie to you," she said softly, brushing her fingertips over his lips.

Instantly, he felt himself getting hard. She hadn't touched him in the weeks since he'd spent the night in her bed. But now was not the time.

He nodded once, and then tightened his hold on her as they continued to walk up the porch. Then he knocked.

"Why do you knock at your parents' house?"

"I don't live here."

The door opened, and his mother appeared, looking between the two of them, her eyes searching.

"Isaiah? Poppy."

"Hi," Poppy said, not moving away from his hold.

"Hi, Mom," Isaiah said.

"I imagine you have something to tell us," his mom said, stepping away from the door.

Isaiah led Poppy into the cozy room. His father was sitting in his favorite chair, a picture of the life he'd had growing up still intact. The feeling it gave him… It was the kind of life he wanted.

"We have something to tell you," Isaiah said.

Then the front door opened again and his brother Devlin and his wife, Mia, who was heavily pregnant, walked into the room.

"We brought chips," Mia said, stopping cold when she saw Isaiah and Poppy standing together.

"Yay for chips," Poppy said.

Then Joshua, Danielle and baby Riley came in, and with the exception of Faith, the entire audience was present.

"Do you want to wait for Faith?" his mom asked.

"No," Isaiah said. "Poppy and I are engaged."

His mother and father stared at them, and then his mother smiled. "That's wonderful!" She closed the distance between them and pulled him in for a hug.

She did the same to Poppy, who was shrinking slightly next to him, like she was her wilting namesake.

His father made his way over to them and extended his hand; Isaiah shook it. "A good decision," his dad said, looking at Poppy. And then, he hugged her, kissing her on the cheek. "Welcome to the family, Poppy."

Poppy made a sound that was somewhere between a gasp and a sob, but she stayed rooted next to his side.

This was what he wanted. This feeling. There was warmth here. And it was easy. There was closeness.

And now that he had Poppy, it was perfect.

* * *

Poppy didn't know how she made it through dinner. The food tasted like glue, which was ridiculous, since Nancy Grayson made the best food, and it always tasted like heaven. But Poppy had a feeling that her taste buds were defective, along with her very soul. She felt…wonderful and awful. All at once.

The Graysons were such an amazing family, and she loved Isaiah's parents. But they thought Isaiah and Poppy were in love. They thought Isaiah had finally shared his heart with someone.

And he didn't understand their assumptions. He thought they wanted marriage for him. A traditional family. But that wasn't really what they wanted.

They wanted his happiness.

And Isaiah was still… He was still in the same place he had always been, emotionally. Unwilling to open up. Unwilling to take a risk because it was so difficult. They thought she'd changed him, and she hadn't.

She was…enabling him.

She was enabling him and it was terrible.

After dinner, Poppy helped Nancy clear the dishes away.

"Poppy," she said. "Can I talk to you?"

Poppy shifted. "Of course."

"I've always known you would be perfect for him," Nancy said. "But I'm hesitant to push Isaiah into anything because he just digs in. They're all like that to a degree… But he's the biggest puzzle. He always has been. Since he was a boy. Either angry and very emotional, or seemingly emotionless. I've always known that wasn't true. People often find him detached, but I think it's because he cares so much."

Poppy agreed, and it went right along with what she'd been thinking when he'd given her the ring. That there were hidden spaces in him he didn't show anyone. And that had to be out of protection. Which showed that he did feel. He felt an awful lot.

"He's a good man," Nancy continued. "And I think he'll be a good husband to you. I'm just so glad you're going to be the one to be his wife, because you are exactly what he needs. You always have been."

"I don't... He's not difficult." Poppy looked down at her hands, her throat getting tight. "He's one of the most special people I know."

Nancy reached out and squeezed Poppy's hands. "That's all any mother wants the wife of her son to think."

Poppy felt even more terrible. Like a fraud. Yes, she would love Isaiah with everything she had, but she wasn't sure she was helping him at all.

"I have something for you," Nancy said. "Come with me."

She led Poppy back to the master bedroom, the only room in the house Poppy had never gone into. Nancy walked across the old wooden floor and the threadbare braided rug on top, moving to a highboy dresser and opening up a jewelry box.

"I have my mother's wedding band here. I know that you like...old-fashioned things. It didn't seem right for Danielle. And I know Faith won't want it. You're the one it was waiting for." Nancy turned, holding it out to Poppy.

Poppy swallowed hard. "Thank you," she said. "I'll save it until the... Until the wedding."

"It can stay here, for safekeeping, if you want."

"If you could," Poppy said. "But I want to wear it. Once Isaiah and I are married." Married. She was going to marry Isaiah. "Thank you."

Nancy gave Poppy another hug, and Poppy felt like her heart was splintering. "I know that your own mother won't be at the wedding," Mrs. Grayson said. "But we won't make a bride's side and a groom's side. It's just going to be our family. You're our family now, Poppy. You're not alone."

"Thank you," Poppy said, barely able to speak.

She walked back out into the living room on numb feet to find Isaiah standing by the front door with his hat on. "Are you ready to go?" he asked.

"Yes," she said.

She got another round of hugs from the entire family, each one adding weight to her already burdened conscience.

When they got out, they made their way back to the car, and as soon as he closed the door behind them, Poppy's insides broke apart.

They pulled out of the driveway, and a tear slid down her cheeks, and she turned her face away from him to keep him from seeing.

"I can't do this."

Chapter 8

"What?"

"I can't do this," she said, feeling panic rising inside her now. "I'm sorry. But your parents think that I've... transformed you in some way. That I'm healing you. And instead, I'm enabling you to keep on doing that thing you love to do, where you run away from emotion and make everything about..."

"Maybe I just don't feel it," he said. "Maybe I'm not running from anything because there isn't anything there for me to run from. Why would you think differently?"

"Because you loved Rosalind..."

"Maybe. Or maybe I didn't. You're trying to make it seem like I feel things the exact same way other people do, and that isn't fair. I don't."

"I'm not trying to. It's just that your parents think—"

"I don't give a damn what my parents think. You

were the one who wanted them to believe this was a normal kind of courtship. I don't care either way."

"Of course you don't."

"This is ridiculous, Poppy. You can't pull out of our agreement now that everybody knows."

"I could," she said. "I could, and I could quit. Like I was going to do."

"Because you would find it so easy to leave me?"

"No!"

"You're doing this because you feel guilty? I don't believe it. I think you're running away. You accuse me of not dealing with my feelings. But you were a twenty-eight-year-old virgin. You've refused to let me touch you in the time since we first made love, and now that you've had to endure hugs from my entire family suddenly you're trying to escape like a feral cat."

"I am not a feral cat." The comparison was unflattering.

And a little bit too close to the truth.

"I think you are. I think you're fine as long as somebody leaves a can of tuna for you out by the Dumpster, but the minute they try to bring you in the house you're all claws and teeth."

"No one has ever left me a can of tuna by a Dumpster." If he wanted claws, she was on the verge of giving them to him. This entire conversation was getting ridiculous.

"This isn't over." He started to drive them back toward his house.

"It is," she protested.

"No."

"Take me back to *my* house," she insisted.

"My house *is* your house. You agreed to marry me."

"And now I'm *un*agreeing," she insisted.

"And I think you're full of shit," he said, his tone so sharp it could have easily sliced right through her. "I think you're a hypocrite. Going on about what I need to do. Worrying about my emotional health when your own is in a much worse place."

She huffed, clenching her hands into fists and looking away from him. She said nothing for the rest of the drive, and then when they pulled up to the house, Isaiah was out of the car much quicker than she was, moving over to her side and pulling open the door. Then he reached into the car, unbuckled her and literally lifted her out as though she were a child. Holding her in his arms, he carried her up the steps toward the house.

"What the hell are you doing?" she shouted.

"What I should have done weeks ago."

"Making the transformation from man to caveman complete?"

He slid his hand down toward her ass and heat rioted through her. Even now, when she should be made of nothing but rage, she responded to him. Dammit.

"Making you remember why we're doing this."

"For your convenience," she hissed.

"Because I can't want another woman," he said, his voice rough, his eyes blazing. "Not now. And we both know you don't want another man."

She made a poor show of kicking her feet slightly as he carried her inside. She could unman him if she wanted to, but she wouldn't. And they both knew it.

"You can't do this," she protested weakly. "It violates all manner of HR rules."

"Too bad for you that I own the company. I *am* HR."

"I'm going to organize an ethics committee," she groused.

"This is personal business. The company has nothing to do with it."

"Is it? I think it's business for you, period, like everything else."

"It's personal," he ground out, "because I've been inside you. Don't you dare pretend that isn't true. Though it all makes sense to me now. Why you wanted me to stay away from you for the past few weeks."

"Because I'm just not that into you?" she asked as he carried her up the stairs.

"No. Because you're *too* into it."

She froze, ice gathering at the center of her chest. She didn't want him to know. He had been so clueless up until this point.

"You're afraid that I'll be able to convince you to stay because the sex is so good."

Okay. Well, he was a little bit onto it. But not really.

Just a little bit off base, was her Isaiah.

"You're in charge of everything," she said. "I didn't think it would hurt you to have to wait."

"I don't play games."

"Sadly for you, the rest of the world does. We play games when we need to. We play games to protect ourselves. We play games because it's a lot more palatable than wandering around making proclamations like you do."

"I don't understand games," he said. He flung open the door to his bedroom and walked them both inside. "But I understand this." He claimed her mouth. And she should have... She should have told him no. Because of course he would have stopped. But she didn't.

Instead, she let him consume her.

Then she began to consume him back. She wanted him. That was the problem. As much as everything that had happened back at the Grayson house terrified her, she wanted him.

Terrified. That wasn't the word she had used before. Isaiah was the one who had said she was afraid. And maybe she was. But she didn't know what to do about it.

It was like the time she had gone to live with a couple who hadn't been expecting a little girl as young as she was. They had been surprised, and clearly, their house hadn't been ready for a boisterous six-year-old. There had been a list of things she wasn't allowed to touch. And so she had lived in that house for all of three weeks, afraid to leave feet print on the carpet, afraid of touching breakable objects. Afraid that somehow she was going to destroy the beautiful place she found herself in simply because of who she was.

Because she was the wrong fit.

That was what it had felt like at the Graysons' tonight. Like she was surrounded by all this lovely, wonderful love, and somehow, it just wasn't for her. Wasn't to be.

There was more to it than that, of course, but that was the *real* reason she was freaking out, and she knew it.

But it didn't make her *wrong*.

It also didn't make her want to stop what was happening with Isaiah right now.

She was lonely. She had been a neglected child, and then she had lived in boisterous houses full of lots of children, which could sometimes feel equally lonely. She had never had a close romantic relationship as an adult. She was making friends in Copper Ridge, but moving around as often as she had made it difficult for her to have close lifelong friends. Isaiah was that friend, essentially.

And being close to him like this was a balm for a wound that ran very, very deep.

"You think this is fake?" he asked, his voice like gravel.

He bent down in front of her, grabbing hold of her skirt and drawing it down her legs without bothering to take off her shoes. Her shirt went next.

"Sit down," he commanded, and her legs were far too weak to disobey him. He looked up at her, those gray eyes intent on hers. "Take your bra off for me."

With shaking hands, she found herself obeying him.

"I imagine you're going to report me to HR for this too." The smile that curved his lips told her he didn't much care.

"I might," she responded, sliding her bra down her arms and throwing it onto the floor.

"Well, then I might have to keep you trapped here so you can't tell anyone."

"This is a major infraction."

"Maybe. But then again. I am the boss. I suppose I could choose to reprimand you for such behavior."

"I… I suppose you could."

"You're being a very bad girl," he said, hooking his fingers in the waistband of her panties and pulling them down to her knees. "Very bad."

Panic skittered in her stomach, and she had no idea how to respond. To Isaiah being like this, so playful. To him being like this and also staring at her right where he was staring at her.

"You need to remember who the boss is," he said,

moving his hands around her lower back and sliding them down to cup her ass. Then he jerked her forward, and she gasped as he pressed a kiss to the inside of her thigh.

Then he went higher, and higher still, while she trembled.

She couldn't believe he was about to do this. She wanted him to. But she was also scared. Self-conscious. Excited. It was a whole lot of things.

But then, everything with Isaiah was a lot.

He squeezed her with both hands and then moved his focus to her center, his tongue sliding through her slick folds. She clapped her hand over her mouth to keep from making an extremely embarrassing noise, but she had a feeling he could still hear it, muffled or not.

Because he chuckled.

Isaiah, who was often humorless, chuckled with his mouth where it was, and his filthy intentions were obvious even to her.

And then he started to show her what he meant by punishment. He teased her with his tongue, with his fingers, with his mouth. He scraped her inner thigh with the edge of his teeth before returning his attention to where she was most needy for him. But every time she got close he would back off. He would move somewhere else. Kiss her stomach, her wrist, her hand. He would take his attention off of exactly where she needed him.

"Please," she begged.

"Bad girls don't get to come," he said, the edge in his voice sharp like a knife.

Those words just about pushed her over the edge all on their own.

"I thought you said you didn't play games," she choked out.

"Let me rephrase that," he said, looking up at her, a wicked smile curving his mouth. "I only play games in the bedroom."

He pressed two fingers into her before laughing at her again with his tongue, taking her all the way to the edge again before backing off. He knew her body better than she did, knew exactly where to touch her, and where not to. Knew the exact pressure and speed. How to rev her up and bring her back.

He was evil, and in that moment, she felt like she hated him as much as she had ever loved him.

"Tell me what you want," he said.

"You *know*."

"I do," he responded. "But you have to tell me."

"You're mean," she panted.

"I'm a very, very mean man," he agreed, sounding unrepentant as he slid one finger back through her folds. Tormenting. Teasing. "And you like it."

"I don't," she insisted.

"You do. Which is your real problem with all of this. You want me. And you want this. Even though you know you probably shouldn't."

"Well, what about you?" she asked, breathing hard. "You want it too. Or you wouldn't be trying so hard to convince me to go through with this marriage. Maybe *you* should beg."

"I'm on my knees," he said. "Isn't that like begging?"

"That's not—"

But she was cut off because his lips connected with that most sensitive part of her again. She could do nothing but feel.

She was so wet, so ready for him, so very hollow and achy that she couldn't stand for him to continue. It was going to kill her.

Or she was going to kill him. One of the two.

"Tell me," he whispered in her ear. "Tell me what you want."

"You," she said.

"Me?"

"You. Inside me. Please."

She didn't have to ask him twice.

Instead, she found herself being lifted up, brought down onto the bed, sitting astride him. He maneuvered her so her slick entrance was poised just above his hardness. And then he thrust up, inside her.

She gasped.

"You want to be in charge? Go ahead."

It was a challenge. And it gave her anything but control, when she was so desperate for him, when each move over him betrayed just how desperate she was.

He knew it too. The bastard.

But she couldn't stop, because she was so close, and now that she was on top she could…

Stars exploded behind her eyes, her internal muscles pulsing, her entire body shaking as her orgasm rocked her. All it had taken was a couple of times rocking back and forth, just a couple of times applying pressure where it was needed.

He growled, flipping her over and pinning her hands above her head. "You were just a bit too easy on me."

He kissed her then, and it was like a beast had been unleashed inside him. He was rough and untamed, and his response called up desire inside her again much sooner than she would have thought possible.

But it was Isaiah.

And with him, she had a feeling it would always be like this.

Always?

She pushed that mocking question aside.

She wasn't going to think about anything beyond this, right now.

She wasn't going to think about what she had told him before he carried her upstairs. About what she believed she deserved or didn't, about what she believed was possible and wasn't.

She was just going to feel.

This time, when the wave broke over her, he was swept up in it too, letting out a hoarse growl as he found his own release.

And when it was over, she didn't have the strength to get up. Didn't have the strength to walk away from him.

Tomorrow. Tomorrow would sort itself out.

Maybe for now she could hang on to the fantasy.

Poppy woke up in the middle of the night, curled around Isaiah's body. Something strange had woken her, and it wasn't the fact that she was sharing a bed with Isaiah.

It wasn't the fact that her resolve had weakened quite so badly last night.

There was something else.

She couldn't think what, or why it had woken her out of a dead sleep. She rolled away from him and padded into the bathroom that was just off his bedroom. She stood there for a moment staring at the mirror, at the woman looking back at her. Who was disheveled and had raccoon eyes because she hadn't taken her makeup off before allowing Isaiah to rock her world last night.

And then it suddenly hit her.

Because she was standing in a bathroom and staring at the mirror, and it felt like a strange kind of déjà vu.

It was the middle of the month. And she absolutely should've started her period by now.

She was two days late.

And she and Isaiah hadn't used a condom.

"No," she whispered.

It was too coincidental.

She went back into the bedroom and dressed as quickly and quietly as possible. And then she grabbed her purse and went downstairs.

She had to know.

She wouldn't sleep until she did. There were a few twenty-four-hour places in Tolowa, and she was going over there right now.

And that was how, at five in the morning in a public restroom, Poppy Sinclair's life changed forever.

Chapter 9

When Isaiah woke up the next morning, Poppy wasn't in bed with him. He was irritated, but he imagined she was still trying to hold on to some semblance of control with her little game.

She was going to end up agreeing to marry him. He was fairly confident in that. But what he'd said about her being like a stray cat, he'd meant. She might not like the comparison, but it was true enough. Now that he wanted to domesticate her, she was preparing to run.

But her common sense would prevail. It didn't benefit her *not* to marry him.

And she couldn't deny the chemistry between them. He wasn't being egotistical about that. What they had between them was explosive. It *couldn't* be denied.

When he got downstairs, he saw Poppy sitting at the kitchen table. She was dressed in the same outfit she'd been wearing last night, and she was staring straight ahead, her eyes fixed on her clenched fists.

"Good morning," he said.

"No, it isn't," she responded. She looked up at him, and then she frowned. "Could you put a shirt on?"

He looked down at his bare chest. He was only wearing a pair of jeans. "No."

"I feel like this is a conversation we should have with your shirt on." She kept her gaze focused on the wall behind him.

He crossed his arms over his chest. "I've decided I like the conversations I have with you without my shirt better."

"I'm not joking around, Isaiah."

"Then you don't have time for me to go get a shirt. What's going on?"

"I'm pregnant." She looked like she was delivering the news of a death to him.

"That's..." He let the words wash over him, took a moment to turn them over and analyze what they made him feel. He felt...calm. "That's good," he said.

"Is it?" Poppy looked borderline hysterical.

"Yes," he said, feeling completely confident and certain now. "We both want children."

It was sooner than he'd anticipated, of course, but he wanted children. And...there was something relieving about it. It made this marriage agreement feel much more final. Made it feel like more of a done deal.

Poppy was his.

He'd spent last night in bed with her working to affirm that.

A pregnancy just made it that much more final.

"I broke up with you last night," she pointed out.

"Yes, you did a very good impression of a woman who was broken up with me. Particularly when you cried out my name during your... Was it your third or fourth orgasm?"

"That has nothing to do with whether or not we should be together. Whether or not we should get married."

"Well, now there's no question about whether or not we're getting married. You're having my baby."

"This is not 1953. That is not a good enough reason to get married."

He frowned. "I disagree."

"I'm not going to just jump into marriage with you."

"You're being unreasonable. You were more than willing to jump into marriage with me when you agreed to my proposal. Now suddenly when we're having a child you can't *jump into* anything? You continually *jump into* my bed, Poppy, so you can't claim we don't have the necessary ingredients to make a marriage work."

"Do you love me?" There was a challenge in her eyes, a stubborn set to her chin.

"I care very much about you," he responded.

It was the truth. The honest truth. She was one of the most important people in his life.

"But you're not in love with me."

"I already told you—"

"Yes. You're not going to do love. Well, you know what? I've decided that it feels fake if we're not in love."

"The fact that you're pregnant with my child indicates it's real enough."

"You don't understand. You don't understand anything."

"You sound like a sixteen-year-old girl having an argument with her parents. You would rather have some idealistic concept that may never actually happen than make a family with me?"

"I would rather… I would rather none of this was happening."

It felt like a slap, and he didn't know why.

That she didn't want him. Didn't seem to want the baby. He couldn't sort out the feeling it gave him. The sharp, stabbing sensation right around the area of his heart.

But he could reason through it. He was right, and her hysterics didn't change that.

There was an order to things. An order of operations, like math. That didn't change based on how people felt.

He understood…nothing right now. Nothing happening inside him, or outside him.

But he knew what was right. And he knew he could count on his brain.

It was the surest thing. The most certain.

So he went with that.

"But it is happening," he said, his voice tight. "You are far too practical to discard something real for some silly fantasy."

Her face drained of color. "So it's a *fantasy* that someone could love me."

"That isn't what I meant. It's a fantasy that you're going to find someone else who can take care of you like I can. Who is also the father of your child. Who can make you come the way that I do."

"Maybe it's just easy for me. You don't know. Neither do I. I've only had the one lover."

That kicked up the fire and heat in his stomach, and

he shoved it back down because this was not about what he felt. Not about what his body wanted.

"Trust me," he bit out. "It's never this good."

"I can't do this." She pressed a balled-up fist to her eyes.

"That's too bad," he said. "Because you will."

Resolve strengthened in him like iron. She was upset. But there was only one logical way forward. It was the only thing that made sense. And he was not going to let her take a different route. He just wasn't.

"I don't have to, Isaiah."

"You want your child growing up like you did? Being shuffled between homes?"

She looked like he'd hit her. "Foster care is not the same as sharing custody, and you know that. Don't you dare compare the two. I would have been thrilled to have two involved parents, even if I did have to change houses on the weekends. I didn't have that, and I never have had that. Don't talk about things you don't understand."

"I understand well enough. You're being selfish."

"I'm being *reasonable*!"

Reasonable.

Reasonable to her was them not being together. Reasonable to her was shoving him out of her life now that he'd realized just how essential she was.

"How is it reasonable to deny your child a chance at a family?" he asked. "All of us. Together. At my parents' house for dinners. Aunts and uncles and cousins. How is it unreasonable for me to want to share that with you instead of keeping my life and yours separate?"

"Isaiah…"

He was right, though. And what he wanted wasn't really about what he wanted. It was about logic.

And he wasn't above being heavy-handed to prove that point.

"If you don't marry me, I'm going to pursue full custody of our child," he said, the words landing heavily in the room.

Her head popped up. "You what?"

"And believe me, I'll get it. I have money. I have a family to back me up. I can make this very difficult for you. I don't want to, Poppy. That's not my goal. But I will have my way."

The look on her face, the abject betrayal, almost made him feel something like regret. Almost.

"I thought you were my friend," she said. "I thought you cared about me."

"I do. Which is why I'm prepared to do this. The best thing. The right thing. I'm not going to allow you to hurt our child in the name of friendship. How is that friendship?"

"Caring about someone doesn't just mean running them over until they do what you want. Friendship and caring goes both ways." She pressed her hand to her chest. "What I feel—*what I want*—has to matter."

"I know what you *should* want," he insisted.

If she would only listen. If she could, she'd understand what he was doing. In the end, it would be better if they were together. There was no scenario where their being apart would work, and if he had to play hardball to get her there, he damn well would.

"That isn't how wanting works. It's not how feelings work." She stood up, and she lifted her fist and slammed it down onto his chest. "It's not how any of this works, you robot."

He drew back, shock assaulting him. Poppy was one of the only people who had never looked at him that way before. Poppy had always taken pains to try to understand him.

"I'm a robot because I want to make sure my child has a family?" he asked, keeping his voice low.

"Because you don't care about what I want."

"I *want* you to want what *I* want," he said, holding her fist against his chest where she had hit him. "I want for this to work. How is that not feeling?"

"Because it isn't the *right feeling*."

Those words were like a whip cracking over his insides.

He had *never* had the right feelings. He already knew that. But with Poppy his feelings hadn't ever felt wrong before. *He* hadn't felt wrong before.

She'd been safe. Always.

But not now. Not now he'd started to care.

"I'm sorry," he said, his voice low. "I'm sorry I can't open up my chest and rearrange everything for you. I'm sorry that you agreed to be engaged to me, and then I didn't transform into a different man."

"I never said that's what I wanted."

"It *is* what you wanted. You wanted being with me to look like being with someone else. And you know what? If you weren't pregnant, I might've been able to let you walk away. But it's too late now. This is happening. The wedding is not off."

"The wedding *is* off," she insisted.

"Look at me," he said, his voice low, fierce. "Look

at me and tell me if you think I was joking about taking custody."

Her eyes widened, her lips going slack. "I've always cared about you," she said, her voice shaking. "I've always tried to understand you. But I think maybe I was just pretending there was a heart in your chest when there never was."

"You can fling all the insults you want at me. If I'm really heartless, I don't see how you think that's going to make a difference."

Then she let out a frustrated cry and turned and fled the room, leaving him standing there feeling hollowed out.

Wishing that he was exactly what she had accused him of being.

But if he were heartless, then her words—her rejection—wouldn't feel like a knife through his chest.

If he were a robot, he wouldn't care that he couldn't find a way to order his feelings exactly to her liking.

But he did care.

He just had no idea what to do about it.

Chapter 10

Ultimately, it wasn't Isaiah's threats that had her agreeing to his proposal.

It was what he'd said about family.

She was angry that it had gotten inside her head. That it had wormed its way into her heart.

No. Angry was an understatement.

She was *livid*.

She was also doing exactly what he had asked her to do.

The date for their wedding was now Christmas Eve. Of all the ridiculous things. Though, she supposed that would give her a much stronger association with the holiday than she'd had before.

His family was thrilled.

Poppy was not.

And she was still sleeping in her own room.

After that lapse when she had tried to break things

off with him a week earlier, she had decided that she really, *really* needed Isaiah not to touch her for a while.

For his part, he was seething around the house with an intensity that she could feel.

But he hadn't tried to change her mind.

Which was good. Because the fact of the matter was he *would* be able to change her mind. With very little effort.

And besides the tension at home, she was involved in things that made her break out in hives.

Literally.

She had been itchy for three days. The stress of trying to plan a wedding that felt like a death march was starting to get to her.

The fact that she was going wedding-dress shopping with Isaiah's mother and sister was only making matters worse.

And yet, here she was, at Something New, the little bridal boutique in Gold Valley, awaiting the arrival of Nancy and Faith.

The little town was even more heavily decorated for the holidays than Copper Ridge. The red brick buildings were lined with lights, wreaths with crimson bows on every door.

She had opted to drive her own car because she had a feeling she was going to need the distance.

She sighed heavily as she walked into the store, the bell above the door signaling her arrival. A bright, pretty young woman behind the counter perked up.

"Hi," she said. "I'm Celia."

"Hi," Poppy said uncomfortably. "I have an appointment to try on dresses."

"You must be Poppy," she said.

"I am," Poppy said, looking down at her hands. At the ring that shone brightly against her dark skin. "I'm getting married."

"Congratulations," Celia said, as though the inane announcement wasn't that inane at all.

"I'm just waiting for…" The words died on her lips. Her future mother-in-law and sister-in-law. That was who she was waiting for.

Isaiah's family really would be her family. She knew that. It was why she'd said yes to this wedding. And somehow it hadn't fully sunk in yet. She wondered if it ever would.

The door opened a few moments later and Faith and Nancy came in, both grinning widely.

"I'm so excited," Faith said.

Poppy shot her an incredulous look that she hoped Nancy would miss. Faith of all people should not be that excited. She knew Isaiah was only marrying Poppy because of the ad.

Of course, no one knew that Isaiah was also marrying her because she was pregnant.

"So exciting," Poppy echoed, aware that it sounded hollow and lacking in excitement. She was a great assistant, but she was a lousy actress.

Celia ushered them through endless aisles of dresses and gave them instructions on how to choose preferred styles.

"When you're ready," Celia said, "just turn the dresses out and leave them on the rack. I'll bring them to you in the dressing room."

Poppy wandered through her size, idly touching a few of the dresses, but not committing to anything.

Meanwhile, Faith and Nancy were selecting styles left and right.

She saw one that caught her eye. It looked as though it was off the shoulder with long sleeves that came to a point over the top of her hand and loops that would go over her middle finger. It was understated, sedate. Very Grace Kelly, which was right in Poppy's wheelhouse. The heavy, white satin was unadorned, with a deep sheen to it that looked expensive.

She glanced at the price tag. *Incredibly* expensive.

It was somewhat surprising that there was such an upscale shop in the small community of Gold Valley, but then the place had become something of a destination for brides who wanted to make a day of dress shopping, and the cute atmosphere of the little gold rush town, with its good food and unique shops, made for an ideal girls' day out.

"Don't worry about that," Nancy said.

"I can't not worry about it," Poppy said, looking back at the price.

"Isaiah is going to pay for all of it," Nancy said. "And he made sure I was here to reinforce that."

"I know it's silly to be worked up about it," Poppy said. "Considering he signs my paychecks. But the thing is… I don't necessarily want to just take everything from him. I don't want him to think that…"

"That you're marrying him for his money?" Faith asked.

"Kind of," Poppy said.

"He isn't going to think that," Nancy said with authority. "He knows you."

"Yes," Poppy said slowly. "I just…" She looked at them both helplessly. "He's not in love with me," she said. Faith knew, and there was no reason that Poppy's future mother-in-law shouldn't know too. She'd thought she wanted to keep it a secret, but she couldn't bear it anymore, not with the woman she was accepting as family.

"I love him," Poppy said. "I want to make that clear. I love him, and I told him not to let on that this was…a convenient marriage. For my pride. But I can't lie to you." She directed that part to his mother. "I can't lie to you and have you think that I reached him or changed him in a way that I haven't. He still thinks this marriage is the height of practicality. And he's happy to throw money at it like he's happy to throw money at any of his problems. He's not paying for this wedding because he cares what I look like in the wedding dress."

She swallowed hard. "He's paying for it because he thinks that making me his wife is going to somehow magically simplify his life."

Nancy frowned. "You love him."

"I do."

"You've loved him for a long time, haven't you?"

Poppy looked down. She could see Faith shift uncomfortably out of the corner of her eye.

"Yes," Poppy confirmed. "I've loved him ever since I met him. He's a wonderful person. I can see underneath all of the… Isaiah. Or maybe that's not the right way of putting it. I don't even have to see under it. I love who he is. And that…not everybody can see just how wonderful he is. It makes it like a secret. My secret."

"I'm not upset with you," Nancy said, taking hold of the wedding dress Poppy was looking at and turning it outward. "I'm not upset with you at all. You love him, and he came barreling at you with all of the intensity that he has, I imagine, and demanded that you marry him because he decided it was logical, am I right?"

"Very."

"I don't see what woman in your position could have resisted."

If only his mother knew just how little Poppy had resisted. Just how much she wasn't resisting him…

"I should have told him no."

"Does he know that you love him?" Faith asked.

"No," Poppy said.

And she knew she didn't have to tell either of them to keep it a secret. Because they just would.

"Maybe you should tell him," Faith pointed out.

Poppy bit back a smart remark about the fact that Faith was single, and had been for as long as Poppy had known her, and Faith maybe didn't have any clue about dealing with unrequited love.

"Love isn't important to him," Poppy said. "He *likes* me. He thinks that's enough."

Nancy shook her head. "I hope he more than likes you. Otherwise that's going to be a cold marriage bed."

Faith made a squeaking sound. "Mom. Please."

"What? Marriage is long, sweetheart. And sometimes you get distant. Sometimes you get irritated with each other. In those times all you've got is the spark."

Faith slightly receded into one of the dress racks. "Please don't tell me any more about your spark."

"You should be grateful we have it," Nancy said pointedly at her daughter. "It's what I want for you in your marriage, whenever you get married. And it's certainly what I want for Poppy and Isaiah."

Poppy felt her skin flushing. "We're covered there."

"Well, that is a relief."

She wasn't going to tell them about the baby. Not now. She was just going to try on wedding dresses.

Which was what they did.

For the next two hours, Poppy tried on wedding dresses. And it all came down to The One. The long-sleeved beauty with the scary price tag and the perfect train that fanned out behind her like a dream.

Celia found a veil and pinned it into Poppy's dark hair. It was long, extending past the train with a little row of rhinestones along the edge, adding a hint of mist and glitter.

She looked at herself in the mirror, and she found herself completely overwhelmed with emotion.

She was glowing.

There, underneath the lights in the boutique, the white dress contrasted perfectly with her skin tone. She looked like a princess. She felt like one.

And she had...

She looked behind her and saw Nancy and Faith, their eyes full of tears, their hands clasped in front of them.

She had a family who cared about this. Who was here watching her try on dresses.

Who cared for her. For her happiness.

Maybe Isaiah didn't love her, but she loved him. And... His mother and sister loved her. And that offered Poppy more than she had ever imagined she might have.

It was enough. It would be.

Nancy came up behind Poppy and put a hand on Poppy's shoulder. "This is the one. Let him buy it for you. Believe me, he'll cause enough trouble over the course of a lifetime with him that you won't feel bad about spending his money this way."

Poppy laughed, then wiped at a tear that fell down her cheek. "I suppose that's true."

"I'm going to try to keep from hammering advice at you," Nancy said. "But I do have to say this. Love is an amazing thing. It's an inexhaustible resource. I've been married a long time. And over the course of that many decades with someone, there are a lot of stages. Ebbs and flows. But if you keep on giving love, as much as you have, you won't run out. Give it even when it's not flowing to you. Give it when you don't feel like it. If you can do that… That's the best use of love that I can think of. It doesn't mean it's always easy. But it's something you won't regret. Love is a gift. When you have it, choosing to give it is the most powerful thing you can do."

Poppy looked back at her reflection. She was going to be a bride. And more than that, she was going to be Isaiah's wife. He had very clear ideas about what he wanted and didn't want from that relationship. He had very definite thoughts on what he felt and didn't feel.

She had to make a decision about that. About what she was going to let it mean to her.

The problem was, she had spent a lot of years wanting love. Needing love. From parents who were unable to give it for whatever reason. Because they were either too captivated by drugs, or too lost in the struggle of life. She had decided, after that kind of childhood, after the long years of being shuffled between foster homes, that she didn't want to expose herself to that kind of pain again.

Which was exactly what Isaiah was doing.

He was holding himself back. Holding his love back because he'd been hurt before. And somehow…somehow she'd judged that. As if she was different. As if she was well-adjusted and he was wrong.

But that wasn't true.

It was a perfect circle of self-protection. One that was the reason why she had nearly broken the engagement off a week ago. Why she was holding herself back from him now.

And they would never stop.

Not until one of them took a step outside that self-created box.

She could blame her parents. She could blame the handful of foster families who hadn't been able to care for her the way she had needed them to. She could blame the ones who had. The ones she had loved deeply, but whom she had ultimately had to leave, which had caused its own kind of pain.

She could blame the fact that Isaiah had been unavailable to her for all those years. That he had belonged to Rosalind, and somehow that had put him off-limits.

But blame didn't matter. The reasons didn't really matter.

The only thing that mattered was whether or not she was going to change her life.

No one could do it for her.

And if she waited for Isaiah to be the first to take that step, then she would wait forever.

His mother was right. Love was a gift, and you could either hoard it, keep it close to your chest where it wouldn't do a thing for anyone, or you could give it.

Giving her love was the only thing that could possibly open up that door between them. If she wanted him to love her, wanted him to find the faith to love her, she'd have to be the first one to stop protecting herself.

Poppy would have to open up her arms. Stop holding them in front of her, defensive and closed off.

Which was the real problem. Really, it had been all along.

That deeply rooted feeling of unrequited love that she'd had for Isaiah had been incredibly important to her. It had kept her safe. It had kept her from going after anyone else. It had kept her insulated.

But she couldn't continue that now.

Not if she wanted a hope at happiness. Not if she wanted even the smallest chance of a relationship with him.

Someone was going to have to budge first. And she could be bitter about the fact that it had to be her, but there was no point to that.

It was simple.

This wasn't about right or wrong or who should have to give more or less. Who should have to be brave.

She could see that she should.

And if she loved him… Well. She had to care more for him and less for her own comfort.

"I think I might need to give a little bit more love," Poppy said softly.

"If my son doesn't give back to you everything that you deserve, Poppy, you had better believe that I will scar him myself."

"I do believe it," Poppy said.

And if nothing else, what she had learned in that moment was invaluable.

Somebody was in her corner.

And not only had she heard Nancy say it, Poppy believed it. She couldn't remember the last time that had been true.

This was family.

It was so much better than she had ever imagined it could be.

Chapter 11

It was late, and Isaiah was working in his home office. His eyes were starting to get gritty, but he wasn't going to his room until he was ready to pass out. It was the only way he could get any sleep at all these days.

Lying in bed knowing she was just down the hall and he couldn't have her was torture. Distance and exhaustion were the only things he could do to combat the restlessness.

He looked up, catching his reflection in the window, along with the reflection of the lamp on his desk.

It was dark out. So dark he couldn't see anything. But he knew the view well. The mountains and hills that were outside that window. A view he had carefully curated after growing tired of the gray landscape of Seattle.

Poppy had been out shopping all day, and he hadn't

seen her since she'd left that morning. But he had been thinking about her.

It was strange. The way his feelings for her were affected. A borderline obsession with a woman who should feel commonplace to him in many ways. She had been a part of his office furniture for the past decade.

Except, she'd always been more than that.

Yes. That was true. She always had been.

She was remarkable, smart and funny. Funny in a way he could never really manage to be. More than once, he had wished he could capture that sweetness and hold it to himself just for a little while.

Not that she was saccharine. No. She had no issues taking strips off his hide when it was necessary.

She was also so damn sexy he couldn't think of anything else, and she was starting to drive him insane.

He didn't have any practice with restraint. Over the years, he had been involved mostly in casual hookups, and the great thing about those was they could absolutely happen on his schedule. If the woman didn't matter, then all that was needed was time spent in an appropriate location, and a woman—any woman—would eventually indicate she was available.

But now, he was at the point where not just any woman would do. He needed Poppy.

She was still withholding herself from him, and he supposed he could understand. What with the fact that he had made threats to take her child away if she didn't fall in line. It was entirely possible he wasn't her favorite person at the moment.

That bothered him.

He wasn't very many people's favorite person. But Poppy liked him. At least, she had always seemed to.

And now, he had found a very unique way of messing that up.

He'd had a lot of friendships not go the distance. Admittedly, this was quite the most creative way he'd had one dissolve. Proposing, getting that same friend pregnant, and then forcing her to marry him.

Not that he was *forcing* her. Not *really*. He was simply giving her a set of incredibly unpleasant options. And forcing her to choose the one she found the least unpleasant.

He supposed he could take some small measure of comfort in the fact that he wasn't the *least* pleasant option.

But then, that had more to do with the baby than with him.

He sighed heavily.

He'd never felt this way about a woman before. The strange sense of constant urgency. To be with her. To fix things with her. The fact that she was angry with him actively bothered him even when she wasn't in the room displaying that anger.

He could feel it.

He could actually feel someone else's emotion. Stronger than his own.

If he wasn't so fed up, he might marvel at that.

He didn't know what was happening to him.

He was obsessing about the desire. Fixated on it. Because that he understood. Sex, he understood.

This need to tear down all the walls inside him so that he could...

He didn't know.

Be closer to her? Have her feel him, his emotions, so difficult and hard to explain, as keenly as he felt hers?

They'd been friends for ten years. Now they were lovers.

His feelings were like nothing he'd ever felt for a friend or a lover.

The door opened behind him, and he didn't have to turn to see that it was Poppy standing in the doorway. She was wearing her favorite red coat that had a high collar and a tightly belted waist, flaring out at her hips. Her hands were stuffed in her pockets, her eyes cast downward.

"How was your day?"

Her voice was so soft it startled him. He turned. "Good. I wish it were over."

"Still working?"

"Yes. Faith is interested in taking on a couple more projects. I'm just trying to make sure everything balances out."

"I chose a wedding dress."

He had half expected her to say that she had chosen a burlap sack. Or nothing at all. As a form of protest.

"I'm glad to hear it," he said, not quite sure what she wanted him to say. Not quite sure where this was leading at all.

"I've missed you."

The words landed softly, then seemed to sing down deep into his heart. "I've seen you every day for the past week."

"That isn't what I meant." A small crease appeared between her brows as she stared at him. "I'm not going to say I miss the way we used to be. Because I don't. I like so much of what we have now better. Except...we don't have it right now. Because I haven't let you get close to me. I haven't let you touch me."

She pushed away from the door jamb and walked slowly toward him. His eyes were drawn downward, to the wicked, black stilettos on her feet. And to her bare legs. Which was odd, because she was wearing a coat as if she had been outside in the cold, and he would have thought she would have something to cover her skin.

"I've missed you touching me," she said, her voice growing husky. "I've missed touching you."

She lifted her hands, working the button at the top of her coat, and then the next, followed by the next. It exposed a V of brown skin, the soft, plump curve of her breasts. And a hint of bright yellow lace.

She made it to the belt, working the fabric through the loop and letting the coat fall open before she undid the button behind it, and the next button, and the next. Until she revealed that she had nothing on beneath the coat but transparent yellow lace. Some sort of top that scooped low around her full breasts and ended above her belly button, showing hints of dark skin through the pattern, the darker shadows of her nipples.

The panties were tiny. They covered almost nothing, and he was pleased with that. She left the heels on, making her legs look impossibly long, shapely and exactly what he wanted wrapped around him.

"What did I do to deserve this?" he asked.

It wasn't a game. Not a leading question. He genuinely wanted to know.

"Nothing," she said. She took a step toward him, lifted the delicate high heel up off the ground and pressed her knee into the empty space on the chair, just beside his thigh.

She gripped the back of the chair, leaning forward. "You haven't done anything at all to deserve this. But I

want it. I'm not sure why I shouldn't have it. I think…
I think this is a mess." Her tongue darted out, slid over
her lips, and he felt the action like a slow lick. "*We* are
a mess. We have been. For a long time. Together. Apart.
But I'd rather be a mess with you than just a mess who
lives in your house and wears your ring. I'd rather be a
mess with you inside of me. We're going to get married.
I'm having your baby. We're going to have to be a family. And I don't know how to…fix us. I don't know how
to repair the broken spaces inside of us. I don't know if
it's possible. But nothing is going to be fixed, nothing at
all if we're just strangers existing in the same space. If
I'm still just your personal assistant when I'm at work."

"What are you going to be when you're at work?"

"Your personal assistant. And your fiancée. And
later, your wife. We can't separate these things. Not
anymore. We can't separate ourselves."

She pressed her fingertips against his cheek and
dragged her hand back, sliding her thumb over his lower
lip. "I'm so tired of being lonely. Feeling like…nobody
belongs to me. That I don't belong to anyone."

Those words echoed inside him, and they touched
something raw. Something painful. He felt… He felt as
if they could be words that were coming out of his own
mouth. As if she was putting voice to his own pain, a
pain he had never before realized was there.

"I want you," she said.

He reached out, bracing his hands on her hips, marveling at the erotic sight of that contrast. His paler hand
over the deep rich color of her skin.

A contrast. And still a match.

Deep and sexual and perfect.

He leaned forward and pressed a kiss to her breast,

to the bare skin just above the edge of lace. And she gasped, letting her head fall back. It was the most erotic sight. Perfect and indulgent, and something he wanted to hold on to and turn away from with matching intensity.

He wanted her to make him whole. He wanted to find the thing that she was talking about. That depth. That sense of belonging.

Of not being alone.

Of being understood.

He had never even made that a goal. Not even when he'd been with Rosalind. He'd never imagined that a woman might…understand him. He didn't quite understand himself. No one ever had.

He was different. That was all he knew.

He didn't know how to show things the way other people did. Didn't know how to read what was happening right in front of him sometimes.

Was more interested in the black-and-white numbers on a page than the full-color scene in front of him.

He couldn't change it. Didn't know if he would even if he could. His differences were what had made him successful. Made him who he was. But there were very few people willing to put up with that, with him.

But Poppy always had.

She had always been there. She had never—except for the day when she'd hit him in the chest and called him a robot—she had never acted like him being different was even a problem.

Maybe she was the one who could finally reach him. Maybe she was the one he could hold on to.

"I want you," he said, repeating her words back to her.

"I'm here," she said, tilting his face up, her dark eyes

luminous and beautiful as she stared down at him. "I'm giving myself to you." She leaned forward, her lips a whisper from his. "Can I be yours, Isaiah?"

"You already are."

He closed the distance between them and claimed her mouth with his.

It was like a storm had exploded. He pulled her onto his lap, wrapping his arms around her tightly as he kissed her. As he lost himself in her. He wanted there to be nothing between them. Not the T-shirt and jeans he was wearing, not even the beautiful lace that barely covered her curves.

Nothing.

Nothing but her.

A smile curved his lips. She could maybe keep the shoes. Yes, he would love for her to have those shoes on when he draped her legs over his shoulders and thrust deep inside her.

"I want you so much," he said. The words were torn from him. Coming from somewhere deep and real that he wasn't normally in touch with. "I think I might die if I don't have you."

"I've been in front of you for ten years," she whispered, kissing the spot right next to his mouth, kissing his cheek. "Why now?"

Because he had seen her. Because she had finally kissed him. Because...

"I don't see the world the way everyone else does," he whispered. "I know that. Sometimes it takes an act of God for me to really notice what's happening in front of me. To pull me out of that space in my head. I like it there. Because everything makes sense. And I put people in their place, so I can navigate the day with everything just where I expect it. I can never totally do that with you, Poppy. You always occupied more spaces than you were supposed to.

"I hired you, but you were never only my assistant. You became my friend. And then, you wouldn't stay there either. I put control above everything else. I always have. It's the only way to... For me to make the world work. If I go in knowing exactly what to expect, knowing what everything is. What everyone is. And that's how I didn't see. But then...the minute our lips touched, I knew. I knew, and I can't go back to knowing anything different."

"You like blondes," she pointed out.

"I don't," he responded.

"Rosalind was blonde," Poppy said, brazenly speaking the name she usually avoided at all costs. "And there have been a string of them ever since."

"I told you. I like certainty. Blondes are women I'm attracted to. At least, that was an easy way to think of it. I like to bring order to the world in any way I can."

"And that kept you from looking at me?"

He searched her face, trying to get an idea of what she was thinking. He searched himself, because he didn't know the answer. She was beautiful, and the fact that he hadn't been obsessed with her like this for the past decade was destined to remain a mystery to him.

"Maybe."

She touched his face, sliding her palms back, holding him. "You are not difficult," she said. "Not to me. I like you. All of you."

"No," he responded, shaking his head. "You... You put up with me, I'm sure. And I compensate for the ways that I'm difficult by..."

"No, Isaiah. I like all of you. I always have. There's no putting up with anything."

He hadn't realized how much words like that might mean. Until they poured through him like sunshine dipping down into a low, dark valley. Flooding him with light and warmth.

When he'd been younger, he'd had a kind of boundless certainty in his worldview. But as he'd gotten older—as he'd realized that the way he saw things, the way he perceived interactions and emotions, was often different from the other people involved—he'd started questioning himself.

The older he'd gotten the more he'd realized. How difficult people found it to be his friend. How hard he found it sometimes to carry on a conversation another person wanted to have when he just wanted to charge straight to the point.

How much his brother Joshua carried for him, with his lightning-quick response times and his way with words.

Which had made him wonder how much his parents had modified for him back before he'd realized he needed modification at all.

And with that realization came the worry. About how much of a burden he might be.

But not to Poppy.

He reached up and wrapped his fingers around her slender wrists, holding her hands against his face. He looked at her. Just looked. He didn't have words to respond to what she had said.

He didn't have words.

He had nothing but his desire for her, twisting in his gut, taking him over. Control was the linchpin in his life. It was essential to him. But not now. Now, only Poppy was essential. He wanted her to keep touching him.

Control could wait. It could be set aside for now.

Because letting go so he could hold on to this—to her—was much more important.

It was necessary.

He slid her hands back, draping her arms over his shoulders so she was closer to him, so she was holding on to him. Then he cradled her face, dragging her mouth to his, claiming her, deep and hard and long. Pouring everything that he felt, everything he couldn't say, into this kiss. Into this moment.

He pulled away, sliding his thumb across her lower lip, watching as heat and desire clouded her dark eyes. He could see her surrender to the same need that was roaring through him.

"I always have control," he mumbled, pressing a kiss to her neck, another, and then traveling down to her collarbone. "Always."

He pressed his hand firmly to the small of her back, holding her against him as he stood from the chair, then lowered them both down onto the floor.

He reached behind her and tugged at the top she was wearing. He didn't manage to get hold of the snaps, and he tore the straps, the elastic popping free, the cups falling away from her breasts.

He didn't have to tell her he was out of control. She knew. He could see it. In the heat and fire burning in her dark eyes, and in the subtle curve of her full lips.

She knew that he was out of control, for her. And she liked it.

His efficient, organized Poppy had a wild side. At least, she did with him.

Only for him.

Suddenly, the fact that she had never been with another man before meant everything. This was his.

She was his.

And it mattered.

More than he would have ever thought it could. He had never given thought to something like that before. He didn't know why he did now. Except... Poppy.

Poppy, who had always been there.

She was a phenomenon. Someone he couldn't understand, someone he wasn't sure he wanted to understand. He didn't mind her staying mysterious. An enigma he got to hold in his arms. As long as this burning bright glory remained.

If he stopped to think, she might disappear. This moment might vanish completely, and he couldn't bear that.

She tore at his clothes too, wrenching them away from his body, making quick work of his shirt before turning her attention to his pants.

As she undressed him, he finished with her clothes, capturing her nipple in his mouth, sucking it in deep. Tasting her. Relishing the feel of her, that velvet skin under his tongue. The taste of her.

It wasn't enough. It never would be. Nothing ever would be.

He felt like his skin was hypersensitized, and that feeling ran all the way beneath his skin, deeper. Making him feel...

Making him *feel*.

He pressed his face into the curve of her neck, kissing her there, licking her. She whimpered and shifted beneath him, wrapping her fingers around his thick length, squeezing him. He let his head fall back, a hoarse groan on his lips.

"Not like that," he rasped. "I need to… No, Poppy. I need you."

"But you have me." She looked innocent. Far too innocent for the moment.

She stroked him, sliding her fingers up and down his length. Then she reached forward, planting her free hand in the center of his chest and pushing him backward slightly. He didn't have to give. He chose to. Because he wanted to see what she would do. He was far too captivated by what might be brewing beneath the surface.

Her breasts were completely bare for him. And then she leaned forward, wrapping her lips around the head of his erection, sliding down slowly as she took all of him into her mouth.

He gritted his teeth, her name a curse on his lips as he grabbed hold of her dark curls and held on tightly while she pleasured him with her mouth. He was transfixed by the sight of her. By the way she moved, unpracticed but earnest. By the way she made him feel.

"Have you ever done this before?" He forced the words out through his constricted throat.

The answer to that question shouldn't matter. It was a question he never should have asked. He'd never cared before, if one of his partners had other lovers. He would have said he preferred a woman with experience.

Not with Poppy. The idea of another man touching her made him insane.

She licked him from base to tip like a lollipop, and then looked up at him. "No."

He swore, letting his head fall back as she took him in deep again.

"Does that matter to you?" she asked, angling her head and licking him.

"Don't stop," he growled.

"Does it matter, Isaiah?" she repeated. "Do you want to be the only man I've ever touched like this? Do you want to know you that you're the only man I've ever seen naked?"

His stomach tightened, impossibly. And he was sure he was going to go right over the edge as her husky, erotic words rolled over him.

"Yes," he bit out.

"Why?"

"Because I want you to be mine," he said, his tone hard. "Only mine."

"I said I was yours," she responded, stoking the length of him with her hand as she spoke. "You're the only man I've ever wanted like this."

His breath hissed out through his teeth. "Me?"

"The only one. From the time you hired me when I was eighteen. I could never... I wanted to date other men. But I just couldn't. I didn't want them. Isaiah, I only wanted you."

Her dark eyes were so earnest as she made the confession, so sincere. That look touched him, all the way down. Even to those places he normally felt were closed off.

She kissed his stomach, up higher to his chest, and then captured his lips again.

"I want you," she said. "Please."

She didn't have to ask twice. He lowered her onto her back and slipped his fingers beneath the waistband of those electric yellow panties, sliding his fingers through her slick folds slowly, slowly, drawing out all that slick wetness, drawing out her pleasure. Until she was whimpering and bucking beneath him. Until she was begging him.

Then he slipped one finger deep inside her, watched as her release found her. As it washed over her like a wave. It was the most beautiful thing he'd ever seen.

But it wasn't enough.

He pulled her panties off and threw them onto the floor, positioning himself between her thighs, pressing himself to the entrance of her body and thrusting in, rough and decisive. Claiming her. Showing her exactly who she belonged to.

Just as he belonged to her.

He lost himself completely, wrapped in her, consumed by her. That familiar scent, vanilla and spice, some perfume Poppy had always worn, mingling with something new. Sweat. Desire. Skin.

What they had been collided with what they were now.

He gripped her hips, thrust into her, deep and hard, relishing her cry of pleasure as he claimed her. Over and over again.

She arched underneath him, crying out his name, her fingernails digging into his skin as her internal muscles pulsed around him.

And he let go. He came on a growl, feral and unrestrained, pleasure like fire over his skin, in his gut.

And when it was over, he could only hold her. He couldn't speak. Couldn't move. Didn't want to.

He looked down at her, and she smiled. Then she pressed her fingers to his lips.

He grabbed her wrist, kissed her palm. "Come to bed with me," he said.

"Okay."

Chapter 12

At three in the morning, Isaiah decided that they needed something to eat. Poppy sat on the counter wearing nothing but his T-shirt, watching as he fried eggs and bacon.

She wondered if this was…her life now. She could hardly believe it. And yet, she didn't want to believe anything different.

She ached just looking at this man.

He was so…him. Undeniably. So intense and serious, and yet now, there was something almost boyish about him with his dark hair falling into his eyes, his expression one of concentration as he flipped the eggs in the pan flawlessly without breaking a yolk.

But then, he was shirtless, wearing a pair of low-slung gray sweatpants that seemed perilously close to falling off. His back was broad and muscular, and she enjoyed the play of those muscles while he cooked.

Just that one moment, that one expression on his face, could come close to being called boyish. The rest of him was all man.

He served up the eggs and bacon onto a plate, and he handed Poppy hers, then set his on the counter beside her. He braced himself on the counter, watching her expectantly.

"Do you often have midnight snacks?" she asked.

"No," he said. "But then, tonight isn't exactly routine. Eat."

"Are you trying to fortify me so we can have sex again?"

His lips curved upward. "Undoubtedly."

"This bacon is tainted with ulterior motives," she said, happily taking a bite.

"You seem very sad about that."

"I am." She looked down, then back up, a bubble of happiness blooming in her chest.

"I wanted to make sure you were taken care of," he said, his voice suddenly serious. "Do you feel okay?"

"Yes," she said, confused for a moment.

"No...nausea, or anything like that?"

Right. Because of the baby. So he wasn't only concerned about her. She fought off a small bit of disappointment.

"I feel fine," she said.

"Good," he said.

"Because if I had morning sickness I'd have to miss work?" she asked, not quite certain why she was goading him.

"No. Because if you were sick it would upset me to see you like that."

Suddenly, she felt achingly vulnerable sitting here like this with him.

Isaiah.

She was having his baby. She'd just spent the past couple of hours having wild sex with him. And now she just felt...so acutely aware of who she was. With her hair loose and curly, falling into her face that was free of makeup. Without her structured dresses and killer high heels.

She was just Poppy Sinclair, the same Poppy Sinclair who'd bounced from home to home all through her childhood. Who had never found a family who wanted her forever.

Her throat ached, raw and dry.

His large hand cupped her chin, tilted her face upward. "What's wrong?"

Her heart twisted. That show of caring from him made the vulnerability seem like it might not be so bad. Except...even when he was being nice, it hurt.

She definitely liked a little bit of opposition in her life, and Isaiah was always around to provide that. Either because of her unrequited feelings, or because he was such an obstinate, hardheaded man.

Somehow, all of that was easier than...feeling. It was all part of remaining closed off.

This...opening up was hard, but she had expected that. She hadn't expected it to be painful even when nothing bad was happening.

"I was just thinking," she said.

"About?"

"Nothing specifically," she said.

Just about who she was, and why it was almost ludicrous that she was here now. With him. With so many beautiful things right within her reach.

A family. A husband. A baby.

Passion.

Love.

"You can tell me," he said, his gray eyes searching.

"Why do you *want* me to tell you?" she pressed.

"Because you're mine. Anything that is bothering you… Give it to me. I want to…help. Listen."

"Isaiah…" Her eyes burned.

"Did I make you cry?" He looked genuinely concerned by that. He lifted his hand, brushed his thumb beneath the corner of her eye, wiping away a tear she hadn't realized was there.

"You didn't," she said. She swallowed hard. "I was just… It's stupid."

"Nothing is stupid if it makes you cry."

"I was thinking, while I was sitting here watching you take care of me, that I don't remember what it's like to have someone care for me like this. Because… I'm not sure anyone ever really has. People definitely showed me kindness throughout my life—I'm not saying they didn't. There were so many families and houses. They blur together. I used to remember everyone's names, but now the earlier homes are fading into a blur. Even the people who were kind.

"I remember there was a family… They were going to take me to the fair. And I'd never been before. I was so excited, Isaiah. So excited I could hardly contain myself. We were going to ride a Ferris wheel, and I was going to have cotton candy. I'd never had it before." She took another bite of her bacon and found swallowing difficult.

"The next day, that family found out that the birth mother of a sibling group they were fostering had given birth to another baby. Child services wanted to arrange to have the baby brought in right away. And…that required they move me. The baby had to be with her half siblings. It was right. It made sense."

"You didn't get to go to the fair."

She blinked and shook her head. A tear rolled down her cheek, and she laughed. "It's stupid to still be upset about it. I've been to the fair. I've had cotton candy. But I just… I can remember. How it hurt. How it felt like the world was ending. Worse, I think, is that feeling that nothing in the world is ever stable. That at any moment the rug is going to be pulled out from underneath me. That everything good is just going to vanish. Well, like cotton candy once it hits your tongue."

"I want to take care of you," he said, looking at her, his gray eyes fierce. "Always."

"Don't make promises you can't keep," she said, her stomach churning.

"Don't you trust me?"

She wanted to. But he didn't love her. And if they didn't share love, she wasn't sure what the bond was supposed to be. They had one. She didn't doubt that. And she loved him more than ever.

They would have the baby.

Once they were married it would feel better. It would feel more secure.

"I don't know if you can…understand. But… You've been one of the most constant people I've ever had in my life. Rosalind and I don't see each other very often, but she made sure I was taken care of. She didn't forget me. She's my family. And you… You're my family too."

"If you want to invite Rosalind to the wedding you can," he said.

She blinked. Stunned, because usually any mention of Rosalind's name earned her nothing but stony silence or barely suppressed rage. "She can come to our… wedding?"

"She matters to you," Isaiah said. "And what happened between the two of us isn't important anymore."

"It isn't?" Hope bloomed in her heart, fragile and new, like a tiny bud trying to find its way in early spring. "But she…broke your heart," Poppy finished.

"But now I have you. The rest doesn't matter."

It wasn't the declaration she wanted, but it was something. Better than the promise of a fair or cotton candy or anything like it.

And she wanted to hope.

So she did.

And she leaned forward and kissed him. With each pass of his lips over hers, she let go of a little more of the weight she carried and held on to him a little bit tighter.

Chapter 13

Isaiah had actually taken a lunch break, which wasn't like him, and then it had turned into a rather long lunch. In fact, he had been out of the office for almost two hours, and Poppy couldn't remember the last time he had done that in the middle of the day. She was almost sure he never had, unless he'd taken her with him because it was a working lunch and he had needed somebody to handle the details.

It made her edgy to have him acting out of character.

At least, that's what she told herself. In reality, she just felt a little edgy having him out of her sight. Like he might disappear completely if she couldn't keep tabs on him. Like everything that had happened between them might be imaginary after all.

She tried to relax her face, to keep her concern from showing. Even though there was no one there to see it.

It was just… The situation made her feel tense all over. And she shouldn't. Last night had been…

She had never experienced anything like it. Never before, and the only way she would again was if…

If they actually got married.

If everything actually worked out.

She placed her hand lightly on her stomach and sent up a small prayer. She just didn't want to lose any of this.

She'd never had so much.

She sighed and stood up from her desk. She needed some coffee. Something to clear her head. Something to make her feel less like a crazy lady who needed to keep a visual on her fiancé at all times.

Of course, she *was* a crazy lady who wanted a visual on her fiancé at all times, but, it would be nice if she could pretend otherwise.

Then the door to her office opened and she turned and saw Isaiah standing there in the same black T-shirt and jeans he'd been wearing when he left. But his arm was behind his back, and his expression was…

She didn't think she had ever seen an expression like that on his face before.

"What are you doing?" she asked.

"I went out looking for something for you," he said, his expression serious. "It was harder to find than I thought it would be."

"Because you didn't know what to get me?"

"No. Because it turns out I had no idea where to find what I was looking for."

She frowned. "What's behind your back?"

"Roses would have been easy," he said, and then he moved his hand and she saw a flash of pink. He held out something that was shaped like a bouquet but was absolutely not.

She stood there and just…stared for a moment. Another diamond ring wouldn't have affected her as deeply as this gesture.

Seemingly simple and inexpensive.

To her…it was priceless.

"Cotton candy," she breathed.

"I just wanted to find you some to have with lunch." He frowned. "But now of course it isn't lunchtime anymore."

Isaiah in his most intense state, with his dark brows and heavy beard, holding the pinkest, fluffiest candy in the world, was her new favorite, absurd sight.

She held back a giggle. "Where did you go to get this?"

"There's a family fun center in Tolowa that has it, funnily enough."

"You drove all the way to… Isaiah." She took hold of the cotton candy, then wrenched it from his hand and set it on her desk before wrapping her arms around his neck and kissing him.

"It's going to melt," he said against her lips.

"Cotton candy doesn't melt."

"It shrinks," he pointed out.

"I love cotton candy, don't get me wrong. But I'd rather eat you," she returned.

"I worked hard for that."

She laughed and reached behind her, grabbing hold of the cotton candy and taking a bite, the sugar coating her lips and her tongue. Then she kissed Isaiah again, a sugary, sweet kiss that she hoped expressed some of what she felt.

But not all of it.

Because she hadn't told him.

She was afraid to.

Last night had been a big step of faith, approaching him and giving herself to him like that. It had been her *showing* him what was in her heart. But she knew that wasn't enough. Not really. She needed to say it too.

It had to be said.

She cupped his face and kissed him one more time, examining the lines by his gray eyes, the weathered, rugged look his beard gave him, that sharp, perfect nose and his lips… Lips she was convinced had been made just for her.

Other women had kissed them. She'd seen them do it. But it didn't matter. Because those lips weren't for those women. They were for her. They softened for her. Smiled for her. Only she reached those parts of Isaiah, and she had been the only one for a long time.

And yes, Rosalind had reached something in him Poppy hadn't managed to reach, but if she could do all these other things to him, if she could make him lose control, make him hunt all over creation for cotton candy, then maybe in the future…

It didn't matter. What might happen and what might not. There was only one thing that was certain. And that was how she felt.

She'd loved him for so long. Through so many things. Growing his business, enduring a heartbreak. Long hours, late nights. Fighting. Laughing. Making love.

She'd loved him through all of that.

And she'd love him forever.

Not telling him… worrying about what might happen was just more self-protection, and she was done with that.

"I love you," she said.

He went stiff beneath her touch, but she truly hadn't expected a different reaction. It was going to take him time. She didn't expect a response from him right away; she didn't even want one.

"I've always loved you," she said. "In the beginning, even when you were with Rosalind. And it felt like a horrible betrayal. But I wanted you. And I burned with jealousy. I wanted to have your intensity directed at me. And then when she… The fact that she got to be the only one to ever have it… It's not fair.

"I want it. I love you, Isaiah. I've loved you for ten years, I'll love you for ten more. For all my years. You're everything I could ever want. A fantasy I didn't even know I could create. And I just… I love you. I loved you before we kissed. Before we made love. Before you proposed to me and before I was pregnant. I just… love you."

His expression hadn't changed. It was a wall. Impenetrable and flat. His mouth was set into a grim line, his entire body stiff.

"Poppy…"

"Don't. Don't look at me like you pity me. Like I'm a puppy that you have to kick. I've spent too much of my life being pitied, Isaiah, and I don't want to be pitied by you."

"You have me," he said. "I promise that."

"You don't love me," she said.

"I can't," he said.

She shook her head, pain lancing her heart. "You won't."

"In the end, does it make a difference?"

"In the end, I suppose it doesn't make a difference, but on the journey there, it makes all the difference. *Can't* means there's nothing… Nothing on heaven or earth that could make you change. Won't means you're choosing this. You're choosing to hold on to past hurts, to pain. You're choosing to hold on to another woman instead of holding on to me. You accused me of clinging to a fantasy—of wanting a man who might love me, instead of taking the man who was right in front of me. But what you're doing is worse. You're hanging on to the ghosts of the past rather than hanging on to something real. I think you could love me. I think you might. But you have it buried so far down, underneath all this protection…"

"You don't understand," he said, turning away from her and pushing his fingers through his hair. "You don't understand," he repeated, this time more measured. "It's easy for you. You don't have that disconnect. That time it takes to translate someone's facial expression, what the words beneath their words are, and what it all means. Rosalind was the clumsiest liar, the clumsiest cheat in the entire world, and I didn't know. Because she said she loved me, and so I believed it."

Poppy let out a harsh, wounded breath. "And you don't believe me?"

"I didn't say that."

"But that's what it is. You don't trust me. If you trusted me, then this wouldn't be an issue."

"No," he said. "That isn't true. I felt like a tool when everything happened with Rosalind. She broke places in me I hadn't realized were there to be broken. I don't think you can possibly understand what it's like to be blindsided like that."

Her vision went fuzzy around the edges, her heart pounding so hard she thought she might faint.

"You don't… I just told you one small piece of what it was like to grow up like I did. How anticipating what might happen tomorrow was dangerous because you might be in a whole new house with a bunch of strangers the next day. My life was never in my control. Ever. It was dangerous to be comfortable, dangerous to care. There was a system, there were reasons, but when I was a child all I knew was that I was being uprooted. Again and again."

"I'm sorry. I didn't mean…"

"We've all been hurt. No one gives us a choice about that. But what are you going to do about it? What is the problem? Say it out loud. Tell me. So that you have to hear for yourself how ridiculous this all is."

"It changed something in me," he said. "And I can't… I can't change it back."

"You *won't*. You're a coward, Isaiah Grayson. You're running. From what you feel. From what you *could* feel. You talk about these things you can't do, these things you can't feel. These things you can't understand. But you understand things other people never will. The way you see numbers, the way you fit it all together—that's a miracle. And if your brain worked like everyone else's, then you wouldn't be that person. You wouldn't be the man I love. I don't want you to change who you are. Don't you understand that? That's not what I'm asking for. I'm asking for you to hold on to me instead of her."

He took a step back, shaking his head slowly. "Poppy…"

"Where's my big, scary, decisive boss? My stubborn friend who doesn't back down? Or is this request terrifying because I'm asking for something that's not in your head? Something that's in your heart?"

Her own heart was breaking, splintering into a thousand pieces and falling apart inside her chest. She thought she might die from this.

She hadn't expected him to be able to give her a response today, but she hadn't known he was going to launch into an outright denial of his ability to ever, ever love her.

"Maybe I don't have a heart," he said, his voice hard. "Maybe I'm a robot, like you said."

"I don't think that's true. And I shouldn't have said that in the first place."

"But maybe you were closer to the truth than you want to believe. Maybe you don't love me like I am, Poppy. Maybe you just see things in me that aren't there, and you love those. But they aren't real."

She shook her head, fighting back tears. "I don't think that's true. I've been with you for a decade, Isaiah." She looked at his face, that wonderful, familiar face. That man who was destroying everything they'd found.

She wanted to hit him, rage at him. "I *know you*. I know you care. I've watched you with your family. I've watched you work hard to build this business with Joshua and Faith, to take it to the next level with the merger. You work so hard, and that's not…empty. Everything you've done to support Faith in her dream of being an architect…"

"It's her talent. I can't take the credit."

"Without you, the money wouldn't flow and that

would be the end of it. You're the main artery, and you give it everything. You might not express how you care the way other people do, but you express it in a real, tangible way." He didn't move. Didn't change his expression. "You can love, Isaiah. And other people love you."

He said nothing. Not for a long moment.

"I would never take our child from you," he said finally.

"What?"

"I won't take our child from you. Forcing you to marry me was a mistake. This is a mistake, Poppy."

She felt like that little girl who had been promised a carnival, only to wake up in the morning and have her bags packed again.

The disappointment even came complete with cotton candy.

"You don't want to marry me?"

"I was forcing it," he said. "Because in my mind I had decided that was best, and so because I decided it, it had to be true. But... It's not right. I won't do that to you."

"How dare you? How dare you dump me and try to act like it's for my own good? After I tell you that I love you? Forcing me to marry you was bad enough, but at least then you were acting out of complete emotional ignorance."

"I'm always acting out of emotional ignorance," he said. "Don't say you accept all of me and then act surprised by that."

"Yeah, but sometimes you're just full of shit, Isaiah. And you hide behind those walls. You hide behind that brain. You try to outwit and outreason everything, but life is not a chess game. It's not math. None of this is.

Your actions least of all. Because if you added up every-thing you've said and done over the past few weeks, you would know that the answer equaled love. You would know that the answer is that we should be together. You would know that you finally have what you want and *you're giving it away.*

"So don't try to tell me you're being logical. Don't try to talk to me like I'm a hysterical female asking some-thing ridiculous of you. You're the one who's scared. You're the one who's hysterical. You can stand there with a blank look on your face and pretend that some-how makes you rational, but you aren't. You can try to lie to me. You can try to lie to yourself. But I don't be-lieve it. I refuse."

She took a deep breath. "And I quit. I really do quit this time. I'm not going to be here for your conve-nience. I'm not going to be here to keep your life run-ning smoothly, to give you what you want when you want it while I don't get my needs met in return. If you want to let me go, then you have to let me go."

She picked up the cotton candy. "But I'm taking this." She picked up her coat also, and started to walk past him and out of the room. Then she stopped. "I'll be in touch with you about the baby. And I will pay you back for the wedding dress if I can't return it. Please tell… Please tell your mom that I'm sorry. No. Tell them you're sorry. Tell them you're sorry that you let a woman who could never really love you ruin your chance with one who already does."

And then she walked out of the office, down the hall, past Joshua's open door and his questioning expression, through the lobby area, where Faith was sitting curled up in a chair staring down at a computer.

"Goodbye," Poppy said, her voice small and pained.

"What's going on?" Faith asked.

"I quit," Poppy said. "And the wedding is off. And… I think my heart is breaking. But I don't know what else to do."

Poppy found herself standing outside the door, waiting for a whole new life to start.

And, like so many times before, she wasn't confident that there would be anything good in that new life.

She took a breath. No. There would be something good. This time, there was the certainty of that.

She was going to be a mother.

Strangely, out of all this heartbreak, all this brokenness, came a chance at a kind of redemption she had never really let herself believe in.

She was going to be a mother.

It would be her only real chance at having a good mother-daughter relationship. And yes, she would be on the other side of it. But she would give her child the best of herself.

A sad smile touched her lips. Even without meaning to, Isaiah had given her a chance at love. It just hadn't been the kind of love she'd been hoping for.

But…it was still a gift.

And she was going to cling to it with everything she had.

Chapter 14

Isaiah wasn't a man given to excessive drinking, but tonight he was considering it.

By the time he had gotten home from work, Poppy had cleared out her things. He supposed he should have gone after her. Should have left early. But he had been…

He had been frozen.

He had gone through the motions all day, trying to process what had happened.

One thing kept echoing in his head, and it wasn't that she loved him, though that had wrapped itself around his heart and was currently battering at him, making him feel as though his insides had been kicked with a steel-toed boot.

Or maybe just a stiletto.

No, the thing that kept going through his mind was what she'd said about his excuses.

He had known even as he said it out loud that he

didn't really believe all the things he'd said. It wasn't true that he couldn't love her.

She had asked if he didn't trust her. And that wasn't the problem either.

He didn't trust himself.

Emotion was like a foreign language to him. One he had to put in effort to learn so he could understand the people around him. His childhood had been a minefield of navigating friendships he could never quite make gel, and high school and college had been a lot of him trying to date and inadvertently breaking hearts when he missed connections that others saw.

It was never that he didn't feel. It was just that his feelings were in another language.

And he often didn't know how to bridge the gap.

And the intensity of what he felt now was so sharp, so intense that his natural inclination was to deny it completely. To shut it down. To shut it off. It was what he often did. When he thought of those parts of himself he couldn't reach…

He chose to make them unreachable.

It was easier to navigate those difficult situations with others if he wasn't also dealing with his own feelings. And so he'd learned. Push it down. Rationalize the situation.

Emotion was something he could feel, hear, taste and smell. Something that overtook him completely. Something that became so raw and intense he wanted to cut it off completely.

But with her… He couldn't.

When he was making love with her, at least there was a place for all those feelings to go. A way for them to be expressed. There was something he could do with them. With that roaring in his blood, that sharp slice to his senses.

How could he give that to someone else? How could he... How could he trust himself to treat those emotions the way that they needed to be treated?

He really wanted a drink. But honestly, the explosion of alcohol with his tenuous control was likely a bad idea. Still, he was considering it.

There was a heavy knock on his front door and Isaiah frowned, going down the stairs toward the entry.

Maybe it was Poppy.

He jerked the door open and was met by his brother Joshua.

"What are you doing here?" Isaiah asked.

"I talked to Faith." Joshua shoved his hands in his pockets. "She said Poppy quit."

"Yes," Isaiah said. He turned away from his brother and walked toward the kitchen. He was going to need that drink.

"What did you do?"

"You assume I did something?" he asked.

Isaiah's anger rang a little bit hollow, considering he knew that it was his fault. Joshua just stared at him.

Bastard.

Was he so predictably destructive in his interpersonal relationships?

Yes.

He knew the answer to that without thinking.

"I released her from her obligation," Isaiah said. "She was the one who chose to leave."

"You released her from her obligation? What the hell does that mean?"

"It means I was forcing her to marry me, and then I

decided not to." He sounded ridiculous. Which in and of itself was ridiculous, since *he* never was.

His brother pinched the bridge of his nose. "Start at the beginning."

"She's pregnant," Isaiah said.

Joshua froze. "She's…"

"She's pregnant," Isaiah repeated.

"How…"

"You know exactly how."

"I thought the two of you had an arrangement. Meaning I figured you weren't going to go…losing control," Joshua said.

"We had something like an arrangement. But it turned out we were very compatible. Physically."

"Yes," Joshua said, "I understood what you meant by compatible."

"Well, how was I supposed to know? You were just standing there staring at me." He rubbed his hand over his face. "We were engaged, she tried to break it off. Then she found out she was pregnant. I told her she had to marry me or I would pursue full custody—"

"Every woman's fantasy proposal. I hope you filmed it so you'll always have a memory of that special moment."

Isaiah ignored his brother. "It was practical. But then…then she wanted things I couldn't give, and I realized that maybe forcing a woman to marry me wasn't the best idea."

"And she's in love with you."

Isaiah sighed heavily. "Yes."

"And you said you couldn't love her back so she left?"

"No," he said. "I said I couldn't love her and I told her I wouldn't force her to marry me. And then she left."

"You're the one who rejected her," Joshua said.

"I don't know how to do this," Isaiah said, his voice rough. "I don't know how to give her what she wants while...while making sure I don't..."

He didn't want to say it because it sounded weak, and he'd never considered himself weak. But he was afraid of being hurt, and if that wasn't weakness, he didn't know what was.

"You can't," Joshua said simply, reading his mind. "Loving someone means loving them at the expense of your own emotional safety. Sorry. There's not another alternative."

"I can't do that."

"Because one woman hurt you?"

"You don't understand," Isaiah said. "It has nothing to do with being hurt once. Rosalind didn't just hurt me, she made a fool out of me. She highlighted every single thing that I've struggled with all my life and showed me how inadequate I am. Not with words. She doesn't even know what she did."

He took a deep breath and continued, "Connecting with people has always been hard for me. Not you, not the family. You all...know how to talk to me. Know how to deal with me. But other people? It's not easy, Joshua. But with her I thought I finally had something. I let my guard down, and I quit worrying. I quit worrying about whether or not I understood everything and just...was with someone for a while. But what I thought was happening wasn't the truth. Everything that should've been obvious was right in front of me."

"But that's not your relationship with Poppy. And it isn't going to be. She's not going to change into something else just because you admit that you're in love with her."

"Poppy is different," Isaiah said. "Whatever I thought I felt then, this is different."

"You love her. And if you don't admit that, Isaiah? Maybe you won't feel it quite so keenly, but you won't have her. You're going to…live in a separate place from the woman you love?"

"I won't be a good father anyway," Isaiah said.

"Why do you think that?"

"How am I going to be a good father when I can't… What am I going to teach a kid about relationships and people? I'm not wired like everyone else."

"And maybe your child won't be either. Or maybe my child will be different, and he'll need his uncle's help. Any of our children could need someone there with him who understands. You're not alone. You're not the only person who feels the way that you do."

Isaiah had never thought about that. About the fact that his own experiences might be valuable to someone else.

"But Poppy…"

"Knows you and loves you. She doesn't want you to be someone else."

Isaiah cleared his throat. "I accused her of that."

"Because she demanded you pull your head out of your ass and admit that you love her?"

"Yes," he admitted.

"Being alone is the refuge of cowards, Isaiah, and you're a lot of things, but I never thought you were a coward. I understand trying to avoid being hurt again. After everything I went through with my ex, I didn't want anything to do with a wife or another baby. But now I have Danielle. I have both a wife and a son. And I'm glad I didn't let grief be the deciding factor in my life. Because, let me tell you something, that's easy. It's easy to let the hard things ruin you. It's a hell of a lot braver to decide they don't get to control you."

"It hurts to breathe," Isaiah said, his voice rough. "When I look at her."

"If you aren't with her, it'll still hurt to breathe. She just won't be beside you."

"I didn't want a wife so I could be in love," Isaiah said. "I wanted one to make my life easier."

"You don't add another person to your life to make it easier. Other people only make things harder, and you should have a better understanding of that than most. You accept another person into your life because you can't live without them. Because easy isn't the most important thing anymore. She is. That's love. And it's bigger than fear. It has to be, because love itself is so damned scary."

"Why does anyone do it?" Isaiah asked.

"You do it when you don't have a choice anymore. I almost let Danielle walk away from me. I almost ruined the best thing I'd ever been given because of fear. And you tell me why a smart man would do that? Why does fear get to be the biggest emotion? Why can't love win?"

Isaiah stood there, feeling like something had shifted under his feet.

He couldn't outrun emotion. Even when he suppressed it, there was an emotion that was winning: fear.

He'd never realized that, never understood it, until now.

"Think about it," Joshua said.

Then he turned and walked out of the house, leaving Isaiah alone with his obviously flawed thinking.

He loved Poppy.

To his bones. To his soul.

He couldn't breathe for the pain of it, and he had no idea what the hell he was supposed to do with the damned fear that gnawed at his gut.

This had all started with an ad for a wife. With the most dispassionate idea any man had ever hatched.

Him, divorcing himself from feeling and figuring out a way to make his life look like he wanted it to look. To make it look like his parents' lives. His idea of home.

Only now he realized he'd left out the most important thing.

Love.

It was strange how his idea of what he wanted his life to be had changed. He had wanted to get married. He had wanted a wife. And he'd found a way to secure that.

But now he just wanted *Poppy*.

Whether they were married or not, whether or not they had perfect, domestic bliss and Sunday dinners just like his parents, whether they were in a little farmhouse or his monstrosity of a place… It didn't matter. If she was there.

Wherever Poppy was…that was his home.

And if he didn't have her, he would never have a home.

He could get that drink now. Stop the pain in his chest from spreading further, dull the impending realization of what he'd done. To himself. To his life. But he had to feel it. He had to.

He braced himself against the wall and lowered his head, pain starting in his stomach, twisting and turning its way up into his chest. Like a shard of glass had been wedged into the center of his ribs and was pushed in deeper with each breath.

He'd never lost love before.

He'd had wounded pride. Damaged trust.

But he'd never had a broken heart.

Until now.

And he'd done it to himself.

Poppy had offered him all he needed in the world, and he'd been too afraid to take it.

Poppy had lived a whole life filled with heartbreak. With being let down. He'd promised to take care of her, and then he hadn't. He was just another person who'd let her down. Another person who hadn't loved her like she should have been loved.

He should have loved her more than he loved himself.

He clenched his hand into a fist. He was done with this. With this self-protection. He didn't want it anymore.

He wanted Poppy.

Now. Always.

More than safety. More than breathing.

But he'd broken her trust. She'd already loved and lost so many people in her life, had been let down by parades of people who should have done better, and there was no logical reason for her to forgive him.

He just had to hope that love would be stronger than fear.

Chapter 15

Poppy was a study in misery.

She had taken all her easily moved things and gone back to her house.

She wasn't going to flee the town. She loved her house, and she didn't really have anywhere else to go at the moment. No, she was going to have to sort that out, but later.

She wasn't entirely sure what she wanted. Where she would go.

She would have to find another job.

She could, she knew that. She had amply marketable skills. It was just that… It would mean well and truly closing the door on the Isaiah chapter of her life. Possibly the longest chapter she even had.

So many people had cycled in and out of her life. There had been a few constants, and the Graysons had been some of her most cherished friends. It hurt. Losing him like this. Losing them. But this was just how life went for her. And there was nothing she could do about it. She was always, forever at the mercy of people who simply couldn't...

She swallowed hard.

There was no real furniture left in her house after she'd moved to Isaiah's ranch. She had gathered a duffel bag full of clothes and a sleeping bag. She curled up in the sleeping bag on the floor in the corner of her bedroom and grabbed her cell phone.

There was one person she really owed a phone call.

She dialed her foster sister's number and waited.

"Hello?"

"I hope it's not too late," Poppy said, rolling to her side and looking out the window at the inky black sky.

It had the audacity to look normal out there. Clear and crisp like it was just a typical December night and not a night where her world had crashed down around her.

"Of course not. Jason and I were just getting ready to go out. But that can wait. What's going on?"

"Oh. Nothing... Everything."

"What's going on?" Rosalind repeated, her voice getting serious. "You haven't called in a couple of months."

"Neither have you," Poppy pointed out.

"I know. I'm sorry. I've never been very good at keeping in touch. But that doesn't mean I don't like hearing from you."

"I'm pregnant," Poppy blurted out.

The pause on the other end was telling. But when Rosalind finally did speak, her voice was shot through with excitement. "Poppy, congratulations. I'm so happy for you."

"I'm single," she said as a follow-up.

"Well, I figured you would have altered your announcement slightly if you weren't."

"I don't know what I'm going to do." She pulled her knees up and tucked her head down, holding her misery to her chest.

"If you need money or a place to stay… You know you can always come and stay with me and Jason."

Poppy did know that. Maybe that was even why she had called Rosalind. Because knowing that she had a place with her foster sister made her feel slightly less rootless.

She wouldn't need to use it. At least, she *shouldn't* need to use it. But knowing that Rosalind was there for her helped.

Right now, with the only other anchor in her life removed and casting her mostly adrift, Rosalind was more important than ever.

"Isaiah isn't being a terror about it, is he?" Rosalind asked.

"Not… Not the way you mean," Poppy said slowly. "It's Isaiah's baby."

The silence stretched even longer this time. *"Isaiah?"*

"Yes," Poppy said. "And I know… I know that's… I'm sorry."

"Why are you apologizing to me?" Rosalind sounded genuinely mystified.

"Because he's your…your ex. And I know I don't have a lot of experience with family, but you're the closest thing I have to a sister, and I know you don't… go dating your sister's ex-boyfriends."

"Well. Yes. I suppose so. But he's my *ex*. From a long

time ago. And I'm with someone else now. I've moved on. Obviously, so has he. Why would you keep yourself from something you want just because…just because it's something other people might not think was okay? If you love him…"

Poppy realized that the guilt she felt was related to the fact that her feelings for Isaiah had most definitely originated when Isaiah had not been Rosalind's ex.

"I've had feelings for him for a long time," Poppy said quietly. "A really long time."

"Don't tell me you feel bad about that, Poppy," Rosalind said.

"I do," Poppy said. "He was your boyfriend. And you got me a job with him. In that whole time…"

"You didn't *do* anything. It's not like you went after him when were together."

"No."

"I'm the cheater in that relationship." Rosalind sighed heavily. "I didn't handle things right with Isaiah back then. I cheated on him, and I shouldn't have. I should have been strong enough to break things off with him without being unfaithful. But I wasn't."

They'd never talked about this before. The subject of Isaiah had always been too difficult for Poppy. She'd been so angry that Rosalind had hurt him, and then so resentful that her betrayal had claimed such a huge part of his heart.

But Poppy had never really considered…how Rosalind's past might have informed what she'd done.

And considering happiness had made Poppy act a lot like a feral cat, she should have.

"He was the first person who treated me really well, and I felt guilty about it," Rosalind continued. "But gratitude isn't love. And what I felt for him was gratitude. When I met Jason, my whole world kind of turned over, and what I felt for him was something else. Something I had never experienced before.

"I caused a lot of trouble for Isaiah, and I feel bad about it. But you certainly shouldn't feel guilty over having feelings for him. You should… You should be with him. He's a great guy, Poppy. I mean, not for me. He's too serious and just…not *right* for me. But you've known him in a serious way even longer than I have, and if you think he's the guy for you…"

"We were engaged," Poppy said. "But he broke it off."

"What?"

"It's a long story." Poppy laughed. "A very Isaiah story, really. We got engaged. Then we slept together. Then I broke up with him. Then I got pregnant. Then we slept together again. Then we kind of…got back engaged… But then he…broke up with me because I told him I was in love with him."

"We really need to not have so much time between phone calls," Rosalind said. "Okay. So… You being in love with him…scared him?"

"Yes," Poppy said slowly.

She wasn't going to bring up Rosalind's part in the issues between Poppy and Isaiah. Mostly because Poppy didn't actually believe they were a significant part. Not specifically. The issues that Isaiah had with love and feelings were definitely on him.

"And you're just going to…let him walk away from what you have?"

"There's nothing I can do to stop him. He said he doesn't love me. He said he doesn't… He doesn't want a relationship like that. There's nothing I can do to change how he feels."

"What did you do when he said that?"

"I yelled at him. And then… I left."

"If I was in love with a guy, I would camp out on his doorstep. I would make him miserable."

"I have some pride, Rosalind."

"I don't," Rosalind said. "I'm a crazy bitch when it comes to love. I mean, I blew up a really good thing to chase after Jason."

"This is… It's different."

"But you love him."

"How many times can I be expected to care for someone and lose them? You know. Better than anyone, you understand what growing up was like for me. For us. People were always just…shuffling us around on a whim. And I just… I can't handle it. Not anymore."

"There's a really big difference between now and then," Rosalind pointed out. "We are not kids. This is what I realized, though a little bit late with Isaiah. I wasn't a child. I didn't have to go along. I had a choice. Child services and foster families and toxic parents don't get to run our lives anymore, Poppy. We are in charge now. You're your own caseworker. You are the one who gets to decide what kind of life you want to have. Who you want to live with. What you'll settle for and what you won't. You don't have to wait for someone to rescue you or accept it when someone says they can't be with you."

"I kind of do. He said…"

"What's the worst that could happen if you fight for him one more time? Just one more?"

Poppy huffed out a laugh. "I'll die of humiliation."

"You won't," Rosalind said. "I guarantee you, humiliation isn't fatal. If humiliation were fatal, I would have died twice before Jason and I actually got married. At *least.* I was insecure and clingy, and a lot of it was because of how our relationship started, which was my own fault. My fear of getting him dirty and losing him dirty, that kind of thing. But…now we've been married for five years, and…none of that matters. Now all that matters is that we love each other. That we have each other. Everything else is just a story we tell and laugh about."

"You know Isaiah. He was very certain."

"I don't actually know Isaiah as well as you do. But you're going to have a baby with him. And… Whether or not you get him in the end, don't you think what you want is worth fighting for? Not for the sake of the baby, or anything like that. But for you. Have you ever fought for *you* before, Poppy?"

She had started to. When Isaiah had broken things off. But…

She didn't know if she really had.

Maybe Rosalind was right. Maybe she needed to face this head-on. Again.

Because nobody controlled the show but her. Nobody told her when to be done except for her.

And pride shouldn't have the last word.

"I love you," Poppy said. "I hope you *know* that. I know we're different. But you've been family to me. And… You're responsible for some of the best things I have in life."

"Well, I'm going to feel guilty if Isaiah breaks your heart."

"Even if he does… I'll be glad he was in my life for

as long as he was. I love him. And…being able to love someone like this is a gift. One I don't think I fully appreciated. With our background, just being able to admit my love without fear, without holding back… That's something. It's special. It's kind of a miracle."

"It really is," Rosalind said. "I had a rocky road to Jason. I had a rocky road to love, but Poppy, it's so worth it in the end. I promise you."

"I just hope Isaiah realizes how special it is. How amazing it is. His parents always loved him. He grew up in one house. He…doesn't know that not everyone has someone to love them."

"He might have had all of that, Poppy, but he's never had you. Don't sell yourself short."

Poppy tried to breathe around the emotion swelling in her chest. "If it all works out, you're invited to the wedding," Poppy said decisively.

"Are you sure?"

"Of course. You're my family. And the family I've created is the most important thing I have."

"Good," Rosalind said. "Then go fight for the rest of it."

Poppy would do that. She absolutely would.

Isaiah didn't know for sure that he would find Poppy at her house. He could only hope that he would.

If not, he would have to launch a search of the entire town, which everyone was going to find unpleasant. Because he would be getting in faces and asking for access to confidential records. And while he was confident that ultimately he would get his way, he would rather not cut a swath of rage and destruction through the community that he tried to do business in.

But, desperate times.

He felt like he was made entirely of feelings. His skin hurt from it. His heart felt bruised. And he needed to… He needed to find Poppy and tell her.

He needed to find her and he needed to fix this.

It was 6:00 a.m., and he had two cups of coffee in his hand when he pounded on the door of her house with the toe of his boot.

It took a couple of minutes, but the door finally opened and revealed Poppy, who was standing there in baggy pajama pants with polar bears on them, and a plain shirt. Her hair was exceptionally large and sticking out at all angles, one curl hanging in her face. And she looked…

Not altogether very happy to see him.

"What are you doing here?"

"I brought you coffee."

"Yesterday you brought me cotton candy, and you were still a dick. So explain to me why I should be compelled by the coffee." She crossed her arms and treated him to a hard glare.

"I need to talk to you."

"Well, that works, because I need to talk to you too. Though, I was not going to talk to you at six in the morning."

"Were you asleep?"

"Obviously. It's six in the morning." Then her shoulders slumped and she sighed, backing away from the door. "No. I wasn't sleeping."

He found himself relieved by that.

"I couldn't sleep at all," she continued. "Because I kept thinking about you. You asshole."

He found that extraordinarily cheering.

"I couldn't sleep either," he said.

"Well, of course not. You lost your assistant. And you had to get your own coffee as a result. Life is truly caving in around you, Isaiah."

"That isn't why I couldn't sleep," he said. "I talked to my brother last night."

"Which one?"

"Joshua. Who was not terribly impressed with me, I have to say."

"Well, I'm not sure who could be terribly impressed with you right at the moment."

She wasn't letting him off easy. And that was all right. He didn't need it to be easy. He just needed to fix it.

"I do feel," he said, his voice coming out so rough it was like a stranger's. "I feel a lot. All the time. It's just easier when I don't. So I'm very good at pushing down my emotions. And I'm very good at separating feelings from a moment. That way I have time to analyze what I feel later, instead of being reactionary."

"Because being reactionary is bad?"

"Yes. Especially when… When I might have read a situation wrong. And I do that a lot, Poppy. I'm a perfectionist. I don't like being wrong."

"This is not news to me," she said.

"I know. You've also known me long enough that you seem to know how to read me. And I… I'm pretty good at reading you too. But sometimes I don't get it right. Feelings are different for me. But it doesn't mean I don't have them. It does mean that sometimes I'm wrong about what's happening. And… I hate that. I hate it more than anything. I hate feeling like everything is okay and finding out it isn't. I hate feeling like something is wrong only to find out that it's not."

"You know everyone makes those mistakes," she said gently. "Nobody gets it completely right all the time."

"I do know that," he said. "But I get it wrong more often than most. I've always struggled with that. I've found ways to make it easier. I use organization. My interest in numbers. Having an assistant who helps me with the things I'm not so great at. All of those things have made it easier for me to have a life that functions simply. They've made it so I don't have to risk myself. So I don't have to be hurt.

"But I'm finding that they have not enabled me to have a full life. Poppy, I don't just want easy. That was a mistake I made when I asked you to find me a wife. I thought I wanted a wife so I could feel the sense of completeness in my personal life that I did my professional life. But what I didn't realize was that things felt complete in my professional life because I was with you every day."

He took a step toward her, wanting to touch her. With everything he had.

"I had you in that perfect space I created for you. And I got to be with you all the time," he continued. "Yours was one of the first faces I saw every morning. And you were always one of the last people I saw before I went home. There was a rightness to that. And I attributed it to…the fact that you were efficient. The fact that you were organized. The fact that I liked you. But it was more than that. And it always has been. It isn't that I didn't think of you when I decided to put an ad in the paper for a wife. You were actually the reason I did it. It's just that… I'm an idiot."

He paused and watched her expression.

"Are you waiting for me to argue with you?" She blinked. "I'm not going to."

"I'm not waiting for you to argue. I just want you to… I want you to see that I mean this. I want you to understand that I didn't do it on purpose. There's just so many layers of protection inside me, and it takes me days sometimes to sort out what's happening in my own chest.

"You are right. I hated it because it wasn't in my head. I hated it because it all comes from that part of me that I find difficult. The part that I feel holds me back. It is amazing to have a brother like Joshua. Someone who's a PR expert. Who seems to navigate rooms and facial expressions and changes in mood seamlessly. I've had you by my side for that. To say the right thing in a meeting when I didn't. To give me your rundown on how something actually went so that I didn't have to."

"I already told you it's not hard for me to do that for you. The way you are doesn't bother me. It's just you. It's not like there's this separate piece of you that has these challenges and then there's you. It's all you. And I could never separate it out. I wouldn't even want to. Isaiah, you're perfect the way you are. Whether there is a label for this or not. Whether it's a disorder or it isn't. It doesn't matter to me. It's all you."

"I bet you resented it a little bit yesterday."

"You hurt me. You hurt me really badly. But I still think you're the best man I know. I still… Isaiah, I love you. You saying terrible things to me one day is not going to undo ten years of loving you."

The relief washing through him felt unlike anything he'd ever experienced before. He wanted to drop to his knees. He wanted to kiss her. Hold her. He wanted to unlock himself and let everything he felt pour out.

Why wasn't he doing that? Why was he standing there stiff as a board when that wasn't at all what he felt?

So he did.

He dropped down to his knees and he wrapped his arms around her, pressing his face against her stomach. Against Poppy and the life that was growing inside her.

"I love you," he whispered. "Poppy, I love you."

He looked up at her, and she was staring down at him, bewildered, as he continued, "I just… I was so afraid to let myself feel it. To let myself want this. To let myself have it. I can't help but see myself as an emotional burden. When I think of everything you do for me… I think of you having to do that in our lives, and it doesn't feel fair. It feels like you deserve someone easier. Someone better. Someone you don't have to act as a translator for."

"I've had a long time to fall in love with other men, Isaiah. But you are the one I love. You. And I already told you that I don't see you and then the way you process emotion. It's all you. The man I love. All your traits, they can't be separated. I don't want them to be. You're not my project. You… You have no idea what you give to me. Because I've never told you. I talked with Rosalind last night."

"You did?"

"Yes." Poppy crouched down, so that they were eye to eye. "She told me I needed to fight for you. That we are not foster children anymore, and I can't live like someone else is in control of my destiny. And she's right. Whether or not you showed up at my house this morning, we were going to talk. Because I was going to come find you. And I was going to tell you again that I love you."

"I'm a lot of work," he said, his voice getting rough.

"I don't care. It's my privilege to have the freedom to work at it. No one is going to come and take me away and move me to a different place. No one is controlling what I do but me. If I choose to work at this, if I choose to love you, then that's my choice.

"And it's worth it. You mean everything to me. You hired me when I was an eighteen-year-old girl who had no job experience, who had barely been in one place for a year at a time. You introduced me to your family, and watching them showed me how love can function in those kinds of relationships. Your family showed me the way people can treat each other. The way you can fight and still care. The way you can make mistakes and still love."

"That's my family. It isn't me."

"I haven't gotten to you yet." She grabbed hold of his chin, her brown eyes steady on his. "You've told me how difficult it is for you to navigate people. But you still do it. You are so loyal to the people in your life. Including me.

"I watched the way you cared for Rosalind. Part of that was hiring me, simply because it meant something to her. Part of that was caring for her, and yes, in the end you felt like you made a mistake, like she made a fool out of you, but you showed that you had the capacity to care deeply.

"You have been the most constant steady presence in my life for the past decade. You've shown me what it means to be loyal. You took me with you to every job, every position. Every start-up. You committed to me in a way that no one else in my life ever has. And I don't know if you can possibly understand what that means for a foster kid who's had more houses than she can count."

Poppy stroked his face, her heart thundering hard, her whole body trembling. She continued, "You can't minimize the fact that you taught me that people can care that deeply. That they might show it in different ways, but that doesn't mean they don't care.

"I *do* know you have feelings, Isaiah. Because your actions show them. You are consistent month to month, year to year. It doesn't matter whether I misinterpret your reaction in the moment. You're always in it for the long haul. And that seems like a miracle to me." Her voice got thick, her eyes shiny. "You are not a trial, Isaiah Grayson. You are the greatest gift I've ever been given. And loving you is part of that gift."

The words washed over him, a balm for his soul. For his heart.

"I was afraid," he said. "Not just of being too much for you—" the words cut his throat "—but of losing you. I wish I were that altruistic. But I'm not. I was afraid because what I feel for you is so deep… I don't know what I would do if I lost you. If I… If I ruined it because of… Because of how I am."

"I *love* how you are." Poppy's voice was fierce. "It's up to me to tell you when something is wrong, to tell you when it's right. It doesn't matter how the rest of the world sees things, Isaiah. It matters how *we* see things. Here. Between us.

"Normal doesn't matter. Neither of us is normal. You're going to have to deal with my baggage. With the fact that I'm afraid I don't know how to be a mother because I never had one of my own. With the fact that sometimes my first instinct is to protect myself instead of fighting for what I feel. And I'm going to have to learn your way of communicating. That's love for everyone. Sometimes I'll be a bigger burden. And sometimes you will be. But we'll have each other. And that's so much better than being apart."

"I think I've loved you for a very long time. But it felt necessary to block it out. But once I touched you... Once I touched you, Poppy, I couldn't deny it. I can't keep you or my feelings for you in a box, and that terrifies me. You terrify me. But in a good way."

She lifted her hand, tracing a line down the side of his face. "The only thing that terrifies me is a life without you."

"Will you marry me? This time I'm asking. Not because you're pregnant. Not because I want a wife. Because I want you."

"I will marry you," she said. "Not for your family. Not in spite of you, but because of you. Because I love you."

"I might be bad when it comes to dealing with emotion, but I know right now I'm the happiest man in the world."

His heart felt like it might burst, and he didn't hide from it. Didn't push it aside. He opened himself up and embraced all of it.

"There will have to be some ground rules," Poppy said, smiling impishly.

"Ground rules?"

"Yes. Lines between our personal and professional lives. For example, at home, I'm not making the coffee."

"That's a sacrifice I'm willing to make."

"Good. But that won't be the only one."

He wrapped his arms around her and pulled them both into a standing position, Poppy cradled against his chest. "Why don't I take you into your bedroom and show you exactly what sorts of sacrifices I'm prepared to make."

"I don't have a bed in there," she protested as he carried her back toward her room. "There's just a sleeping bag."

"I think I can work with that."

And he did.

Epilogue

December 24, 2018

WIFE FOUND—

Antisocial mountain man/businessman Isaiah Grayson married his assistant, his best friend and his other half, Poppy Sinclair, on Christmas Eve.

She'll give him a child or two, exact number to be negotiated. And has vowed to be as tolerant of his mood as he is of hers. Because that's how love works.

She is willing to stay with him in sickness and in health, in a mountain cabin or at a fancy gala. As long as she is with him. For as long as they both shall live.

She's happy for him to keep the beard.

They opted to have a small, family wedding on a mountain.

The fact that Poppy was able to have a family wedding made her heart feel like it was so full it might burst. The Grayson clan was all in attendance, standing in the snow, along with Rosalind and her husband.

Poppy peeked out from around the tree she was hiding behind and looked at Isaiah, who was standing next to Pastor John Thompson. The backdrop of evergreens capped with snow was breathtaking, but not as breathtaking as the man himself.

He wasn't wearing a suit. He was wearing a black coat, white button-up shirt and black jeans. He also had on his black cowboy hat. He hadn't shaved.

But that was what she wanted.

Him.

Not some polished version, but the man she loved.

This would be her new Christmas tradition. She would think of her wedding. Of their love. Of how her whole life had changed because of Isaiah Grayson.

For her part, Poppy had on her very perfect dress and was holding a bouquet of dark red roses.

She smiled. It was the fantasy wedding she hadn't even known she wanted.

But then, she supposed that was because she hadn't known who the groom might be.

But this was perfectly them. Remote, and yet surrounded by the people they loved most.

There was no music, just the deep silence of the forest, the sound of branches moving whenever there was a slight breeze. And Poppy came out from behind the tree when it felt like it was time.

She walked through the snow, her eyes never leaving Isaiah's. She felt like she might have been walking down a very long aisle toward him for the past ten years.

And that each and every one of those years had been necessary to bring them to this moment.

Isaiah didn't feel things the way other people did. He felt them deeper. It took longer to get there, but she knew that now she had his heart, she would have it forever.

She trusted it. Wholly and completely.

Just like she trusted him.

He reached out and took her hand, and the two of them stood across from each other, love flooding Poppy's heart.

"I told you an ad was a good idea," he whispered after they'd taken their vows and the pastor had told him to kiss the bride.

"What are you talking about?"

"It's the reason I finally realized what was in front of me the whole time."

"I think we would have found our way without the ad."

"No. We needed the ad."

"So you can be right?" she asked, holding back a smile.

He grinned. "I'm always right."

"Oh, really? Well then, what do you think is going to happen next?"

He kissed her again, deep and hard and long. "I think we're going to live happily-ever-after."

He was right. As always.

* * * * *

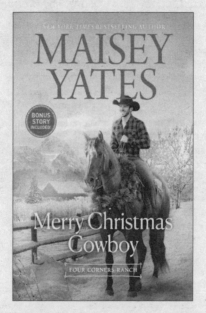

Love Harlequin romance?

DISCOVER.

Be the first to find out about promotions,
news and exclusive content!

Facebook.com/HarlequinBooks

Twitter.com/HarlequinBooks

Instagram.com/HarlequinBooks

Pinterest.com/HarlequinBooks

YouTube.com/HarlequinBooks

ReaderService.com

EXPLORE.

Sign up for the Harlequin e-newsletter and
download a free book from any series at
TryHarlequin.com

CONNECT.

Join our Harlequin community to
share your thoughts and connect
with other romance readers!
Facebook.com/groups/HarlequinConnection

HARLEQUIN

Heartfelt or thrilling, passionate or uplifting—Harlequin is more than just happily-ever-after.

With twelve different series to choose from and new books available every month, you are sure to find stories that will move you, uplift you, inspire and delight you.

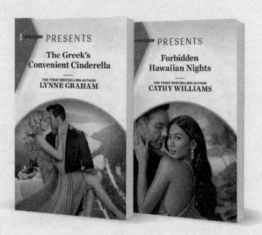